The Romanov Dynasty ... What if

Diana E. Linn

Diana Linn's Publishing, LLC
Tucson, Arizona

Diana Linn's Publishing LLC
6398 S. Wheaton Dr.
Tucson AZ 85747

Ordering Information:
Sales
For details, contact the publisher at the address above. Copies may be purchased via e-mail: amazon.com or
http://www.barnesandnobles.com/

Printed in the United States of America
Category of the Book: Historical Mystery. Narrative with a message.
ISBN 978-0-9980819-8-4
First Edition

DEDICATION

This book is especially dedicated to my husband, Dr. Robert T. Linn. During the months, it took me to write this story that in part I started in my mind many decades ago but had only written a few pages until now. He was my reader, encourager as I passionately wrote on.

IN LOVING MEMORY

I dedicate this book to my beloved mother who gave me the inspiration for this manuscript. She was born in Russia and experience first-hand these incidences told of in The Romanov Dynasty ... What if.

ACKNOWLEDGMENTS

Cover Illustration Copyright © 2017 by Bert Linn,
Photographer
Cover design by Diana E. Linn, Photographer
Book design and production by Diana E. Linn
Editing by Bert & Diana Linn
Author photograph by Bert Linn, Photographer
Book printing by Ingram Sparks

FOREWORD

A note from the author. Other books authored by Diana E. Linn such as *Can Anyone Tell me* is a novel written with a message. Its experiences are taken from real life situations that are usually not shared with anyone for fear of being ostracized. It doesn't matter where we are in our lives that we can step out and allow God to help us change our destination.

It has been said by readers that they couldn't put the book down until they had read every word of it.   -   Norma Jones

Also, a family read the book and decided to call a pastor to dispel of evil spirits in their home and they came to know the Lord because of the book.

-   Doris Crawford

Abducted and Lost, is a murder mystery also written with a message. When our attempt is to defy regulations to do everything our own way, we often have to pay bitterly. It is written so that the reader can experience how God makes the path straight in spite of where we come from in our lives.

PREFACE

This novel, *What If ... The Romanov Dynasty,* a novel as told to the
author, is a historical recap in the time when Russian propaganda
was at its worse. Further examination shows that the demise of the
Romanov Dynasty could very well have become the "Great
Escape" of that decade. Thus, the Novel, *The Romanov Dynasty...
What If,* an exciting read from start to finish.

Contents

The Romanov Dynasty
Diana E. Linn

Copyright Page
Dedication
In Loving Memory
Acknowledgements
Forward
Preface

What If? The Romanov Dynasty

Chapter 1
Not to Be Accepted

"Jacob, what has happened to you?" He couldn't escape his Mother's notice of his bruises and scrapes.

"The same as always, people hate the Jews."

His father knew his son could take care of himself. "How are your attackers?"

"They'll be fine. I had to forcefully give them a few punches that I don't think they'll brag about. That wasn't the problem. I can take care of myself, but Bruno, one of the thugs, was about to use a knife on me."

"Oh, my dear son. What happened then?" His mother was visibly shaken.

"Luckily, when they saw Matthew coming, they *took off* into the woods and because Matthew isn't Jewish, they didn't want to be seen doing what they were about to do. They said every time they fight other Jewish kids I break it up so today was *payday* for me. They were ready to kill me."

"Dear, God. Spare our Son, please spare our son." His

mother was in tears.

"Martha, he'll be okay. God will take care of him." His Dad couldn't begin to comprehend what had just happened.

"Son, go clean up." Their parents always insisted they eat together as a family, the dinner Jacob's three sisters had prepared. Peter and Jessie, his brothers, were also home after having worked in the vineyard all day. Though it wasn't yet the fall season, dinner needed to be hot or at least warm after a long day of working. This was especially common in the cooler weather, after working on the farm. Today it was stew cooked over a hot stove.

With a full stomach the family retired to the living room, as normally they would. This was the time of evening they would be ready to share together the events of the day. Today wasn't to be an exception.

Their bungalow was a comfortable six-bedroom home with enough room for the entire family. His father and all four of his sons had much to do with how comfortable it was. There was a fireplace that separated the living room from the kitchen, open enough to see from one room to the other.

"Son, tell us then, how did you get out of it?

"Like I said, Matthew came along."

"Thank God for Matthew. I've always really liked him even if he isn't a Jew." His Mother spoke in earnest.

"Tell us how your studies went with your instructor? You know our greatest wish for you is to have an excellent education. Be more than we could be and really make a difference in your generation. Maybe you could be a lawyer and stop all this nonsense." His Dad knew what he wished for his son.

"I think Peter will be your lawyer, right? Jessie will probably be your Doctor. You should be proud of them." His brothers sat there in silence. They hung on every word Jacob was saying. They as their Father, kept busy in the vineyard away from the city where assailants tended to hide out.

"Jacob, you are always the advocate for those who haven't a chance."

"That won't make me a lawyer."

"What about you becoming our Rabbi?"

"You know, Dad, it is very hard. I have no problem with the learning and I do well with all of that. Yet, when I leave to come home, there isn't a day that I don't have to defend myself somehow or even some other lad. Today was the worst. I know if I'm not careful it will get out of hand, and then they will kill someone. That was the intent today. I fear for you, my parents and my family. What will happen? It's getting worse here every day."

"Son, don't worry. We will be fine. Things will settle down and soon we will have our freedom back again without conflict."

"You really believe that, don't you? I don't and I really want to leave this place for Russia and I wish you all would come with me. You know that there was a Manifesto in 1789 signed by Crown Prince Peter III in Russia inviting people to come and settle in the Southern part of the Ukraine."

"Son that Manifesto went out almost a century ago. It wasn't for us. No, they didn't want us, only Christians."

"Maybe, but their people can believe and live as they want."

"Not the Jews, remember?"

"Dad, I want to take advantage of that and make a difference in that Country. Please say you will come with me."

"You can't leave everything here, Son. You will lose out on all you've worked for."

"If I stay, I'll be killed eventually. Bastian and Bruno are not the only haters of the Jews. Oh, sure, I can defend myself right now but for how long? You have to believe me. I have to leave."

His Mother begged him not to say that.

"There is one more thing I must tell you. This is hard for me because I love you and after all, you are my parents. I respect you." Jacob shared his acceptance of Jesus as his Savior but his Mother said instantly, "We do *not* allow those words to be spoken in this house."

His sisters and brothers sat there listening but made no comment. His Dad spoke, "As long as you live in our house, you will follow our God!"

"I am following your God, and I have made my decision to follow Christ but I want to tell you I have also made the decision to leave for Russia with or without you. You should come because it is not safe here anymore. Now you do not understand but you will. Soon you will see and you will be glad I went."

His Dad continued to complain, "How can you leave?" He spoke as though his son had just slighted him. "You are a Jew. I know they persecute us here but you are only 17 years old. How can you turn your back on your God and your family?"

"I'm not turning my back on God. I've found the Messiah and I don't intend to look back."

"The Messiah! How can you say that? We are waiting for our King to come as the Messiah."

"Dad, Jesus came as the Savior to save us from our sins. He will come as King when He comes back again for us."

"You talk foolishness. You have been fed nonsense. You are deceived and you are stubborn. I forbid you to go!"

"I cannot turn my back on God and what Jesus has done for me. As you say, I am 17 and I have decided it is time for me to make this change in my life. I am truly sorry, but I have to go. You think only the Jewish people are being persecuted but so are the Christians. They are being murdered every day for their belief in God. As God is my witness, I have seen that as well."

"Jacob," his mother was insistent, "you are no longer our

Son, and you have disgraced us. If you follow through on that decision, we no longer know you."

So, it was to be.

Jewish law had an institution called shunning and excommunication but the goal was to exclude people from the Jewish community who seek to dissent from central tenets. However, it was not used as a form of punishment, it was designed to encourage people to conform to communal norms or cease to be part of the religious sub-society. When Jacob's Mother wanted him to feel disinherited it was in hopes that he would see the folly of his ways and return to his original heritage as a Jew.

Emperors Theodosius II and Valentinian III decreed that Jewish parents and grandparents could not disinherit any children and grandchildren who converted to Christianity. Clearly the Roman emperors didn't want Christians to suffer any disadvantages from being Christian, not even within one's own family. People who converted to other religions could still be disinherited, but not those who converted from Judaism to Christianity.

Jacob was not a crypto-Jew. He was sure of what he believed and there was no altering his mind and heart for any reason. Arguments ensued but Jacob had decided he had found what Christ preached in the Scriptures and he didn't intend to give that up. With a new location, a new country he felt he could go anywhere. His Savior would see him through. The country to where he was going was now offering the freedom he wanted. It still wasn't easy for him to leave all and follow Christ, but his decision was made.

The initial step to joining the Wagon Train Caravan wasn't going to be just a *done deal* and Jacob knew that. To start with, he had no wagon with which to join the Caravan. If he were going to make this trip, he would have to find employment. Then the important issue would be whether the Wagon Train Caravan

Captain would find him to be ably suitable to the safety of the Caravan. Jacob knew he had the physical strength but he prayed that he could be one of the hired help on this trip through the rugged terrain. He was an able body man and knew he could easily work his way through this long journey.

The Wagon Train Caravan Captain sat down on a nearby log with Jacob to see if he could be of value in his trek across the country. Jack was quick to inform Jacob, "This group of folks are mostly followers of Meno Simons. You would need to understand that they call themselves Christians but some of those people are not necessarily pro Jewish."

"Might I just interject. I may not be a follower of Meno Simons but I have indeed given my life to God and do profess Jesus as my Savior. Yes, I am a born Jew and for that I don't apologize. I am also a Christian Jew. Shouldn't that help me?"

"It certainly should, but if you found it in your being, finding a bride along the way would help you immensely when we cross the border into the Ukraine. You must know Russia is open for new immigrants, they specifically claim that no Jews are allowed. However, you are a professing Christian. They are saying Christian Jews will do just fine living in Russia and hopefully they mean what they say. Having said that, if you can accept and put up with the arduous task, I could use your help. As far as the pay is concerned, it should take about two months to get to the Ukraine so we are paying minimal amounts of money in earnings. If you own a wagon I would be willing to pay more. However, if you need to use one of mine, your pay will be all the grub you can eat and you will get to your destination. It is important that we keep to our schedule since we want to get there before the snow flies. It will be too cold if it takes us any extra time. If that happens, and things do happen on any trek, we will be dealing with health problems."

"You expect us to arrive in the Ukraine, in October?"

"This is now early August? The beginning of October we should be there. By the time, we get into Ukrainian terrain, the weather will be tolerable there. To get through the higher elevation, is the problem. Are you with me?"

"I am."

When winter arrived, the weather would require changes in the modes of transportation. Deep snow on trails made walking impossible and wagon wheels often got stuck. People couldn't travel by boat on frozen lakes so they travelled in sleighs in the winter. Sleighs were similar to carts but had no wheels. Two flat metal bars called runners slid easily over snow.

Thick snow made traveling in a sleigh a smoother ride than traveling in a wagon. Most sleighs were not covered, so the ride could be very cold. People kept warm by covering themselves with fur blankets and with heavy coverlets called *lap robes*. Lap robes were designed to cover a rider's legs and feet. They came in many kinds of designs and could be surprisingly bright and colorful. People also used foot warmers to keep warm in a sleigh or carriage. These were metal boxes filled with hot coals and placed on the floor inside the wagon.

"I haven't a wagon. Do you have one I might be able to buy?"

"I do have a wagon you can use."

"May I see it?"

"Of course. Let's head over to it."

Live-in wagons first came into prominence in the early 1800s in Europe. Gypsy wagons had extensive hand-carvings and were brightly painted in colors such as yellow, green, and maroon. Most had a standard interior layout but some came equipped with a set of beds across the back, built-in dressers and lockers for storage, plus a small wood or coal stove. They were frequently constructed with fine woods by custom coachbuilders. Some were often decorated with gold leaves. Wagons could cost as much as a small house because it really was a house-on-wheels. Often, they could be equipped with windows and some even had china hutches.

They walked along side of the wagons as people milled about preparing for the journey. Some were more elaborate with the idea, once they would arrive in the Ukraine, the families would be living in their Mobil coach until they managed to construct their homes.

"Our wagons on the whole, are simply constructed but amply supplied with all the needs of a small home. Your wagon would be bringing up the rear, so you would be last in line."

"I think I can handle that. Everything I might need seems to be here. Again, my question to you would be, do you suppose I could work to buy it from you?"

"Now, that might just be possible. You certainly look able body and if you become my *right-hand man*."

"I think I will need it when we arrive at our destination."

"I'm sure you will need it. Let's shake on it." The deal was sealed.

'I am prepared to make you the Wagon master."

"Why, thank you for that vote of confidence. I aim to prove my worth."

As far back as the 1880s, the handshake or the *gentleman's agreement* was legal and binding if you could prove an offer was made, the offer was accepted, consideration was exchanged, and both parties had the intention to enter into a legally binding contract, it then could be upheld in court.

Jacob found the coach to be a fine home on wheels to get him to his destination and then to live in until he could build a home.

At first coaches were used only by the rich. Coaches for hire were as early as 1625, when stagecoaches also appeared. It was very costly to travel by coach, and the roads were so bad that most people preferred to ride a horse. Only the coming of the Industrial Revolution at the end of the eighteenth century really spurred the demand for faster, cheaper transportation. Few people could afford to feed and take care of more than one horse, so the coach-for-hire industry developed.

From the end of the eighteenth century into the nineteenth century, the horse-drawn vehicle was a key element in the evolving transportation system that increasingly linked urban and rural parts of the country. Private carriages and commercial vehicles also played a vital role in the growth of cities. Horse-drawn vehicles contributed to moving goods and people to and from urban centers, encouraging the settling of rural areas, the growth of cities, the creation of wealth, and the rise of consumer culture.

Stagecoaches designed to carry passengers across the country to heavy wagons developed to haul industrial goods and horse-drawn vehicles once fulfilled most of the needs. They moved people around cities. They allowed farmers to get their raw goods to train stations and city markets. They also enabled large manufacturers to get their products from the factory to the consumer. Carriages played a key role in the transportation revolution transforming almost all areas of life. In turn, changes in transportation influenced the design, production, and use of horse-drawn vehicles.

"The rough train and rutted roads make it almost impossible for wagon travel. That being complicated by falling timber, your help to keep the roads clear will earn you your wagon. A deal."

"You'll find I will be your man for the journey."

In the 1800s, most country roads were dirt paths with two

ruts worn by wagon wheels and a grassy strip in the middle. These roads were often hard and bumpy. In warm months, they were dry and dusty, while in the spring they were wet and muddy. In winter, they could be covered with ice and snow. Most roads were so narrow that if two buggies met, one might be forced into a ditch along the side of the road. In those days, there were few bridges, so drivers simply drove their wagons through rivers and streams.

It had been a few days now since Jacob had his last conversation with his parents. Jacob was a determined young man and now he was here with the rest of the people in the Caravan preparing for the long journey. Soon they would be on their way and he wouldn't even be able to say a good bye to his own parents. If that meant he was following God, then that was how it had to be. It didn't seem to matter much though because his heart was heavy. He kept himself busy working. He had to prepare the provisions for his wagon. He wanted to set up the compartments into a sleeping area, an eating area and a reading section to make the lengthy journey more tolerable.

Jacob was preparing his coach when he heard rustling in the bushes. His first thought went back to the fight he had just a few days earlier. "Please, God, not that again. If you aren't my helper now God, I'll be thrown out of this Caravan because of my behavior. Please send protection," he was praying in earnest. Finally, he turned around to face his accuser, if that was who it had to be.

Chapter 2
Preparing for the Journey

Turn he did. His fear was unconscionable to the feelings he was experiencing. First it was shock, then surprise and finally delighted. It was his Dad!

"I'm surprised to see you."

"I had a hard time finding which wagon was yours. They all look alike."

"From the outside, possibly, but the inside is usually different."

"Here," He handed Jacob a strong box and a small basket with food, "I know you are not my eldest son but because I may never see you again I want you to have what I have decided should be yours."

"I don't expect anything from you. You don't need to be dividing up an inheritance for me. I don't deserve anything. I have simply chosen to leave Germany to begin a new life for myself."

"You are our son and we wish the very best for you. You must take what I'm giving you. Be careful with the gold bar, it is heavy but your inheritance. There is plenty for the rest of the family. Some of it you may need along the journey."

Jewish custom dictated that the father's firstborn son would inherit twice as much as his other children. However, it normally stayed in the possession of the father until he would be on his dying bed. He could, however write up a will and assign his property while he was still living to prevent his heirs from fighting, but this was always to be done on his free will. However, should he have chosen to do this, his heirs couldn't sell that property until the death of their Father. In Jacob's situation, he would carry the gold bar with him never to use it. Eventually it would be handed down to his own son.

As in the case of the prodigal son, who wished his father dead and though his elder brother should have been there to stand with his father, he didn't for whatever reason. Then, to make things worse, the prodigal son sold his inheritance for his wild living, instead of keeping it until his father's death.

Jacob's Dad didn't just want to let Jacob go. "You and I know what we believe as a Jew but if you want to be called a Christian, then at least go with God. Your Mother can't say that yet, but she still loves you very much. You are our son and we are not disinheriting you, so please when you can, let us know where you are and how you are doing. If you really believe yourself to be a Christian, who knows, just maybe we will find you are right. Should it get better here, you can always come back. We will be here for you. You must believe that."

"Thank you, Dad. I will pray for you. I will write you from the first city stop we make."

"Write the letters to me. I will be sure that Mother reads them but I don't want her to return them unanswered."

"I'm praying that God spare you and that eventually you will know and ask Jesus to be your Savior. Here, I have an extra Bible that is translated in Hebrew. It was given to me from the University. You can have it. Please take it. Even if you only read it to understand me."

"I'll have to hide it."

"Read it when you can and you will understand."

They hugged one another and then parted. By this time both men had tears in their eyes.

Travel wasn't easy and while the Caravan was being prepared for the journey, Jacob knew this would be a grueling trip that would take many days to achieve. He knew his strength and ability for endurance but also was very aware that he must be of considerable help during the trip. The dirt roads would be long and lonely with only horses and Jack as their leader to guide the people to their promised land of freedom. Jack was well acquainted with the task on hand. He had accomplished this trip, over the mountains and through the brush, many times before. With the cooler fall season soon approaching they would have to have clothing suitable for traveling so that the cold nights would be tolerable to them.

Finally, the day came when they were on their way. Jacob caught up with Jack on his horse, "How many people on this Caravan, Jack?"

"Last count, about a hundred people including children in twenty carriages. That is my limit for traveling purposes. Some Wagon Train Caravans have up to as many as 200 people. My preference is around 100. Easier to keep together and less confusing. When I get back we will start over with another group of people. When we move out, another encampment will begin their preparations to be ready for me when I return."

On any trek across the country the wagon master's job, when stopping for the night, was to have the train form a corral. This was usually done by the lead wagon of the train stopping, and then the following wagons in succession pass slightly inside and ahead of the preceding wagon thus forming a circle. The stock and all members of the train were ordered inside so that they might be better protected from the attack of wild animals or bands of robbers. On such occasions, all grown people, both men and women and young boys, would prepare for the defense.

There were about thirty teams of oxen, each team consisting of four yoke of cattle to each wagon. In all, there were about 420 work cattle, 100 head of stock cattle, and a large number of horses. About 100 hundred men and women and many children were entrusted to the guidance and care of these two men, the Captain and Wagon master.

The road was dusty and the path wasn't always open enough for so many carriages to pass through. "Here, let me clear the way." Jacob would stop his horses and jump down with a few other men and clear the brush away. "Okay, I think we have it." So, on they continued.

By 1870 about 9000 people had immigrated to Russia, mostly to the Mennonite Colonies of Chortitza and Molotschna, with a population increase numbering about 45,000 in the Southern part of the Ukraine. This wasn't going to be an easy run up the mountains, by the river and through strange Countries, but Jacob was on the journey now.

The Caravan was working its way southeast and so It was hot and dusty as they continued to follow the stream alongside the gravel road. Jacob rigged a wheel with blades he had carved wide enough to catch the blowing wind with the movement of the Caravan. It created a pleasant breeze throughout his wagon.

During the journey, they had to break often for the people. Everything was continuing easily enough until one of the wagons in the middle of the Caravan stopped. Apparently, the metal on the wheel of the wagon began to come loose. When the Caravan wasn't moving from the center, Jack came back to see where the problem was. Jacob, just as quickly jumped from his wagon to check on the people in the Caravan. Jack and Jacob met at the offending Wagon with the broken wheel to decide what had to be done. To continue without addressing the problem of the wheel, meant it would certainly splinter apart. Repair the wheel, was their only option.

Attempting to find parts was never easy. The Caravan was now near a small town where Jacob and the owner of the wagon, Tom, sought out a blacksmith shop.

"What do you think, Jacob? Buy a new wheel?"

"You could see if the one you have is repairable but then buy a new one and if any of the other wheels have a problem you may have enough parts to make it to our destination."

"I think your idea could save the day. Let's see how much this will set me back."

They set out to walk through an open meadow that led them to a small town. Strolling along the City's wooden sidewalk, Jacob noticed and said, "Here we are Tom, a blacksmith shop, just what we need."

As they entered the shop they saw an old hunched-back older man with a black beard, no more than five feet tall. He had all the features of a man that had been through much in his lifetime. Dressed in well-worn pants with a slightly tattered shirt, and a pipe in the corner of his mouth. Standing over an open fire, he was hammering away on a piece of metal that lay on his anvil. Looking up at Jacob and Tom, "How can I help you men?"

Tom had been distracted by all the tools he saw hanging on the wall. "It looks as if you are a busy man."

"Horses need shoes and wagons need repair so I guess you could say that."

"I have a wheel I brought with me for my wagon that is showing excess wear and won't make another mile. Can you help me? Here is the wheel, what do you think?"

"I'll repair it, young man, but it won't take many more

miles. It would make for a good spare."

"How 'bout I buy one and you repair this? How soon can you do that?"

"It'll take a few hours but why don't you visit the bar next door while I get this done for you?"

Jacob asked, "Is it a rowdy bar?"

"Not at this time of day. The roughnecks come out at night. They need a few too many drinks to become annoying. Then there is a restaurant just two doors down. Get a good cup of coffee. That might be more to your liking than the bar."

"Ah, what do you say Jacob? Try the Bar?"

"Surely, I'm game for that if you are."

Both men entered through the swinging doors and were about to sit at the bar when they were confronted with someone who had already had too many. Jacob couldn't help but notice that he was dressed in black pants, leather vest and tattered hat that hung over his head making it difficult to make eye contact. His large burly left hand was resting on his holster.

"Let's leave, Tom."

"Not so fast." Blurted the burley, unshaven man.

"What is it we can do for you, Sir?" Jacob asked.

"You're not going anywhere until you tell me what business you have in my town?"

The bar tender interrupted, "How many times have I told you this is not your town. It is our Town. Just sit yourself down in the corner and behave yourself."

Jacob and Tom weren't exactly accustomed to people who had too many beers let alone the stench of a man who had not bathed in months and then the smell of a cheap cigar hanging out the side of his mouth.

"It's okay, we'll just go across the street and have coffee at the restaurant. Didn't think it would be so bad this early in the morning."

"Don't pay any attention to him. He's all threats but never yet has he done anyone in."

The drunk didn't intend on backing off for anyone. "Just try me." He pulled his gun and fired a shot through the roof. "State your business, men!"

"Tom, let's go."

"Don't run out on me! I'm talking to you."

Jacob turned to face him, "You think you're tough. Do as the bar tender told you, sit!"

"Let's fight it out in the back ally!

"Get a life, man." Jacob remembered, only too well, his last fight. It made him shudder.

"Shaking, are you? Stand up like a man and prove your worth!"

"Shoot an unarmed man? What are you a left-handed bandit? You surprise me."

"I can whip anybody with that hand. My right arm was shot off years ago in a brawl."

Jacob looked at him. "Come again, you want to lose your other arm? I'd never do that to another man.

"Let's fight it out. I can beat you to a pulp with one hand."

"You only think that." Jacob caught Tom's glance, "We're out of here. You may not value life but I do. I even care for yours. Fighting is out so don't try to make something of it. I have a Caravan to care for and you aren't part of that group."

The guy sauntered to the end of the bar. "He won't fight me. He cares? Who would ever care for anybody? Never heard such stupidity." This was not what he had anticipated. He just wanted a good old fashioned bar fight but Jacob didn't intend to comply.

"Well, that's a first. I've never seen him so subdued. We

need more of your kind around here. Aiming to settle in these parts?"

"No, Tom and I are on our way to the Ukraine to settle."

"Why?"

"Just because we chose to." Tom said it just as it was.

"Tom, let's go to the hotel and have some dinner." Turning again to the bartender, "Do they serve food there?"

"They do. The best in these parts but it might cost some money."

"We'll handle it."

Chapter 3
The Broken Wheel

"Well, I must say, Jacob, you know how to handle yourself. I, for one, am glad you are with us."

"Let's go get some grub or just coffee, whatever, Tom." The restaurant at this point seemed the better choice. Together the two men sat enjoying their coffee and reminiscing about the past and why they were on the journey to the Ukraine.

Tom seemed to recognize Jacob as a handsome young man. "Tell me, why are you traveling alone? Are you not a Jew?"

"As a Jew, it is hard to remain anonymous. It seems, no matter what, if you look like a Jew, then that makes us fair game to be hunted down, at least in my town." Jacob went on to share his faith and how he came to believe in Jesus the Christ.

"My family and I didn't have an encounter like you had, at least in Germany. We did in Holland, turning away from the traditional church as well as from the Priests. We literally had to go into hiding. Couldn't even stay more than a couple of months in any one place. As a group, we moved to Germany hoping it would be better and it was but if we don't want to bear arms and fight for the country we had to pay extra tariff. We did this but recently they raised the levy so high it was beginning to take away from our livelihood. Sometimes we didn't even have enough food on the table."

"That was because you wouldn't join the armed forces?"

"That's right. We don't believe in taking another man's life. We would rather just walk away or turn the other cheek."

"From what I hear, it was likely that your clan made that decision because your founding leader, Meno Simon's brother, or it was assumed to be his brother, was killed by fighting between Catholics and Christians over doctrinal issues. Meno searched the Scripture to validate that doctrine."

"Don't you adhere to our belief of nonviolence?"

"Anabaptists? I don't have a problem with it but I'd bear arms if my country demanded it of me. Please, don't misunderstand what I'm saying, I would not choose that way of life but for those who do, I'd say, "Go with God.""

"Then why are you traveling with us?"

"I would've been killed. I felt I had to leave but I came to know the Savior just as you did. I don't know everything as of yet, I am still learning. I too want the *free world* and I would much rather follow as you do. However, I will defend my family, no matter what. God will have to be my judge on that account."

"Well, Jacob, I'm glad you are with us and we will pray that you learn to know the Scriptures as we do. I have seen you defend the Caravan and I know you will be the man of God you need to be. Thank you for being with us."

A shadow appeared in the doorway, "Your wheel is as good as new and ready to go."

"Where do you suppose, I could mail my letter?" Jacob had not forgotten his family.

"Here, next door."

The journey continued and all seemed well as the miles

began to drag on. The evening breeze was pleasant but Jacob's heart was lonely. He had left everything behind. His friends, his parents, and even his Education, still, he had brought his books to enable him to read and study using the course plans he acquired from his instructors.

Sitting around the campfire proved interesting as people shared their testimony. How they came to the decision to take this journey and how God was leading them. Each of them had no doubts that they needed to make this journey. Singing and the playing of instruments kept everyone together. Every evening one of the men shared God's Word and taught a lesson of encouragement for their lives.

The weather was still unusually pleasant. Jacob knew that soon it would begin to cool with the colder season on the horizon. Though he also knew from geography lessons, in the Southern part of the Ukraine, it would again be very pleasant. It made sense to settle in a country such as that.

They had been on the journey for a few weeks already and so far, there wasn't anything exciting outside of deer in the thickets. Most wild animals kept their distance from the large Caravan with so many people and cattle.

Jacob decided he had to make an effort to get acquainted with other young people traveling with families. There had to be more than just a few more broken wheels to be repaired.

He was spotted wondering about alone, "Jacob, where's your family? By the way, my name is Katharina."

Jacob did an about turn and to his amazement couldn't help but notice the young woman with red auburn hair. As she spoke, her deep blue eyes glowed with the sparkle of the stars. He shook his head as he brought himself back to reality.

"Sorry Katharina. You startled me. I'm on my own. I've come to begin a new life in the Ukraine. How about you?"

"I'm with my family. We've come a long way."

"Where from?"

"My family left Holland when I was young. We kept going from place to place because my Father is an ex-priest. Martin Luther's translating of the Bible, made it possible for us to read it for ourselves. My father realized he could no longer follow tradition. More than once, I heard him say he could understand why the Scriptures affected Luther as it did."

"Don't the priests know Latin? Couldn't they have read it even then?"

"Surely, they could but who are they going to speak with in Latin? Another priest that has already decided he doesn't want to break with ritualism? They have too much to lose to break tradition. No one speaks of dissatisfactions, especially if they want to keep their head on their shoulders. Besides, their way of life is quite comfortable. Why change that?"

"What do you mean? I know the Jewish people are always being bullied but you guys?"

"Think for a moment. The churches livelihood was being threatened. The church makes good money from the fees for absolution. Now you have Christians that say you don't have to confess to the priest, let alone pay for your sins. Instead you can ask God's forgiveness directly. So, murder they did, whomever they could accuse and ensnare. You'd think it was back in the days of the Apostle Paul when he had a decree to kill all the followers of Christ."

"I guess you're right, Katharina. I've always believed in God and of course I still do. Being a Jew, trying to swallow the thought of Christ coming to save us from our sins, didn't seem possible."

"People have tried to stamp out believers from the very beginning. Look at Moses and how his parents put him in a basket to stop him from being murdered. Then the Queen rescued him. Even Saul or Paul as he was later called, came and wanted to exterminate the Christians. He really believed he had to do that. He believed he was doing the right thing in the sight of God. How could anyone be the son of God and God all at the same time?"

"I had a problem with that, but even in the book of Genesis, God talks about *us* in the plural in the very beginning. Well, you know, God cannot be defeated. I'm not sure the Roman Diocese's instructions to its clergy have that excuse. It didn't do much good then or now. Fighting against God? I don't think that's even possible but it is so great to finally be on our way to a free country."

"Well, Jacob, Russia has had its problems but just maybe we can be free to worship and believe our God in our lifetime."

"Katharina, should I marry, I would wish the same for my children. I'm still praying for my parents as they wait at home in Germany. Maybe they'll be okay but I don't think it will be long now. It's getting too violent over there, or at least it was for me."

Katharina's long curls bounced around as she shook her head. "From what you are saying, it was you they were after?"

"Right. A couple of guys had pegged me. I just didn't think it was what I wanted. I wouldn't fight except to defend myself but if it continued. I don't think I had a chance."

Katharina couldn't help herself, "But you are so muscular, like you've been working out for years. Who would dare to stand in your way? I find that hard to believe." She hesitated for a moment, "Sometimes God wants us to spread out. Bring more people into the Kingdom of God. When you step back and look at all this, you really can see how God is reaching people around us for the Gospel just because we are scattered. Think about it, if all goes well, we are satisfied with the people we know. We don't want anything different anymore."

The two strolled together around the edge of the encampment talking. "Katharina, look, there's a deer."

"I see it by the stump. Look a fox! Looking for food?"

"I've seen many rabbits, so hopefully they'll get what they want."

Soon it was back to the Wagons as everyone began to bunk down for the night. Jacob couldn't help but allow his mind to wonder into the future. To find a plot of land suitable for building a cabin or dare he dream for a real house? He couldn't just do it for himself. Surely, he could find a girl but she would have to be the most beautiful woman in the world. Could there even be such a person for him? Then he pictured that lovely red auburn hair. No, it couldn't be. He wouldn't allow himself to think that. She had her family and no way would that be possible. Anyone could easily see he was of Jewish decent. No, it can't be but maybe someday there would be someone. Having worked hard during the day, sleep was soon to overtake him.

The last thoughts he could remember was, 'I wonder what it will be like when we get there? I'll need to stake out a claim and a plot of land to work and then eat from the labor of my hands.' There had to be more for him than just repairing a few more broken wheels. All he could think of was *a few more wheels.* Maybe instead, he should be dreaming about Katharina? Soon he was off to sleep.

Chapter 4
Dreaming of The New Life

Just as the sun came up, everyone was again preparing food and getting ready for the rest of the journey. There was activity everywhere. Breakfast wasn't what Jacob was used to when his parents made it, but it would do. He began building a fire with scrap kindling, hoping it would get hot enough for his water to boil.

He couldn't believe what he saw. It had to be Katharina. He turned quickly, he didn't want to be caught staring. Tending to the fire, stoking the wood, not to make eye contact seemed the better choice for the moment. He hadn't considered looking at a woman at this point in his life so why would the image of her not leave him? Life would be too busy for him at the present and he surely had no time for such thinking.

"Jacob, come here! Join us, we have more food than we know what to do with, would like you to share it with us. Meet my Mother and Father."

His heart desired nothing more. "Pleased to meet you. No, I couldn't eat with you, I have plenty and you'll need all that you have to complete this journey."

"No, no. We insist. God always provides for our needs and even more if we share what we have. You must join us." Mr. Janzen insisted, "We are glad that you have been visiting with our daughter."

"Thank you. I guess I could join you."

Jacob was overwhelmed by the visit he had with such a wonderful family. Katharina. She had already made an imprint in his heart. He couldn't forget her for that entire day.

The Caravan travelled for some miles over an almost unbearable road. The country, though very mountainous, was covered with forests. As the Caravan travelled along the roadway, Jacob spotted droves of pigs in the fields. Sometimes they could see herds of sheep, goats and cattle. Here and there they also saw some signs of cultivation. Trees had been cut down, yet some appeared to be burned while others were left standing. There also were fields of corn and massive vineyards that appeared to be entwined among the weeds and brushwood that abundantly grew among them. From his experience, he knew vines shouldn't be left to trail on the ground. Jacob was convinced they had been severely neglected. To know anything about vineyards, surely the inhabitants had either vacated the land or didn't want them anymore. However, the vineyards reminded Jacob of home, making him feel homesick.

They crossed a wooden bridge over the mighty Morava River, where the Caravan came upon a series of small towns. Sometimes they saw inhabitants, both men and women who seemed to be weaving on looms out in the open.

Crossing another wooden bridge at Parachin, ascending Mount Jouor, they were able to get a marvelous view of the Bosnian Mountains, the lofty Jaskevatz, with the Stara Flanina near Nissa, and the magnificent ruin of the Stalatch. The highest peaks of these mountains were covered with snow as the wind blew from that direction, the change in the temperature was far too sudden to be agreeable.

To increase their discomfort, a violent storm of rain poured down like a deluge, which had been very much dreaded by the people in the Caravan, not only because of the personal inconvenience but the slough-like state to which the roads were reduced. They had to wait these storms out for safety reasons.

However, the days progressed as they travelled. Sometimes it was harder than other times as each had to endure the long ride journeying with the Caravan. It was the duty of each of the elders to keep everyone occupied with the duties at hand especially in the disagreeable weather.

Jacob believed that living under oppression of leadership was now all behind him for the present as he was going with the hope of a future. It felt like they were finally going to get to the *Promised Land*. Going somewhere to find a place they could call home, to live as they pleased.

The sun had just begun to appear in the distance, filtering through the Caravan settlement when suddenly the scream of a woman pierced through the silence of the early morning. Jacob wasn't yet fully awake but he, with every man in the encampment, hurriedly arrived at the scene.

"A bear!" The woman shouted. He's eating our food!"

Jacob grabbed his rifle, racing to get a closer look. It was a brown bear. Taking aim, he hit the bear on target, between the eyes. Another shot, just moments later also hit the bear, this time on the side of his head, as the bear slumped down. Suddenly there was nothing but silence.

"Come on men," Jacob didn't intend to leave food lying there. "Let's carve this carcass up and feed the crowd. The meat won't keep and if we leave it, wild animals will be here sooner than you think. We don't want to meet any more of them, so let's get with it."

Preparing the food brought all the women together to begin the preparations for a feast. This was a welcome change for the families. There was no mistaking that they had only brought food that would keep. Often yearning for the day when they would live with some normality.

Jacob stood there after he had done the skinning and cleaning with the other men but now he was taken back. Why hadn't he allowed himself to notice Katharina this way before? They had talked together and he dreamed about her but he hadn't realized how much he cared. Now it was like he didn't want to be without her. Their eyes met and locked but neither could break away. 'Oh, dear God, I didn't notice how beautiful she looked in the sunrise behind her. I just hadn't noticed her short slender body. How could I not have noticed her this way before?'

Soon the day's activities would be over. Tired from the work and again it would be time to bed down so that they could move out in the morning. He was dreaming, dreaming of a life he could share with Katharina.

For Katharina, sleep came in spurts as she lay there thinking. "Could this really be?" She dismissed her thoughts and gave it up for the night.

Morning came with the sun shining brightly. Katharina sat before her makeshift mirror.

"How come all the fussing, Katharina? You are always such a contented daughter. I dare say I've never seen you fuss so much."

"Don't know, Mom. Maybe the journey doesn't feel so out of sorts if I fuss with my hair."

"Do you think that young handsome man has something to do with it?"

"Don't know. There are many women in this Caravan he could care about."

"You are our daughter and I have a sense that tells me he cares."

"Think so?"

"Know so."

"Mothers always have that sixth sense, you suppose? Maybe we should plan a party and pull out all the musical instruments. Wouldn't that be fun? What do you think, Honey?" Both Katharina's parents were enthusiastic at even just the idea.

"You would like that, Dad?"

"It would be great. After today's journey we will be tired and worn out but I think the next day will be a Sunday. Usually we stop for a day of rest and worship. We could come up with much singing and dancing."

"On this rough ground? Well, if we find a meadow on the way."

Across the dusty roads the Caravan continued with the excitement of planning a party in the air as the breeze whisked through the Wagon Train. Sometimes the men walked beside their wagons as the women would hold the reigns. Jacob had an extra horse harnessed to the back of his wagon so that he could ride his horse through the meadows for exercise when they stopped for a break. It was a way of meeting with people and being sociable. Life could be hard and boring if no one ever showed any care. It was also a way of checking on the girl Jacob suddenly had feelings for. Somehow, this journey made for good excuses to gather at any opportunity.

Jacob jumped off his horse, next to Katharina. "Hop on with me, Katharina, okay?"

"I'd love that."

Off they rode, out of direct sight of the Caravan. "Here's a place, Katharina. Want to stop for a while?"

"Love it."

Together they strolled through the grass leisurely.

"What are your plans when we get to the Ukraine, Jacob?" They sat down on the meadow grass, resting. Jacob messed with the green soft grass. It was comfortable as they both looked up into the blue sky filled with white billowy clouds.

"Have done much thinking about that. I knew I wanted to leave where we lived in Germany but I didn't know how that would ever happen until I heard about this wagon train coming through. What do you think you wanted to do?"

"I suppose I would live with my parents for a while. Help them put everything together. I'm sure I'd be of some help. Someday, I'd like to try my hand at painting. Like painting scenery. Maybe add adventure to my pictures, like a cabin in the woods by a brook. When the snow flies, be content with candles on the table and a fire in the fireplace. Bake bread in the oven."

"Hmm, homemade bread! Wouldn't I love that? I can just taste that fresh bread. My Mother used to bake a lot. I wish I knew how they were."

"When was the last time you wrote them?

"In the last town we came through. I always do that and then I'm sure they are hearing from me but I won't hear from them until I find a place of my own."

"How did you come to join the Caravan?"

"Well, not a long story, really. I have a little education, which I am grateful for. My parents are the best and of course you know we are Jewish. I had this friend, Matthew. We hung out a lot but he was a Christian. We enjoyed one another's company and he was always sharing things about Jesus with me. After one of my classes a couple of guys jumped me and were about to knife me. Matthew came along and they took off. Matthew is a gem, he saved my life that day, but he was in earnest about sharing the Gospel with me. When he explained it like he did, Scripture suddenly made sense and I could see that Jesus had died for my sins but I had to accept that and ask His forgiveness. Well, I accepted Jesus as my Savior and I shared it with my parents but they would have nothing of it.

I had heard for some time that the Caravan was about to be leaving and you guys were on your way to the Ukraine. I just felt the urging of the Lord to join with you people. I almost think I know why now."

"You do?"

"Yes, you."

"You flatter me. I like that. Can't say I'm disappointed. You should know that my parents aren't my real parents. They adopted me as a baby because my parents were killed in a house fire. I was the only one that was rescued by a neighbor. That neighbor is my Father now. As I understand it, I am of Jewish decent but my adoptive parents insisted I should be reared with them so I could be taught in the ways of Jesus. Can't say that is a bad thing. They did help me understand the Scriptures for which I am very grateful. That's where the red in my hair comes from. I have all the physical looks but I do know the Lord. I must say I have the best parents on earth, I'm sure. To think I was chosen just like we are when we come to know Jesus as our Savior. If I have a choice I will always want to be available for them, no matter what."

"That explains your beautiful dark eyes and your Roman

nose. We almost match on that account."

"Well, maybe when we arrive to our destination, we can settle close to them."

"What are you saying, Jacob?"

That was about all Jacob could say when the Wagon Captain appeared. "Hey, you guys, everyone is waiting on you. We have to be on our way!" Jacob didn't have time to explain.

―――――――――

For Katharina, it was as if a tidal wave just swept over her. *Oh Lord, don't let Jacob leave without me.* How could he leave so abruptly without finishing that thought? He could have at least promised a future meeting. How could he be so thoughtless? She shook her head to bring herself back to reality. Katharina had only a few short steps to join up with her Parent's Wagon.

Chapter 5
The Engagement

The Caravan pulled out to continue the journey.

"Just a few more miles and we've made it again, Jacob."

"I really appreciate you hiring me on Jack. I don't know how I will ever thank you."

"Well, you have been a great help. I'll tell you what, if you want to be hired on for permanent, I surely could use your help. You've certainly proven yourself. I would increase your pay if that would seal the deal. I don't want an answer now, but think about it. When we get to our destination, it'll be a couple of weeks or more before I'll head back. Then I'll want an answer."

"I'm certainly grateful for that offer. Isn't the weather going to work against us going back?"

"I always carry gliders to attach to the wagons to get us across the snow should we need that. We'd be back in Germany for Christmas. That's a couple of months on the other side, coming back this way we will be in the spring. That's much more manageable when we travel with so many people."

"Who knows what God has for me in a few weeks. For now I'm hoping I can settle in the Ukraine. We'll see, but this offer of a job would mean I could see my family again."

"I'd love to have you on board, for sure. Let me know one way or another so I know if I have to scout for another hired hand, I would need plenty of time."

"That's a promise."

As they road on down the path, Jacob began to think. It had been days, since the last time he was anywhere near Katharina. It had been a very busy time. They were nearing the end of the journey, it would be only days but it would finally end, barring any more catastrophes. Babies had been born during the journey as well as illnesses being spread throughout the encampment. It hadn't exactly been uneventful. It became extremely trying to get through all the rough terrain. Under Jack's direction, the Caravan was well prepared with Doctors and nurses traveling in their midst. They helped where they could but in spite of everything the journey had taken its toll.

"Ashes to ashes and dust to dust." There had been one such funeral that had just recently been completed. Traveling with Pastors and Elders made these responsibilities more comforting for the families.

Then there was the problem with food storage. Every time a family neglected to deal with food properly bear would interrupt their encampment. As the Caravan continued through the higher elevation, people often wanted to store their extra food in the cold just outside their wagons. Wild animals could smell the contents and invariably visit the campsite. As a result the men in the encampment would be called upon to deal with the threat.

Busying the children was intensified when the Caravan was faced with wild animals attempting to enter the camp. It had been necessary to have the fear of God planted in the children's minds as the excitement of the *new world* grew. Children could not be subdued sufficiently, so they had to be told often what could happen should they choose not to heed authority.

Everyone needed a challenge to keep from becoming discouraged. Fortunately, there were not only doctors that wanted to relocate in the new world but there were plenty of teachers. Teachers were kept busy as they engaged the children in classes every day.

Amidst all the work and patrol to keep people safe, Jacob hadn't forgotten about Katharina. His duties had kept him extremely busy that sometimes it appeared he was the only man in the Caravan that could accomplish anything. He finally decided he had one too many emergencies. Katharina was now paramount on his mind and he knew he must deal with her next.

He couldn't bear to have Katharina think he didn't love her. He hadn't even told her and that couldn't be good. His mind began to torment him. What if some other man had already appealed to her as well? If all else failed, he could join the Caravan with Jack but that wouldn't be his choice. He just knew he had to deal with his heart, not just his head. Things would fall into place if he would deal with what he knew he needed to do.

With Jacob's intensity, he was not to be waylaid. The needs would be there now or later and maybe he would have to pay his dues, but he needed to do what he had to do immediately. He couldn't wait.

"Hey, Jacob, I could use your help."

It was his job, so help he did. "Here, Bill, let's reinforce your home on wheels. You're going to need it when we get to our destination. Do you have any tools?"

"I do."

Together they spent the next few hours repairing the wagon.

"Well, Bill, I think you should be good to go."

"Thanks. You just have saved us from having to worry if we would make the last few miles. I think there are a few others who could use your help. I think Albert is in the next wagon to me and I heard him saying he had a problem."

"I'll tell you what, I have an errand to run and if you guys haven't found a solution to your dilemma when I'm done, I'll be glad to help."

Jacob didn't wait for an answer. He simply excused himself to explore the matters of the heart. He needed to be persistent for there would always be needs. There would always be people that wanted something. This time he would not be deterred. So he went looking. He knew her wagon was closer to the front of the Caravan.

Jacob hadn't forgotten. He couldn't forget the girl he knew he loved. Did she know that? He had to tell her before other men might tell her first. There were plenty of good looking other men in this encampment that could find her as attractive. He needed to do something no matter how busy he had become. He dared to entertain the thought of having her joining him to work with the Caravan. Would she be willing? They could earn the money to build their dream home in the Ukraine. Not only that, but she could meet his family as well. If not, would she be willing to wait for him as he earned the money? She had wanted to help her parents get situated.

I think I just need to find her now. The answers will be there when I need them. God is always faithful, why do I worry about that? I need Katharina. I know I need her.

It wasn't long before he located the girl he loved. She stood there alone, facing the sun as it outlined her figure. Without hesitation he called to her, "There you are, Katharina. I've been looking everywhere for you."

"Been busy and then kind of preparing for the end of the journey. A little excited about finding our new home, aren't you?"

"I am but I want you to share that with me."

"You do? How?"

Jacob sensed aloofness. "Have I lost you to someone else? Oh, please, Katharina. I've been thinking about you all day and night. Don't say I'm not in your future."

For a moment, each of them just stared at one another. Katharina turned to look ahead of the caravan almost not hearing anymore.

Jacob, without hesitating, knelt in front of Katharina. "Please marry me."

Katharina wasn't saying anything, just staring into the distance. Then she turned with a deep smile on her face. "I will."

"Thank you, thank you. I don't want to live without you. I want you to share with me and together we will make a home. Have children and rear them and pray they will find it in their hearts to follow the Lord."

"That was a mouthful, like the Scripture says, *as for me and my household, we will serve the Lord*. I would like that."

"Why don't we see if we can find a minister that would marry us here?"

"In God's green landscape? I'd like that."

They walked together, hand in hand and blissfully to be sure. "You know, Katharina, I was thinking. Jack said I could stay hired on with him in bringing people back. He would give me a raise if I chose to do that. Then we could earn enough money to build ourselves a dream home. What do you think?"

Katharina didn't answer. They continued their stroll into the empty fields not far from the Caravan.

"I take it," Jacob said, "not a good idea? I would want you to stay with me. I wouldn't consider it if you wouldn't come with me."

"I don't know. I want to help my parents get situated. If we are to be married, I want to find that plot of land and begin to work it."

"You are probably right. The journey would possibly be too hard on you and if I went alone we would be apart four months at a time. Maybe you could go with me in the good seasons and meet my parents?"

"I hadn't considered you being gone most of the time."

"I have a feeling Jack won't want to leave right now with the bad weather approaching, traveling through the mountains."

"Do you want to put the wedding off for a while?"

"Absolutely not. I couldn't bear the thought of you not being with me and sharing my life. I can't let that happen."

"Are you really sure?"

"Absolutely!"

"I don't want to make that journey again. I want to settle either with my parents or near to them."

Katharina was about to show who she really was. In her mind it was settled. The love of her life would need to make those concessions. She hadn't considered an alternative, and Jacob knew for certainty what his lot would be with his new bride.

"I think I'm okay with that. I've sort of dreamt of planting a vineyard by our house. My Dad already taught me all about that. If I have to, there will be a nearby town that I can find work in. Shall we find a preacher to do the job?"

"What about my father?"

From there the plans began to find formulation. Excitement spread throughout the encampment. This would be the first wedding for this group of people to experience together on the road.

They planned for a feast. Someone would have to find some eatable wild life delectable to the taste for such an occasion.

"That's an easy problem, Jacob. Just leave some food out that has a lasting odor to it. Surely, a bear might be tempted to devour it."

"That's a dangerous proposition. We might get in deeper than we want to."

"Imagine, Jacob. Finally, we will be together and we'll plot out our land."

"We'll be sure to make it near enough to your parents. Do you realize we are already in the Ukraine? This is to be our home now."

"It is, Jacob. A wedding and a place to live."

The country of Ukraine has a diverse landscape that results in providing a number of habitats that supports a variety of species. Beech trees are found throughout the western area of the forest. In the northern part of the forest region there are pine, linden and oak trees. Spruce is common in the Northeast region. In the country the grassland is fringed with trees such as oak.

Much of the wildlife of Ukraine is home to squirrel, deer, elk, wild boar, foxes and wolves as well as brown bears and lynx. The bird life also constitutes an important part of the wildlife in this region and the forested areas have birds like cranes, black cock, wood grouse, starling and blue titmouse.

Jacob sought out one of the Caravan members whom he had noted was a wood carver. "Chester, I understand you carve wood."

"I do."

"Can you carve rings for Katharina and me?"

"I'd love to do that. Shouldn't take too long, I'll get right on it."

"I'll be forever indebted to you."

"Not at all. I'd love to do that."

Wooden wedding rings were usually carved out of a lasting wood such as oak, cutting them down to the approximate size, then with much sanding, staining and finally rubbing them with oil. A good artisan could make these as an original artistic piece any bride and groom would be thrilled to wear.

With the decorations in place, the party was about to begin.

Wedding plans were formulated. Preparing God's canopy seemed to add to the joyous occasion. The Wagon Train Caravan this time was prepared in a semi-circle to encompass the forest for the backdrop. As long as the sun shone everything was in its fresh beauty as they stood before the people.

"You look beautiful Katharina. The sparkles in your eyes are indeed from heaven." Her Dad was pleased that he could have such a privilege and honor to marry his daughter.

_____   .

During the first year of their marriage, both Jacob and Katharina decided it would be appropriate for Jacob to work the Caravan to earn enough money to build their home they were wanting for their future family. It wasn't long before Jacob was able to start a small vineyard from which he harvested mostly grapes for Jams and Jellies.

Their first child was about to be born when Jacob arrived home from his last trek to and from Germany. "I'm so sorry, Katharina. So, so sorry."

"Don't be Jacob. She was born and Jesus took her. We had the privilege of giving birth."

"She was to be your name sake, Katharina."

"We will be fine."

These were hard times but Katharina gave birth to another child whom they called Martha. She grew to become a helper especially for Katharina. Times were fun but both parents wanted a son. Soon a son was born whom they called Abraham.

"He is to be our first son. Let's call him Abraham."

Again, God had other plans for this newborn baby. God

knew the beginning from the end. He also, went to be with Jesus.

"It's been two years, Jacob."

"Two years for what?"

"I'm going to have another baby."

"Wonderful. If he's a boy, let's name him Abraham again."

"We can do that."

Just when they thought nothing could go wrong, they lost another baby. Katharina was devastated and discouraged. "What have I done, Jacob? I keep losing my babies?"

"You haven't done anything. We don't yet have the kind of medical treatment you need. It will be years until our Doctors are able to help us through the difficult birth. At least our lost babies are not lost but they get to be with Jesus."

Child bearing was never very easy in the early days. It wasn't practical for the family physician to be present at most of the births due to the distance from town to the farms. Midwives attended almost all births in the homes. The skills they brought with them were passed from one woman to another informally. With complications often present, many babies died at birth as well as mothers. Midwives often practiced without government control as late as into the nineteen-twenties.

Not until 1915, Dr. Joseph DeLee, declared that birth should be properly viewed as a labor-intensive suffering process that can very easily damage both mothers and babies much of the time. From that time on interventions began to include routine use of sedatives, ether, episiotomies, and forceps designed to save women from at least some of the pain of labor in childbearing.

A few years went by and Katharina was pregnant again. "A baby girl! Let's call her Julia. She will be our Julia."

Soon they were blessed with another baby boy. "This time he will be called Jacob. I am begging God to let me keep him."

The very next child was called Joann. This was now their

complete family.

"My dear Katharina, sitting here, makes me think I must ride out to Massandra vineyard and just see if I can't get a job there."

"Why, honey, with all the experience you have already acquired not only from your father but also, you've been doing so well in our own vineyard. I would be thrilled if you would like to work for the Czar."

"I don't think I would have a problem. You know we've been praying that God would lead us. Today, it feels as though God wants me to try. If that doesn't work out maybe something will from there. You know we've spent all the money we earned from the Wagon Train Caravan to build this house. I don't think I want to do that back and forth traveling anymore. It was good to visit with my parents but my brothers and sisters are taking good care of them. I want to be with you and our children now. Working for the Czar will make that possible."

"The house is lovely. Our children love it. I feel you are right, that is probably what you should do. Go in safety. We will pray that it all works out well. Maybe your son will be able to work with you."

"Exactly, I must think about him now. I'm not getting any younger, dear."

"None of us are."

Chapter 6
The Vineyard

Jacob prepared his horse for the ride to the Crimean Peninsula in search of the job. The scenery was beautiful with its soaring mountains sweeping sharply all the way down to the Black Sea. There it was, the Massandra winery.

I must find whom I can see. Surely, they should need some extra help.

From afar, Jacob could see the adobe looking brick hut and so he rode on to the building where he saw a worker standing.

"Sir, can you tell me where the vineyard keeper is?"

"His Highness is meeting with him. If you look up ahead, you can see them."

"Do you think they need a helper?"

"They always need someone. Why don't you ask?"

History has proven that the Massandra winery has produced some of the finest wines over the course of the last century and survived some of the most turbulent events. It was built between 1894 and 1897 to cater for the day-to-day needs of the Czar, Nicholas II and his court. Once a year the Romanov's would secretly leave for their summer Palace in Livadia near Yalta. The Czar had appointed a very gifted winemaker, Prince Golitzin who was able to produce the finest wine in all of Europe. He planted vines that suited the warm climate using his incredible talent for blending wines. His style of fortified and sweet wines was influenced by the hot climate of the Crimean coast.

Jacob introduced himself. "I would love to be a part of your hired men to work in such a vast vineyard as yours. I worked with my father back in Germany, learned what I could while attended the University there. My own land has a considerable number of grape vines but certainly nothing in comparison to yours. I would be pleased if I could be a part of your crew."

Jacob was hired. The vineyard was not far from his home and as a result, his family often joined him. The children played in the vineyard running through the groves. It wasn't long before the Czar came with his own family to join with Jacob's children.

Years flew by quickly. Prince Golitzin taught Jacob all the techniques he had learned by trial and error to accomplish the best vineyard in all of Europe. He chose to pass it on to both Jacob and his son Jacob. Nicholas II was delighted to know he now had not only Prince Golitzen but also Jacob who could assist and be his right-hand man. They were taught not only how to grow the best grapes but also how to care for the groves. Much work went into how the grapes tasted. They had to know the precise time to harvest the crop.

Some years a frost would come too early, before the harvest. It was at these times that torches had to be lit. It was so important to keep these crops in excellent condition for the production the Czar demanded of his vineyard. During these days the entire family would spend nights walking through the groves carrying torches attempting to keep the berries from the frost.

Jacob continued the work in the Czar's vineyard and he took his work serious. He was doing his job with his workers in the fields, pruning the crops, and cutting away the dead branches. He

wanted to keep the groves healthy and producing. It was an
arduous task but for the Russian Czar it was not just worth the
effort, he demanded excellence. His crops were still consistently
producing the best wine in the country if not in the world.

"Your Highness, I didn't expect you."

"It is okay. I have come to taste the grapes. I have been
told, you make the best wine in all of Europe, and I want to know
what they taste like."

"Here, let me wash them for you."

"No need."

Emperor Nicholas II sampled the grapes with much
enthusiasm. "They are indeed, as you say, the best ever. I want you
to know, they are a better crop than even your father could
produce."

"Your Highness, our weather has been much more
favorable the last few years. I do nothing different from what
Prince Golitzin or my Father would have done."

The Czar and Jacob continued to ride on horseback through
the fields, in and out, as he looked at the trees and lifted a few
branches loaded with grapes with his hand.

"Jacob, I think I shall bring my son and daughters out to
this vineyard again so they can see what it is all about, the next
time I'm out this way." The Emperor loved coming out to the
Crimea. It was as if he would sneak away from his responsibilities
any time he could.

It wasn't long until the entire family descended on the
Vineyard. Jacob's family was picnicking in the field on a favorable
sunny afternoon when the Nicholas with his family joined them.

The children never needed introductions as they excitedly
ran off to play in the open meadow nearby. Soon, Jacob pulled out
his Violin and began playing. It didn't take Anastasia but a minute
to stand beside him singing. She sang to her delight as Jacob

continued to play.

Most Sundays, the two families would come to picnic, tell stories, and play cards in the large shaded area next to the winery. Since visiting from the Palace to the vineyard and the vineyard to the palace was a common occurrence, Nicholas often had Jacob stay with Alexei in his illness since Jacob's daughters were devoted to the youngest two. Their children's illnesses were never made public. It was better for the nation to feel that their country was in the hands of a strong leader not overloaded with personal concerns. As a result, Jacob's and the Czar's families became inseparable.

Soon history was about to repeat itself, not unlike that faced Jacob and Katharina when they fled to Germany. The very next generation, which included their son, Jacob, was about to face a similar but more severe situation because Russia was now in the middle of a Revolution. They country was in devastating circumstances for this time it would include both the Czar's family as well as his.

Chapter 7
Country in Turmoil

Chaos had now broken out in all of Russia, although the Revolution already began back in July 1914. By January 1, 1917, the revolution was in full force. It was shortly after this a stranger found the business center in Pushkin almost destroyed by violence and pillaging, leaving windows not only broken but riddled with bullet holes in the immigration office. All hope of seeing through the broken glass was gone and it was hard to see the faint glimmer of yellow light still flickering in the ruins. There were spikes of shattered glass laying everywhere. It didn't matter where you looked, but what had happened put the building in a war zone. The plunder was over and so, except for that faint light, there was nothing, not even any people. The town itself appeared to be in a state of pure hell. A beautiful city lay in ashes.

The town was located on the Neva lowland, on the left bank of the River Neva with a landscape that varied from hills, ridges and terraces that was intermixed with valleys, plains, forests and farmland. With an average of 240 days of sunshine and 19 hours of daylight in the summer, it should have been a pleasant day.

The stranger, dressed in a black cape, jumped from his

47

horse. Pausing for a brief moment, looking in every direction to be sure there were no armed soldiers. Every step had to be calculated as he dared to tread between the debris. Stumbling, then attempting to regain his balance, approached the front entrance of the building. He was now standing in front of the huge iron door that had been ripped off its top hinges, was now resting against the devastated exterior brick building. Any miss step or carelessness would cause serious injury to anyone attempting to walk through the carnage. It was hard to tell if the building would be inhabitable again. The stranger nudged the door just enough for him to make his way through.

He carefully walked down the hallway following that faint yellow light to the entry of the immigration office. He entered the large room that obviously had employed many but now was void of workers except for one. The clerk, sitting behind a large desk full of scattered papers, was a man of short stature and balding head with round brimmed spectacles resting on his nose. He was dressed in a brown suit and vest with a white shirt soiled and ripped by all the devastation.

The stranger spotted what he thought to be a nameplate lying on the floor. Picking it up, he read the imprint, "Are you Ronald Mikolvich?"

The clerk was visibly stunned that anyone could find his way into the secluded office. "Yes." He was about to say more but his eyes caught the sight of the man wearing the black cape and a Fedora hat pinched in front, covering his eyes. Instantly, Mikolvich recognized the man. In some feeling of confusion he tried to regroup his thoughts. Speaking in a squeaky, raspy voice, "Sorry, I haven't had anyone here for months. You startled me, but I didn't think..."

"Please don't say anything. I will explain."

It had been virtually impossible to obtain any kind of

requests to leave Russia for some time. "I didn't recognize you with the black cape. Forgive my insubordination."

The stranger answered and once again said, "Don't say anything," and then handed him a note. He put his hand to his mouth in an effort to muffle his words. He repeated for a third time, "Don't say anything more." Then without hesitation, he leaned over the desk, decidedly knowing his request could not be denied, "Are you in charge? I need immigration papers. It's all there on that paper and everything you need in the envelope."

In a little more than a whisper, the clerk responded, "Sir, I will do whatever you wish. Do you have these people with you?"

"No, Sir. I am alone but must have these passports completed with the information and pictures attached immediately."

Mikolvich continued to whisper, "You could be under surveillance. You are aware that each of these people should be appearing before me however, I will do as you wish."

The stranger in disguise knew for certain he held not only his own life but also the life of his entire family in the balance.

The clerk read every word written on the note handed to him. Mikolvich understood. He read, *Arrangements for sponsorship to Canada anyway for a family of three and six for France. I will need Passports and Visas for all of them.* The note included, pictures and all the pertinent information.

"I will wait for the completed documents," he quietly said.

"You said five for Canada?"

"Yes."

The clerk turned to thumb through a few stacks of paper. "Well, here. I knew I had this. Canada seems to be open with sponsorships accepting those who apply. It is a Christian group that will sponsor whoever identifies with them. I just have to let them know your people will be at the designated area waiting to be received."

"Use my authorization to make the call to confirm it. I need everything to be completed to avoid facing complications." Again, the stranger insisted he would wait.

"Pray that I'm not intercepted and that the phone still works." With a sigh, Mikolvich picked up the hand set as he waited for the operator to answer. "Nothing is quick anymore."

As early as 1898 there was a telephone exchange system that connected St. Petersburg and Moscow. At this time they were using carbon microphones transmitting and receiving telephone tubes with a switchboard managed by telephone operators to complete the connections.

The clerk stated his need and within a few minutes, he hung the phone back on its cradle. "There was much static on that call. I hope that it wasn't wired tapped." Using the official embosser, the seal was set. He handed the documents to the stranger in the black cape.

"There is a ship for Canada that sails out of St. Petersburg at these intervals. They must be in the area at least a week before it leaves to be approved by the Canadian authorities. It will dock around the dates listed on this paper and stay in the harbor a week while it replenishes supplies and loads containers."

"What if there is a lapse of time before they make it to St. Petersburg?"

"Not a problem. The dates will be slightly different but when they arrive and make contact with the vouchers, the process will begin from there. You must know that each of these people will have to have been approved with medical clearance. Only then will they be permitted to board. I have attached the vouchers to the documents with all the information for them to follow. There is also an address where they will need to report when they arrive in St. Petersburg. Lodging will also be provided for them. All the procedures to follow are on this paper."

"Just so you know, I believe there will be no problem for your 15-year-old, should he have to board the ship to France alone. The added paperwork I have included would just need to be given to the Shipmaster. They will see that he arrives safely, however it works for the family. That was five for Canada with vouchers and passports. The six for France really won't matter if they choose another country. It may be France, or anywhere. Like you say, who knows anything for certainty anymore."

"We cannot know anything for certain. They will all have to be split up."

"For a man in your position, with this country in such tremendous turmoil, it has to be extremely hard."

The man in the black cape had been a soldier of authority, able to lead militarily and domestically. He had been in charge of an entire nation. He didn't intend to wait for a *few good men* to come to the rescue. He already knew very well the threat of an assassination would be inevitable.

Violence in the streets was now prevalent because virtually no one was listening to the Romanov leadership after 300 years of family rule. Waiting was not an option. Abiding his time for the right moment was what he had to do.

"With all the unrest in Russia, I'm surprised anyone was able to get to you for such a request. I think I have already more than 1500 people on a waiting list wanting to leave and hundreds more on a backup list. I'm certain all the Jews in Russia will want to leave but I have been given strict orders to hold the paperwork for them. That brings me to my next question, are any of these of Jewish decent?"

"No Sir. You are to make that assumption, and you have my word. Check the names, and you will see that should not be a problem."

"You would know," he whispered, "as you know thus far, I have been commissioned to comply with your wishes. You must know better than I, your life is in danger, Sir. I had heard you were under house arrest already? To me you still are in power and I will do as requested."

"I need to have all the paperwork completed and with me when I meet up with these people. I have left instructions for them to wait on me."

"With all the confusion, I hope I am in compliance with the Law?"

"Keep up the good work, Mr. Mikolvich! You have served me well and I shall not forget what you have done for me. Should I need your services in the future, I will send a messenger."

"Okay, Sir, I have put the paperwork in this envelope for your convenience. There are passports for everyone with the names and pictures you gave me." Then turning, "See those cameras in the corner? I had already pulled the plug on all of them, but tried to give the appearance that looters ripped them out. If they buy into that, I don't know." He continued speaking in a whisper. "I don't know if I missed any."

They both stood when the clerk added, "God go with you and keep you safe."

In a matter of moments, he left the office the same way he entered, the black cape over his shoulders, hat over his eyes.

The clerk busied himself sorting paperwork to stash them in some order. He was about to close shop when suddenly, in less than five minutes, he heard a disturbance and then shooting. It had to be on the outside of the building. Though, visibly shaken by the horrifying sounds, not knowing if the man he had just helped might have been killed, he continued to busy himself sorting. What could he do?

Outside the building the stranger in the black cape was

about to mount his horse when he could clearly hear the gunfire whizz by him and then the command was bellowed out.

"Stop! We order you to halt!"

He dared not comply. Making a run for it was his only choice. His life might be in jeopardy but all he had accomplished would be for nothing if he stopped. Swiftly mounting his horse, leaning to the left, another bullet flew by his head. "It missed again." That wasn't the end of flying bullets. Another hit its target as blood ran down his face. The stranger in black held the reins with all of his might. The frightened horse galloped away as he clung to the saddle, praying his horse would know the way. It seemed to be impossible for him to lead.

Chapter 8
Hiding the Evidence

Hearing the commotion of gunfire, Ronald Mikolvich grabbed the paperwork stashing it into an empty box under his desk. If any of the Revolutionaries were to find them, in particular his latest entry, it would mean the end of everything for the stranger and his family. His own life was on the line for granting those passports and visas. To keep calm, Mikolvich continued with the sorting of forms that lay amid the mess he hadn't had time to work through. He heard more commotion. It sounded as though a part of the building was collapsing behind him. Without any warning, three armed Soldiers burst into his office.

The clerk stood up. Surprised at the sight of them, "How did you get in? I thought the only way in anymore was through the front door. The back door has been jammed for months."

"Never mind that. Tell us, who was the man dressed in black? What do you know about him?"

The clerk responded, "The man in the black cape? I advised him there was a freeze on all paperwork to be processed. Then he left."

"We ordered him to stop. He refused, so we shot at him but it appears he left on horseback. In the event he returns because of his injuries, he is to be detained. There should be a red button in the planter, hit it and someone will be here immediately."

The clerk made no response, realizing the soldier hadn't noticed the wires lying beside the planter.

"What kind of information did he come for?"

"Like I already said, I told him there was a freeze on exit visas." He drank the left over cold coffee to keep his nerves steady.

"Have you granted any paperwork recently?"

"I think everyone is beginning to understand. If they insist, I jot down their names with information and promise when the processing begins, they will be notified. I do believe I'm following my orders as given to me."

"You are to grant no more immigration papers to anyone from this time forward. Anyone wishing to leave Russia must register on this new form I'm giving you." The Soldier handed the form to the clerk.

"When all is settled, the papers will be processed. For those who do or have already signed up, transfer that information onto this form. We will be back to take all the information from you and we will personally process them. You heard your orders?"

"I certainly did and will comply. Thank you for your update."

The soldiers sloppily fumbled through the papers on the clerk's desk. Horrified, the clerk tried hard to hide his fear as they continued to pick up the papers. If they were to find the box under his desk, they would know he was lying. They would find everything.

It was apparent the soldiers had no idea what they might be looking for as they threw the papers back on his desk in a heap.

"Can't you be neater than that? This is an order, clean up your desk!" Without hesitation, "We will be back tomorrow and expect the forms completed."

The clerk objected, "All 1500 names and more?"

"Have them completed even if you have to stay overnight to get it done."

One of the soldiers began looking around the room. "What happened to all the cameras?"

"This place had been already looted when I arrived here this morning."

"Get someone in to repair them, tonight. Remember, we will be back tomorrow. Do you understand?"

"You may be assured of my cooperation. You said you'd return tomorrow? Afternoon or evening?"

"Never mind about that. Be ready."

The soldiers left his office the same way they came.

Any more of this and I'm a dead man. I'll probably soon be a dead man anyway, might as well help where I can. Pausing for a moment, *I can't tell if the noise I hear is now them returning or leaving? I need to get out of here!* With the box from under his desk, under his arm, he quickly made his way out of to his car. *I hope that I didn't leave any names behind.* He slid the box on the seat next to him.

Looking from left to right and around the outside of the building, he could see nothing. *They said they shot the man on his horse but the horse took off. I don't see him anywhere. Please God protect him for only you can keep any of us safe now.* The clerk made his way to his only transportation, a badly beat up Russo-Balt. He hadn't been able to fill the gas tank for a long time so he knew there would only be enough to reach his home. This time he hoped it would be enough fuel to take him to the train station. The car sputtered and spat but chugged along as best it could. It bobbed along the bumpy road and then stalled out. In his anxiousness, he flooded the engine. This meant all he could do was wait. He didn't have time for that but wait he did. The last thing he needed was someone to offer assistance, which was just about to happen. *Oh God, let it start! If I'm searched and questioned, they'll find the box of forms completed by people wanting to leave Russia. I won't stand a chance. This time it won't be just me in trouble, it will surely be the Czar and his entire family as well as all the other applicants. Please, God, a soldier is starting to head my way.* On his next try, the car started. It chugged all the way to the train station.

The train station was built between 1914 and 1918 in the Byzantine Revival style situated in the 167-ft. high clock tower. Originally it was named the Bryansk Station. Considered an important landmark of architecture and engineering of the time designed by Ivan Rerberg and Vladimir Shukhov. The station's building was flanked by a gigantic landing platform that was distinguished by its simplicity and constructive boldness. The platform was covered by a massive glass arch structure 1,053 feet long, 157 feet wide and 98 ft. high. The parabola weighed 1250 tons. Somehow this station had been spared from all the destruction.

The clerk knew he could stash the strong box in a corner of such a massive building with the likeliness of it being found very remote. Not only was the army in disarray but so was the inside of this train station. Should the country possibly be given back to the Romanov Dynasty, it wouldn't matter that it would be found. Until then, disarray was an extreme advantage.

It was a welcoming sound to hear the train in the distance for soon he would be boarded and off to Germany where he would reconnect with his relatives. He had no living relative in Russia so this would be a well-timed reunion for him. Carefully, looking in every direction again, for Mikolvich knew that even boarding the train could be dangerous if a soldier wanted to make trouble.

Just as he suspected, a couple Soldiers standing around idly decided to commission themselves the authority to inspect passengers upon boarding the train. This wasn't a good sign. Within minutes, the soldiers attempted to frisk a passenger standing directly in front of him. A scuffle broke out as the man tried to escape the clutches of the two Soldiers. Choosing not to stand by and watch the fight, Mikolvich grabbed his belongings, walked around them and boarded the train. He knew his paperwork was in order since he had done that himself. Attempting to keep out of sight he made his way through the rail cars mingling among the passengers. Looking through the windows it was evident that the scuffle continued as the train began moving. He sighed in relief. He didn't need unauthorized inspectors before he reached his destination. He did know very well there could be more searches before he would reach his own town but only God could help him now.

Chapter 9
Being Detained

The Emperor was nearing the vicinity of Czarskoe Selo when unexpectedly a platoon of Soldiers broke in front of him.

"State your destination!" they shouted.

"I live not far from here, just a few miles, near Czarskoe Selo." Nicholas was fully aware that if these men discovered his identity, the paperwork he had obtained would be nothing more than incriminating evidence including the hope of escape for him and his family. It would include everyone he had involved in his plans for an attempt of a getaway.

"The side of your face is bleeding. How did it happen?"

"Caught in cross fire."

"I'm not surprised if you live near the imprisoned Palace."

The stranger in the black cape hoped his disguise would keep him from being recognized as the Soldiers began forming a circle around him.

"You know it's dangerous."

"As I said, I was caught in cross fire. I was fortunate. It seems to be happening a lot these days."

"I'm surprised you didn't get yourself killed. Do you wish us to escort you to a Doctor?"

"Not necessary, I believe I can take care of myself."

"You are a brave man, that is a serious graze."

The leader of the pack broke up the enclosure, "Let him go." With that, the Soldiers rode off.

That was a close call. Now the problem would be to take his detour to deliver some of the immigration paperwork to his trusted confidant, Jacob, his vineyard right hand man and the very man that took care of his youngest children anytime they were ill. Jacob had known for some time that the assassination was becoming inevitable, the reason a plan had been devised. Jacob had been waiting for the final instructions. This was to be the day but Nicholas needed to be certain that no one had follow him. He held his horse back, waiting until the troops were at a great distance. Finally, everything around him was settled and quiet.

First, he rode off into the city to find a hotel where he could take care of his blood-stained head. Jumping off his horse, he walked to the hotel's horse stall when a stable boy stood there ready to care for his horse.

Nicholas walked through the doors to the entrance, approaching the Hotel attendant behind the desk, "I'm looking for one night."

"Sir, you are bleeding! Can I call a doctor for you?"

"No, just a room and I promise not to contaminate the sheets. I merely have to wash this cut and clean it. An overnight rest would be helpful."

"Your room number is 17, please sign the register. Take this bandage stuff, maybe it will help."

Nicholas signed the register using an alias and paid the bill in advance.

"Enjoy your stay Mr. Aaron. May I ask, with a name like that, are you not Jewish?"

"Would there be a difference? No Sir, I'm not a Jew. Does my name throw you off?"

"Just merely a question."

"Be assured, I'm not a Jew. I'm a faithful Russian. Я Российская."

"You speak excellent Russian. I just wondered about your name. If you need anything more, just call the front desk and we will be glad to assist. I will summon a doctor for you. It is my duty to report that flesh wound."

"Please don't. I will be fine."

Nicholas entered his room when it occurred to him the attendant was unnecessarily concerned. This could not be good. He quickly cleaned his wound when his eyes caught the sight of a tiny blinking red light hidden in an artificial plant on the nightstand next to the bed. He knew instantly the camera was there to see and hear everything that would happen in his room. Had he already been recognized? He determined the best decision would be to leave his room before the doctor would arrive. It didn't take but a few minutes putting the temporary bandage on, sitting for a brief moment. *I can't stay.* He quickly laid the key on the bureau, quietly made his way down the hall to the fire escape staircase. Beginning his decent down the stairs, he turned to look at his door. He hesitated on the stairs catching sight of a man, carrying a leather attaché case, knocking at door number 17. Hesitating for a moment, the man pulled out a revolver.

Not good. Nicholas continued down the stairs, out the back door, undoing his horse without waiting for the stable boy.

"Leaving so soon?" The stable boy stood next to him, watching.

"If anyone asks, tell them you didn't see me leave. You were busy. Here, take this. He handed the boy a few rubles.

Nicholas was off again. This time he needed to get to Jacob's home. It was just a few miles away where he found Jacob working in his own vineyard.

Still mounted on his horse, "Can't stay Jacob, but here is the paperwork you will need."

"What happened to you? Come in, my daughters will see to that wound."

"Can't. Don't have the time. Take a look at the information I just gave you and I'll have to be off."

Jacob opened the envelope, "You don't need to leave me any money. We will be okay. I have an inheritance of a gold bar that should take care of us including Anastasia."

"Here's a map, instructions, and passports. Once you arrive in Canada, you can send Anastasia to meet us in France. You will find that information as well."

"That's for when we arrive in Canada. Okay," Jacob looked up at Nicholas, "but where is the meeting place?"

"At the Opera dinner dance. You will be performing with your violin as you usually do. I just need to know the dates you perform there."

"Here's an extra schedule. Keep it."

"If no one shows, you know I will come looking."

"Don't do that. It is not my intention to involve you in something I can't control and I'm afraid I couldn't protect you. If it is a no show, there will be another way."

"Remember, I have all the paperwork."

"That can't be helped." Nicholas started to turn his horse around to head back to the Palace.

"Just pray that the meeting goes as schedule. Go with God."

Riding back to Czarskoe Selo, he realized if Jacob were to come looking, the likeliness of an escape would be out of the question. He could do nothing more. It must go as planned.

Riding past pockets of protestors who seemed totally disoriented, obviously lacking direction and purpose, he couldn't help but notice a group of men huddled, sitting on the sidewalk next to a vacated factory. Attempting to avoid any contact, cautiously coming near enough to hear bits and pieces of their cussing but nothing of any value. Suddenly he perked up. He nudged just a little closer with his horse. He still wasn't close enough so he jumped off his horse and strolled down the road with the reins in his hand. With his hat over his face, robed in the black cape he slowly strolled past. They hadn't recognized him so he made his way to the edge of the old damaged building. It had not been too long ago, when in that very building, people were employed to build train engine parts. He moved a bit closer. He heard what he feared.

"You heard they plan to pull the plug on the Czar?"

"Oh yeah?"

"They are planning to move them, then eventually the kill."

"No rescue plans?"

"That's not on the agenda. Just an excuse, they've already found executioners who have been hired to get the job done."

"Why would they do that?"

"None of the Russians have the guts to kill their Czar. Hey, that family has ruled us for at least 300 years. Would you?"

"Not on your life. Rasputin is another matter."

"Can you believe a man that used to rule over all of Russia is allowing themselves to be held hostage and then to be killed?"

"Not very smart. Think about it, he did everything Rasputin asked him to do. They couldn't figure out that Rasputin was a traitor and a spy?"

"You could blame the Empress. Everyone knows she believed Rasputin had mysterious healing power so she figured he could do no wrong. She always thought that God told him what was the right thing to do. Instead, spies took that information to defeat our country."

"Don't think Rasputin was a spy. He might have been a traitor but not a spy. I didn't think he was clever enough for that."

"That might be but the spies got him intoxicated and then interrogated him for the information from the Empress."

"The word on the street is that he attempted having an affair with the Empress."

"Do you think she did?"

One of the men answered, "I'll bet she did."

"I don't know and I still feel that they were dealt a bad blow but how could she accept an individual like Rasputin? It's because of that man we have lost our Country."

"I just think they are all corrupt."

That was about enough for Nicholas. He was certainly capable of killing all of those men but what would that get him? He would be as dead as them and surely his family would die as well. He just knew that Alexandra might believe in *a few good men* to rescue them but this time, as much as he loved his wife, he wouldn't succumb to any of her desires. It was time for an ironclad plan.

Chapter 10
The Forbidden Shack

Anastasia's heart felt heavy, she was fully aware that all was not well. She knew that her mother, the Empress, started a hospital to take care of the wounded soldiers and as a result she had been nursing and caring for them day and night. Some of the time she and her sisters would help. She also knew her brother was not well and had a blood disease that might easily take his life. At the moment, she had put all that on the back burner. Being under house arrest for a young woman wasn't her idea of living life to its fullest. A teenager knows very well that life will soon be over if they can't be somewhere, do something or see anyone besides her own family. By now she had found her way into all the places in the Palace she dared go without being caught or discovered. She crept through the hallway, when she heard the noise of drunken men. They had to be close to where she was. '*I must stay away from there.*' Finally, she found a basement exit door that had not been used for decades. '*What's this, a crow bar? That's just what I need.*' She hesitated, '*That's strange, the door doesn't seem locked, just stuck.*' She pushed harder. '*That wasn't so bad. Almost as if someone else was here first to open the door.*'

The basement was always dark with just a faint light

trickling in from a few small windows at ground level. Anyone could be lurking around in the dark corners if they knew about it. However, this was not the time to entertain fear. It would only get her into more trouble. '*I made it. Outside, at last!*' Fresh air was just what she needed. It felt good to feel all her senses.

For a moment, she sat in the grass. The experience was refreshing. She looked around and noticed the vehicle gate was wide open and it didn't seem as though anyone was guarding it. The breeze felt good but her thoughts wouldn't give her any peace knowing the city was in a state of chaos and she really shouldn't be out in this place by herself. It was no place for a young woman and especially the daughter of the Czar. Sitting there in the high grass, she heard more than once the sound of ammunition being fired dangerously close. Should she run back in?

Suddenly, Anastasia felt movement close to where she was sitting. "What's that?" Another ruffle tickled at Anastasia's feet. Impulsively she looked down. "A puppy? Who let you wander into here? Shush, don't bark." She looked around, "You must belong to someone. Come Puppy, follow me." Anastasia yearned for her childhood when she would have paid no attention to the trouble of the day. If only she could go back but it had already passed her by. At 17 years of age, reality had already become a wicked devise with people out to destroy other people. It was now about to destroy her entire family.

She gently played with the puppy, as her thoughts were racing through her mind. She was never one to back away from anyone who could give her insight to the world's events, and now with a dog to accompany her, why not? "Come on, dog. That sounded kind of strange, you must have a real name. I think I must give you a name. How about a name like, Jimmy? Would you come for Jimmy? You look brown like a Spaniel? Your name must be a Jimmy. That's it."

"Follow me, Jimmy, we are going for a little detour."
Jimmy obediently followed but then wanted to walk over to the
guard sleeping on the ground near the open large gate. "Leave him
alone, Jimmy, that guard has had too much to drink. He's as drunk
as a skunk, he won't even know we are here."

In through the overgrown shrubs, the two were now on
their way to see somebody. "It just has to be okay and I've always
wanted to do this anyway. God has sent a dog for a companion,
hasn't He, Jimmy? How can I question that? We'll go together,
okay Jimmy?" Anastasia talked to Jimmy just like he could
understand her words. After all, Jimmy was following obediently
so off they walked together the short distance.

Anastasia could see the shabby black shack now, just a few
yards in front of her. "See, Jimmy? Gypsy Wanda lives there and
Mother tells me she knows stuff. She says she doesn't believe
anything that Wanda says. Well, she doesn't need to because she
has the crazy man, Rasputin. Still she goes to see Gypsy Wanda.
What for? To come and find out what all the rioting was about and
what was going on in and around our world? I don't exactly
believe her. I think she likes to know the future and maybe I do
too, Jimmy. Wouldn't you like to know stuff like that?"

The two approached the little hut that was overgrown by
weeds and shrubs, almost hiding the run-down black wooden
building. "Jimmy, why would anyone paint a building black
anyhow?" It definitely needed repairs that should take place before
the winter would consume the occupant. Gypsies were never in the
habit of staying too long at one location, so maybe this building
was only temporary, it really looked like it. Gypsy Wanda's arrival
always came with the blowing of the wind in the spring and then
she would be gone for the winter. Where to? Who ever knew?

"I do hope, Jimmy, that Gypsy Wanda is home and lets me
to talk with her." Anastasia knocked hesitantly, knowing she had

reached the forbidden shack. She should never have come. It was
getting eerie, more like another time and era. Anastasia tapped
lightly at the door. Then heard the shuffle of feet with the rumpling
of curtains. She saw the shadow of a face in the window. Suddenly
the door creaked opened just a tiny bit, "Anastasia! What are you
doing here?"

"You must be Gypsy Wanda? How would you know who I
am? I've never been to see you before."

Gypsy Wanda repeated herself, "Anastasia what are you
doing here? Everybody knows who you are. It can be dangerous
coming to see me. You'll get yourself killed!"

"Oh, you're not that far from the Palace." Anastasia
answered naively.

"You never know who could come by and find you here!
This is a wicked world, young woman, you need to take your dog
and go home!"

Immediately, as though Jimmy had been given a command
to retreat, he started to run across the field. "Jimmy, come back
here. Jimmy, come back here!" There was no calling Jimmy back
to anything, he didn't intend to obey Anastasia.

"I'm sorry, Anastasia, I didn't mean to scare your dog.
You'll see he'll come back to you on his own. They always do,
animals are just like that."

"Not that dog. He doesn't really belong to me. I just wanted
him to come with me to visit with you. I've never been to a
Soothsayer's home before."

"Don't ever come back, either." Gypsy Wanda looked at
Anastasia puzzled. "Did your Mother send you?"

"Oh, no. She has no idea I'm here. Please don't tell her or I
will be in much trouble. Why do you ask?"

"It's very dangerous, you can't be coming here like this."
Seeing the disappointment on Anastasia's face, Wanda beckoned,

"Come in for a cup of tea and then you really must be off before some of the other people begin to drop by. If they find you here, it'll be over for both of us."

It seemed to be a one-room house with curtains for walls. Everything was brightly colored, many shades of red. In the center of a make shift table stood a huge crystal ball. The room was lit with candles here and there. Gypsy Wanda was dressed in a silky looking robe also colored in reds, orange and yellows. Not colors Anastasia was accustomed to. She sat on the chair at the table as Wanda sat across from her.

"What is going on, Wanda?" Anastasia sounded annoyed. "No one really says anything that makes sense anymore. Just like everything is about to be over soon. Everybody seems to be full of fear. Do you know what's really going on? That's why I came to see you. I want to know what's happening. I hear bits and pieces of things from people who walk outside and around our house. They swear and curse at us all the time when they see us. I heard people on the other side of the wall talking about our family. It was all too noisy to hear the actual words, and when they think we might be listening they whisper. I've even noticed that Dad seems angry all the time. Almost in an incoherent mood, like he thinks nothing will work out well. Oh, he tries to pretend all is well when I make inquiry. He seems to be making plans to go somewhere. He said he thinks we are moving soon so I decided I want to know what's happening. You have to know and now I want to know. How do I stay sane when all around you people seem to have gone mad? No one makes any sense about anything."

"My dear young woman, you shouldn't be concerned. Your Father will surely have plans for his family. Soon all this rioting and fighting will blow over now that Rasputin has been assassinated."

"What did you say? Rasputin is dead?"

"You didn't know? That news just came out a few minutes ago. The local newspaper boy always brings me his first copies. Look, it's all over town that he was killed. People hated him so badly and blamed him for our country getting into this situation. You need to know that if you keep your nose clean and stay out of it, do what your parents tell you, you'll get through everything. Just don't get involved. You can no longer be wondering from house to house." Pausing for a brief moment, "I'm surprised to see you here. The word on the *street* is that your family is under house arrest."

"That can't be, Wanda. Dad hasn't been home for a few days now."

Wanda knew that Anastasia wasn't being comforted by any of her conversation.

"Here, give me your hand and let me tell you about your future." Wanda looked for a moment as though she was studying, but the truth was she needed to find an easy way to get Anastasia out of her home before her other clients found the Czar's daughter in her shack. Anastasia was known to have a mind of her own no matter what she had been instructed to do. This was not the time and place to tarry. It could be certain death for Anastasia and surely it would include herself as well. Worse than that, living through it with blood on her hands was not why she did what she did for a living.

Wanda thought that if she could give Anastasia hope for her future, then she would be willing to leave. Surely, her God could have done that for her. Religious people were always saying that God protects them. If they really believed that stuff, why were they coming to see a Soothsayer? Somehow, people want to think Soothsayers know more than God is willing to reveal. Wanda shook her head in dismay.

With Anastasia's hand in hers, Wanda hesitated for a

moment, as she always did to trick people into sensing that she really was able to connect with the spirit world, "I can see in the palm of your hand that you will be getting married in the future. I can see four people. You with a lady friend will meet two young men. When you greet one another to shake your hands will crisscross. The tall blue-eyed man will become your husband. You won't find him in Russia. You will find him in another country, to be sure. That I see is in your future."

"Oh, Wanda, thank you. So I will live through all this?"

"Yes, Anastasia, of course you will. It might not be easy, but you will. Now you must go, you haven't much time to get out of here before dark. If you hear anything, just get down low in the grass until all is clear. Now, run! Go! Please!" Wanda was begging her to leave.

"Thank you, Wanda. I will run. I'm on my way."

Anastasia ran out the door, back into the tall shrubs. She had run about the length of a short city block when she suddenly heard the sound of gunfire. It made her jump, causing her to lose her footing. She stumbled. "My ankle, ouch, that smarts!" Then she felt a wet nose licking her feet. "Jimmy! You're back. Please stay quiet, those are the sounds of gun shots, we'd better lay flat in these shrubs so that no one can detect us." She started praying, "Oh God, don't let them find us here. Do keep Gypsy Wanda safe. If they find me here, surely they'll figure out where I've been." But her ankle hurt. She had to forget about hurting, this wasn't the time to favor her sore ankle.

Chapter 11
Back to The Palace

Riding cautiously, Nicholas reached his destination undetected. There were numerous guards idly standing around the Palace with no obvious focus. Nicholas rode around carefully to find an unguarded entrance when he spotted a drunken guard sound asleep up against an open gate with his rifle lying on the ground beside him. The army for the most part enjoyed looting more than guarding. Looting was the norm and a needed evil to survive since food and money would never reach them as promised. The gate entrance was large enough for supply vehicles to pass through but if the guard should be suddenly awakened, he risked being shot for no other reason than the guard being startled.

He knew this was probably the only entrance he and his horse could easily get through. Nicholas cautiously looked around and saw that the other soldiers were a great distance away, milling around, far enough not to notice. Snatching the rifle, Nicholas slammed the butt against his skull. Dazed for a moment, he gave a few grunts when Nicholas took the rifle one more time giving him a bullet to his head. Quickly, Nicholas walked his horse into the barn without looking back.

Nicholas crept around to see if he could find an unguarded

entrance. Never having the need to hide in the past he didn't know if there would be a hidden door. Then he remembered, many times he had played with his children on the grounds around the Palace. It was Alexei and Anastasia who had noticed the concealed entrance. There it was, that had to be it!

It was heavily covered in foliage and surrounded by bushes adequately disguising the downward stairs. Nicholas hesitated for a moment, then pulled his precious jewel from his cape, "*This is a good place to hide the jewel I've been carrying with me. Too large to keep with me, I think I'll hide it here.*" With his pocketknife he scratched away at the soil, burying it. "*No one will ever find it. Just something that could lure me back when everything settles down. It will still be here, no one will ever discover it.*" Nicholas grinned. It was like a gold mine, if he couldn't have it, why should anyone else? He walked down and pulled at the door. '*If no one knows about this door, how come it opens so easily?*' What was he about to face now? He hesitated for a moment, turned the handle, opening it slowly. A small amount of light trickled through the tiny basement window as he waited for a moment until his eyes refocused. '*Why did the door appear to have been opened recently?*' He turned to focus on his surroundings when he spotted the crowbar lying next to the door. Carefully he checked the bottom floor, examining empty boxes that had been shoved about. To his satisfaction, there was no one else in the room.

Nicholas had become the Czar of Russia in 1894 inheriting a nation undergoing massive changes. It was a known fact that unlike his father, he preferred to be a family man instead of the Czar of Russia. He had four daughters, of whom Olga was the first born in 1895, Tatiana 1897, Maria 1899, Anastasia 1901, and one son, Alexei 1904.

At this time the French and other European countries had been financing the industrialization of Russia, causing serious social problems in the cities. Czar, Nicholas II had tried to address the concerns of the workers, however, his advisors had chosen to disregard his wishes and ignore the demands of the people. Then, to increase the turmoil of the country Alexandra insisted that Nicholas II follow the advice of Gregory Rasputin, the self-proclaimed healer and womanizer who claimed to know what the will of God was for the Country. Time would tell and now disaster had overtaken the Romanov family.

Rasputin's influence over Empress Alexandra, and consequently the Czar, had grown stronger ever since 1912, when the heir to the Throne, Alexei, nearly died from an injury while the family was on vacation at a hunting lodge. He suffered from what was believed to be hemophilia at the time and later determined to be thrombocytopenia. The bleeding grew steadily worse until it was assumed that Alexei would not survive. Alexandra had heard from a dear friend that a peasant Monk possessed healing powers. Desperate, Alexandra called her close friend, a mistress of Rasputin, to pray for the healing of their son. The reply came back from the Monk, who is quoted as saying, "God has seen your tears and heard your prayers. Do not grieve. The Little One will not die," but with advice that Alexei should be kept still. According to medical belief it is surmised that the hemorrhage stopped the next day when the boy began to recover from the advice to keep the boy still, allowing him to rest rather than constantly moving him in an attempt to relief the accumulation of blood clots. In ignorance, Alexandra took this as a sign that Rasputin was a mystic and that he could perform miracles. As a result, for the rest of her life she would defend him and turn her wrath against anyone who dared to question him. To her, a Monk with such abilities could surely do no wrong.

Alexandra was now satisfied with Rasputin's comforting advice and constant presence over her children, so she convinced

Nicholas II that he should run the country from the front lines. It should be him to receive the glory from the people in the winning of the battles. Since his strong point had always been to be with his troops, he complied. In an autocratic regime, it was assumed then that the spouse would keep the home base together. Usually it would go according to the Czar's instruction but for Alexandra, she implicitly trusted the Monk, Rasputin. Nicholas begged her not to share military secrets with Rasputin but her trust was too intense. She believed he had all the answers and was the instrument for survival through the war.

However, Rasputin lived a double life. He drank heavily, carousing around town with not only beautiful women but also very powerful women. Often, he was accused of seducing important women whose spouses had notable positions in Government. It has been said of him that often when women came to Rasputin to be prayed for, he would seduce them saying they must submit to him in order for their prayers to be answered.

This didn't stop there, on a regular basis, spies would pay for his alcohol consumption, and in turn, he gave them military secrets that Alexandra had confided in him. As the bribery money kept flowing to Rasputin he began challenging Alexandra to heed his demands of how to run the country.

As the war was being fought against Germany, Empress Alexandra, being a German woman, gave cause for skepticism as to her loyalty. Many times, she wavered. As a result, Alexandra would allow Rasputin's demand for unlikely personnel to be put into power in positions they were incapable of commanding. The Empress pleaded with Nicholas II, using the excuse that Rasputin had threatened God's punishment, if he didn't comply. Alexandra would reason, how could a Monk pray for healing and it be granted, not be the wisest man in the world? Surely, he must know best what God's will for the country was.

How could she know that Rasputin had been partying with spies? Her interest in mysticism mentally allowed her to accept anything from him. As a result, she was deceived into destroying the dynasty by heeding to the wishes of Rasputin. By the time Nicholas was ready to work with the wishes of the people through what was called the Duma or the representatives for the voice of the people, the damage was already done.

Eventually Russia was run by incompetent leadership, which in turn brought on the shortage of food supplies. No one cared enough to complete the task of transporting food supplies, not only for the troops but also for the people. The industrial revolution was at a stale mate as people had no jobs and no food. Starvation and diseases broke out everywhere.

Extreme anger at Nicholas's failure to act and the damage that Rasputin's influence had done to Russia and the Monarchy was now causing the Revolution to turn against the Romanov's.

Chapter 12
Where to Turn

It was February 1917 with two Revolutions erupting in
Russia was now changing the entire country from being under
autocratic leadership with the Romanov Dynasty to a Provisional
Government that resulted in the Bolshevik taking power. On
International Women's Day, 90,000 women took to the streets to
demonstrate because of the poor working conditions they had to
endure while their husbands were fighting in World War I. The
very next day another 150,000 workers joined in the protest. It
wasn't very long until the entire city of Petrograd was almost
entirely shut down with no one going to work resulting in factories
being closed. Even the police soon joined in the demonstrations.
Nicholas II was not in Petrograd so he calculated it to be a limited
situation and chose to ignore it. By the time he realized the reality
of the situation and was willing to concede to changes, his cabinet
chose to ignore him. By March 2 the Czar's rule was over with
Nicholas II abdicating the throne for both he and his son. By
October of that year the Bolsheviks started the first Communist
Country in history.

It was under these circumstances that the Czar's family had

been put under house arrest to await the decision of Moscow to allow them to leave for an unknown location to live in exile.

Olga, Tatiana, and Maria were anxious, knowing their situation couldn't improve.

Tatiana broke the silence, "I don't understand that we are just sitting here, doing nothing."

"Remember, we're under house arrest." Maria knew what that meant.

Alexei said, "How things have changed. You can't trust anyone. Everyone is out to kill anyone that might have something to do with us. The rumors on the street claim the Jews are behind all this unrest in the cities. That can't be good for Jacob."

"Can't be true of him. Dad depended on him for more than just his vineyard."

"We had some good times at the vineyard with Jacob and his girls, Tina, Lena, and Susana."

Alexandra was quiet for she knew that if she and Nicholas were to come up with a plan of escape, it would have to be for more than just to save their own family. It would have to include Jacob. She hoped he could become one of the *few good men* that could help to rescue them.

"Nicholas always does what I say, so I'm convinced he will have a plan of escape for us. So far he has been able to get what we need in spite of the so-called *house arrest*."

"I suppose Dad, as the Czar of Russia, could do anything. Then, the other question is where can any of us go and be safe?"

"What do you suppose about the Americas?" was Tatiana's question. "They've already established their freedom from Britain which could make it a safe haven."

"How do we get him to leave with no home for his destination?"

This was to be a serious concern for any Jew, let alone a

man of his stature. He had been an outstanding man that was known to make peace in impossible circumstances. He had been an extremely valuable member of society, especially for the Czar of Russia.

Though he was known to the public as taking charge of numerous responsibilities including the Czar's vineyard, yet the most prominent was the fact that as a revered elder of his church, there was a great demand for him as a counselor. There was no other person who could diffuse the local community as Jacob.

"I have my fears for Nicholas. He has been gone too long." Alexandra continued, "Girls do whatever you can to prepare for what is to come."

"Mother!" Alexandra didn't wait to answer any more questions. She left as though she was busily settling affairs in the household for what might be the last time. Truth was, she knew the soldiers were waiting for Nicholas and he had not yet returned. She didn't want to answer for the family. She had done enough and in reality, no one cared for her opinion any more, nothing up to this point had worked. The answers, this time, would need to come from the Emperor not the Empress.

Olga insisted, "Mother, what do you want us to do now?" Alexandra was already out of the room as the door closed behind her. For the moment, she was safe.

Within minutes, a Soldier appeared in the room unannounced, "Where is the Czar and the Empress?"

In terror, the girls moved to the corner of the room. Olga was the first to answer. "They should be here shortly."

He stormed out of the room. Finally Alexandra returned.

"The Red Army Soldier was just here demanding to see both you and Father. He hasn't returned yet. I'm guessing he should be back soon."

"Nicholas should've been back already. He'll know what to

do." She disappeared again.

The girls continued, "Don't we need to prepare for what is to come? Besides, since we are under house arrest, instead of just sitting here grumbling about our circumstances, let's get busy." Olga was convinced they needed to act accordingly.

"I thought there was an upcoming Opera?" Tatiana asked.

"That has to be out of the question now, don't you think?" Maria responded.

"You could have fooled me. There is no one guarding us, we could just leave for all anyone would know. Why do we wait?" Tatiana was serious.

"Apparently, they aren't very good at watching over anyone under their *infamous house arrest*, otherwise we wouldn't be going and coming. We wouldn't have house guests, like Rasputin." Olga believed she knew what she was talking about.

"I didn't know Rasputin was coming. Are you not feeling well, Alexei?"

"I'm fine."

"Then why is that idiot healer coming?"

"Ask your mother."

Olga just had to say it, "She's probably at the soothsayer finding out our future."

"I call it *Wanda the Gypsy story teller*. That woman will do and say anything for a few coins. You'd be surprised how many people believe in that stuff. Anyone with any common sense would know they give bogus thinking patterns of life then throw in an untruth about future issues and you are a happy person. It's just a way for you to go get rid of all your money." Alexei wasn't a believer in mystics.

"Don't you believe in Rasputin's healing power?"

"No, I don't. I believe in the power of God. I think He is our only Healer."

By now Tatiana was curious, "Then why are we supporting and calling for Rasputin all these years?"

"Don't know, ask your Mother."

Tatiana answered, "I don't know either, but does anyone believe that God can heal, anymore?"

Maria, responded, "Seeing what you, Alexei, go through and knowing that your illness is such that it kills many people, I guess that makes me want to believe that God is still alive and very much in control. It is disappointing, that Mother has to visit soothsayers, though. Surely she should know that God is our refuge and that He will see us through all of this."

Alexei couldn't keep quiet. "Mother's soothsayer is Rasputin. She hangs on to his every word. Anything he says goes. Nothing more, nothing less."

"I've heard her say, she wants to hear what Gypsy Wanda is saying about the climate of the people. Then Mother swoons over Rasputin as though he were God Himself."

"Are they about to kill us now or later?" Olga continued, "I know she wants to know what will happen tomorrow but God just doesn't reveal that to us. Gypsy Wanda pretends to. Problem is, people listen to her and then thinking what she told them will happen, they tend to make it their business and make it happen."

Alexei added, "That makes Satan happy, not us. If we follow that path, we become a very unbelieving people and all it does is put more fear into us. God does not promote fear."

"I hate to bust your sermon, but we need to get on with it. Alexei, how about getting our dresses from the closet and bring them to us. We need to get working." Olga was insistent.

Maria opened the door. Then looked down the corridor where she saw one of the servants coming toward her running, "Someone just broke into the wine cellar!"

"Did you hear that?"

"Now what do we do?"

Alexei piped up, "If they've entered the wine cellar, what are we worried about? That should buy us some time."

Tatiana added, "If they've tasted the wine, they'll all be drunker than skunks and not only that, they will experience the greatest hangover in history."

Maria answered, "If it's the Bolsheviks drinking our wine and doing the pilfering, maybe they are coming to rescue us. I heard they want us alive."

"Don't be so sure about that. I'm not sure about Lenin. He's not a person to be trusted under any circumstances. He'd just as soon get rid of us now rather than later. Every one of them is now a traitor. Going back to that batch of brew, all I can say is that there's enough wine in that cellar to keep the best people with the best intentions, drinking for some time. Sadly enough, that was the best wine we've ever had. The best crop Jacob has ever made. He surely has the knowledge and ability to make the crops produce."

Olga remarked, "Realize how big this house is, the wine cellar is a long way from our section of the Palace. We all know this building has over 1500 rooms and 117 staircases. The front is 500 feet long and 100 feet high. Then there are solid locked doors to break through. No, we can be safe for a while but we better have a plan."

"Here's an idea, we have valuables that we need to keep because whether we like it or not, poor is poor. We have means, so we need to be wise with our possessions."

"How cold, Tatiana. What good are our belongings now?"

"Hold that thought for a moment. Why don't we fasten our jewels into our under garments?"

"Why not just sew them into the hem of our dresses?"

"Using our dresses might not be smart. What if we have to change from what we usually wear? If we have to sneak out of here, we won't be wearing our good clothes. We will need our street clothes and who knows, we may have to wear stuff that's not even fashionable." Maria was convinced.

"God forbid, we will have to stoop to that."

"Get a grip Olga. I want to live so I will do anything to get out of here. If I had my way, we would split up and sneak out already. I just don't trust anyone and I don't know why we are waiting here."

"Get real, Tatiana. With the killing and flowing of blood on the streets, there is no such thing as mercy. Let's just start the sewing. Does anyone know where the needles and thread are without alarming our servants? This has to be top secret. We never know who will talk to the enemy. We don't even know if we are fighting against the Bolsheviks or the Communists."

"Tatiana, I don't really think there is a difference anymore and what makes you think we can get away with this?"

"I don't know, but we need to try. The world has suddenly changed from the rich being filthy rich to the poor wanting everything we have. I've always thought that not heeding to the wishes of the poor would become our downfall. Now the rich are too rich and the poor are too poor. That's what all the demonstrations are all about."

"Think about it, Olga, instead of fighting for individual freedom, they fight for sharing the wealth from the wealthy. Isn't that called redistribution?"

"It started out for better working conditions but no one was listening."

The number of escaped serfs and poor Cossacks was growing quickly. The autocratic rule in society felt the poor lacked the intelligence to deal with better conditions and they should continue to do as they were commanded. In those days, they lacked a leader who could unite them in attacking and plundering the

State. In the past, their man was Stepan Razin, who became to the poor a type of Robin Hood. Now the laborers wanted better working conditions but the same autocratic leadership wasn't listening so as a result in came Stalin and then Communism with all the promises they had wanted.

Tatiana insisted, "Let's get our jewels and money sewn into our under garments in a hurry. Alexei, why don't you find us street clothing, not to our liking but what will wear and last."

It wasn't long before clothing was spread all over the floor. Alexei brought in more than anyone could wear.

"Oh, here comes Mother. She looks rushed or just very worried, something is definitely wrong."

Alexandra, stood still for a moment, "What are you people up to? What is going on?" The Empress was truly disgusted. "You are worried about clothing? Let me tell you something, there is a war out there. We are the prime target and all you can do is gather up clothing?"

"Mother, we know all that but we don't intend to sit here and wait for the inevitable. You just told us to think of something we could do. We are sewing jewels, money and anything we can think of, into our under garments. We are going to escape out of here even if we have to separate and do it one by one." Olga was stating her decision.

"Okay, okay. I get it but I'm sure Father will have a more secure plan when he comes. There just has to be a *few good men* out there to rescue us."

The Empress starting to look around knowing that someone was missing, "Where is Anastasia?"

Chapter 13
Facing the Inevitable

Anastasia came bursting in the door with Jimmy following behind her.

"Anastasia, where have you been? We've looked all over for you. Don't you know we are to stay in the house and in our compound? How did you get out and where did you go?"

"There was no one to stop me so I left, Olga, and so when I was out and about, I found Jimmy. He followed me home."

"Did you ask Mother if you could keep him?"

"Please don't send Jimmy away. He doesn't have a home anymore so that's why he followed me."

Jimmy's wagging tail immediately won everyone over. It changed the mood for the family. A dog was a welcome relief. Dr. Botkin, their long-time family physician, disappeared momentarily returning with a leash he had found. "Here, Anastasia, you can keep track of your dog when you walk him."

"Thank you, Doctor." Turning to her Mother, "Please, Mother, can I keep Jimmy?"

"Just take care of him. See that his needs are met."

Everyone was quite pleased to have a dog join the family. It lifted the black cloud hanging over them, if only for a moment.

That soon changed. "What's that noise? Someone's coming through the door." Maria was frightened to be sure.

"It's your Father." Turning to Nicholas as he came through the door, "What happened to you? You've been shot!" The Empress appeared shaken. She saw the blood seeping through the gauze he had on his head. It was now running down the side of his face. "Oh, God help us! Are you all right?" Trying to catch her breath, "Who shot you? Girls, go ask the servants for first aid bandages."

"Let me take care of him." Dr. Botkin grabbed his medical bag and began pulling out his necessary medical supplies.

"Don't worry, Alexandra. The bullet only grazed my forehead. I'm fine, just needed to wipe the blood off my face."

"Where were you? We've been worried sick about you. Some of the soldiers said that you had been detained."

"Any closer and we would never have seen you again, Dad." Tatiana was seriously concerned.

"Don't worry about me. I've been in more battles than I care to remember but I don't usually get caught this way. When I'm on the front lines, my men do the fighting. This was a little too close but I had to get to the offices before they were shut down totally." Then he told of the incident with the soldiers.

"Fortunately, the Red Soldiers lack experience. That is working to our advantage for now. Once they figure out what house arrest is supposed to mean, we will have something to worry about."

"I have news for you, they have begun to close in on us. We need to prepare for the inevitable. So far they just keep us under surveillance." Dr. Botkin was worried.

Nicholas appeared to be somewhat concerned about what he was to say next. He turned to Dr. Botkin, "Now we have another problem. Typhoid has already broken out and is having devastating effects. It hasn't reached this far north yet, but it certainly could."

"I think that's why we now have a water treatment plant. Wasn't that supposed to curb the outbreak?"

"We do have that, but with the devastation of war all around us it still seems to be causing another very serious outbreak."

Dr. Botkin seemed totally informed, "If the soldiers would pick up the dead and wounded, maybe the outbreak wouldn't be so bad. I know dealing with the wounded and dead is no easy task. There never have been any plans in place to remove those bodies from the streets. The citizens are just beginning to come out to clean up the roads and bury the dead. Fortunately, they look for family members of the dead so that they can be notified. Eventually the disease will affect everyone, even where we are." No one commented about the death threat of the disease.

The servants, as always served dinner for the family and as everyone was seated, the Empress began the discussion, "Nicholas, I did the unthinkable today, I went to see Gypsy Wanda."

"Alix." Privately, Nicholas would call Alexandra, Alix. It was what he called her during their courtship. When she became Empress, her name was changed to Alexandra. "You are out of your mind. We don't need advice from a devil advisor."

Anastasia sat quietly holding on to her newfound friend, Jimmy. She felt guilty with the mention of Gypsy Wanda. She turned her face to focus on Jimmy. No one would be in the mood for another confession coming from her.

"Come on. Many Kings and Queens, even Presidents seek advice from people like Gypsy Wanda merely because they want *road signs* of what might be happening in the future."

"That's no excuse for us. We need to know better. When do you even have time for such a meaningless thing as that?"

"You weren't coming home when I had expected. I didn't know how long you would be detained. I was worried. I left very early this morning to see Gypsy Wanda. I'll have you know that I had to use the crowbar I found in a back corner not far from the door. It was stuck tight, but the crowbar worked well. It seems no one has been through there for quite a while. By the time I came back the girls were preparing themselves in the event you want us to leave from this place."

"Tell me, Alix, you went through that basement door? That's why it opened so easily when I went through there. You know they could just as easily have shot you. They don't care and they would have had an excuse that you were trying to escape." Nicholas was more than just a little annoyed.

"You're just opinionated about Gypsy Wanda, Nicholas. Not only does she see the future which may be true or not, but she sees informants who want to talk about what they know."

At this point, Olga asked, "Mom, tell us, what did she really say?"

"We all know of the unrest among the people and the rioting but the Bolsheviks are making headway and coming our way. It appears that the whole country is in rebellion."

"I believe the people will come around and settle down." Nicholas was insistent, almost challenging. "We've promised the workers almost all they wanted, why would they turn on us now?"

"Nicholas, the word on the street is that your cabinet isn't communicating your decisions anymore. According to Gypsy Wanda, those you trusted have turned on you. The result is that the workers are saying you have ignored them long enough."

"I saw mutiny when I ordered military force to restore order. I even dismissed the Duma three other times because of that."

"Apparently, the mutinies are spreading."

"That's treason!"

"Surely you are correct but it may be too late to deal with." Alexandra was insistent.

"Too late? Is that what your Soothsayer says?"

The stage had been set, everyone waiting for someone to make suggestions for the next approach. It was apparent now that they needed a way out, but to where? Most importantly, how?

"We need another plan, Nicholas. We should think of leaving if we can."

Nicholas still had the presence of being in command. "The Bolsheviks have always said if we have to leave they will help us escape. It's the Communists that want us dead."

"Dad, I've heard the Communists are also on their way here." By now, Olga was very serious.

"Okay. I still can't accept what you are all saying. I just don't believe it. We made all those decisions and concessions just a few days ago. As the information starts to circulate around, the rioting will subside. You'll see. Furthermore, as you already know, I've been told to ready everyone for a photo shoot. They wouldn't be coming to photograph us if what you are saying is true."

"They already did that once. Why would they do that again? I don't trust them Dad. We need to have another way out!" Olga was very serious. "What if the Soothsayer has heard what really is happening? What if they come to kill us? Are we just to sit tight until their guns are drawn? Dad, help us to get out of here! I don't want to die. You can't tell me any of us want to die."

"Stop it, all of you! We are not going to die."

"Dad, are you saying we just sit here and wait? If the writing is on the wall, where do we go from this point? Is there a place to hide until this all blows over?" shrugged Tatiana.

"You know, Dad, soldiers are already in our wine cellar. I know everything is supposed to be secure but if they got in there, who's to say they won't make it up to our part of the Palace?" insisted Alexei.

Nicholas didn't intend to ignore his only son. "I have a telescope in my study. I'm in the habit of watching to see what is going on in the field. I will know if anything turns bad. If it turns sour, I want you, Alexei to leave with Rasputin."

Anastasia couldn't help herself. "Don't you know, Dad that Rasputin was murdered?"

"Where did you hear that?"

"Everybody knows. It was in this morning's Newspaper."

Dr. Botkin added, "I think she is right. I went to town and bought the Newspaper when I heard people talking about him. It seems it only just happened, not more than a few hours ago. It would have happened after your wife came back from Gypsy Wanda's place. Here, I think I still have it. I stuck it in my Jacket pocket."

Nicholas began reading, "I heard there was an attempt for assassination. Apparently, someone tried poisoning him but that didn't work." He paused for a moment, "They stabbed and then drowned him just in case he still wasn't dead," continued Nicholas as he was reading.

Alexandra gave out a scream. "How can that be? He was a Monk!"

Nicholas was ignoring Alexandra's hysterics, "Okay, we need another plan."

––––––––––––––––––

It was already the next morning and with all that had happened thus far, everyone appeared extremely anxious when one of the soldiers entered their living area, unannounced, the norm for them lately.

"If you like, you may attend the Chapel today. Your Dr.

Botkin has requested that you attend a service at least one more time. Solovjev, from the Chapel will come and accompany you."

This was a delightful change in the stagnant situation they were finding they were in. Walking across to the Chapel would mean they could feel the outside air one more time. Listen to the Priest and participate in Mass. The news gave a slight refreshing feeling for the family as they prepared to walk across to the Chapel.

"Thank the Lord, we can at least go to the Chapel for meetings again. It is an outing." Olga was pleased for this latest privilege.

"Don't be too confident. This might be the last time for any good they plan to show us. Be aware." Dr. Botkin knew what he was talking about.

The girls had already entered the church sitting in the pews awaiting the Priest. Dr. Botkin, Soloviev with Nicholas as well as Alexei and Alexandra lagged further behind. Guards were a few feet away and didn't seem to want to follow the entourage into the Chapel.

Soloviev pulled back from the others, handing Nicholas a note with instructions. Nicholas read it intently, "But I don't have all the information. You know I will not leave any of my family behind."

"We know that but it has to be separate. The less any of you know, the better the chance for survival. You must accept it. If at any time you feel someone is in trouble, you must continue on with the plan or you will die, and it won't be just one of you, it will be your entire family."

Alexandra pleaded, "You must let us keep Alexei with us."

"That cannot be. Have I made myself clear?"

Alexandra was in tears, "I will do as you say."

"Please, no second guessing. Again, I say, you will be

responsible for killing your family if you don't obey. Will you do that?"

"Maybe our captors will release us if we just do as they say."

"The plan is assassination. Allow your family to have a chance at life."

Nicholas asked one more time, "Alix, please, can you trust me to get us through this?"

Reluctantly, Alexandra answered, "I will do what is asked of me. I don't want to but I will."

The plan had been conceived. Could they carry it out? Nicholas turned to Alexei, whispering.

"Dad, I can do that."

Mass was long but the family took in every moment of freedom for they knew it would be snapped away when they would be brought back to house arrest.

"Alexei," Alexandra called, "what are you doing? You will hurt yourself if you play on that dirt pile."

"I'll be fine. I'm following you guys, I'll be there."

The family was back from Chapel, sitting at the dinner table. They were about to have their afternoon meal.

"Where's Alexei?" Alexandra thought it was odd that he had not followed them in.

"He was playing with that stuff we set up for winter sledding," Tatiana continued, "you know what he's like, always messing around."

Finally, Alexei came in, hobbling to his cot next to the window.

"So tell me," asked Nicholas, "you were well when we left. What happened now? Didn't you hear Mother say to stay away from that mound of dirt?"

"I was playing like I always do but somehow I slid down

the side. If it hadn't been for the two-foot rock in my path, I would have been fine. I thought I would just slide up against it, but instead I started to pick up speed sliding down. That's all it took." He looked at his family as he continued to groan.

"Who put it there anyhow?"

Alexandra was convinced he was as bad as he had gotten on their camping trip the first time he had experienced the swelling and bruising. "Who can help us now? No one to pray for him anymore."

"We can," Tatiana remarked. "You all know we can pray and that God answers us when we humble ourselves." They hardly had finished speaking about Alexei's accident, when there was an unexpected rap at the door. Not waiting for anyone to answer, the door opened. Still holding the door knob in his hand, the soldier stood there, "I understand that in a few days there will be a couple of wagons with soldiers here to escort you to another location."

"Why another location? Where are you sending us?" Nicholas was noticeably annoyed.

"We are still waiting for Britain to give us directions when they will be coming for you but so far no answer has come. Meanwhile, you are to be moved to Tyumen."

There was nothing but a dead silence.

"We have a problem with moving to a new location." Dr. Botkin was insistent. "Alexei is too ill to be moved. Look at him."

The Soldier asked, "Doctor tell me, how soon will he be able to leave?"

"This disease can't be predicted. As you know, he is a young boy and can't be kept still when he is well, no matter how we try. This latest event happened when he was playing with the mound of dirt we used for sledding down in the snow. I've seen him down for months, he cannot be moved."

"You are very sure he can't be moved?"

"I would stake the fact that I'm a doctor on what I just said."

"How soon can he be moved?"

"We have to wait and see."

"I will wire Moscow and let them know."

Chapter 14
Sent to Tyumen

The Soldier left to send a telegram to Moscow. "Youngest child too ill. Cannot be moved. Please advise."

A day later, he received word back, "Move Czar only. Will send for others later."

Tyumen, the administrative center of Tyumen Oblast, Russia, is located on the Tura River approximately 1060 miles east of Moscow. It was the first Russian settlement in Siberia. Tyumen covers an area of 91 square miles and its primary geographical feature is the Tura River, shallow with extensive marshlands that crosses the city from Northwest to Southeast. The left bank is a floodplain surrounded by gently rolling hills. It usually floods by the middle of May, causing the river to become 8-10 times wider. A dike was built to withstand floods up to 26 feet high protecting the city.

The Soldier returned to relate the message. "Moscow wants the Czar to be moved to Tyumen alone. The others are to follow when the youngest is well enough to travel."

"I will not let you take my husband alone. If he must go, I

will go with him." The Empress was insistent that she would not allow them to take him from her.

"Do as you please. We are leaving in the morning. Be prepared to leave. Dr. Botkin will stay with the family to care for the youngest. If you wish, you can choose one of your daughters to accompany you."

It was decided that Maria would accompany them.

For the first time, the Emperor and Empress with Maria would travel in two rough flatbed horse drawn carriages that would carry them to their next destination. One had a mattress for Alexandra to rest on. Tyakovlev, the coachman of the leading wagon, invited Nicholas to accompany him up front.

They had progressed a few miles when Tyakovlev and his other coachman signaled to one another. Nicholas's heart sank for a moment. What were they about to do with them? Would they become hostages for ransom? Then what, surely the next step was to murder them. They had been told already, that murder was the plan. He prayed.

"We are taking a detour?" Immediately Nicholas's mind ran into overload, "How will our children find us?"

"They won't."

"What will become of them?"

"I am not privy to that. You may know more than I but I know nothing. You will not know if they are dead or alive."

"Will we ever see them again?"

"Everything will always depend on you people as individuals. We can only give you the possibility but each of you must carry it through."

Nicholas was silent. How would his wife react to all of this? Would she wreak havoc with what none of them could control?

Suddenly they began the detour as Tyskoviev began to

detour the wagons. "We're going through the mountains and then on to Moscow. It will be safer that way."

Nicholas gave a sigh. Should he get to Moscow, he could get asylum and move his family out safely. They rode on for a few miles when without warning a troop of soldiers rushed them. Within minutes they were surrounded.

"What is the meaning of this, Tyskoviev? You were to go to Tyumen."

"It is safer to travel this direction, over the mountains."

"You cannot do that, Tyskoviev. Go to Tyumen immediately. Then you will be taken into custody there."

Moscow ordered an investigation and found that Tyskoviev decision wasn't serious and accepted his explanation. He was again assigned to keep Nicholas, Alexandra and Maria under surveillance while on house arrest at the new location.

A few months had gone by. They had been sitting in the parlor with one another having their dinner in the new environment when one of the Soldiers burst into their presence.

"Your children have disappeared. We were to bring them back today but when the guards entered their living quarters there was no one there."

Nicholas was angered now. "You are telling me you couldn't find them?"

"We scoured the place. They are nowhere to be found."

"What have you done with my children? Have you murdered them?"

Alix had tears flowing down her cheeks, "My children! Alexei, he is not well! He can't even walk. Anastasia has always been ill! Where are they?"

"We hoped you would give us insight. You must know."

"You people were the last to be with them. Tell us what you have done with them!"

Finally, the soldiers left in disgust.

Nicholas walked up to the planter with a beautifully planted fern. He pulled back the leaf, motioning to Alix and Maria. In silence, they understood their plight.

It was early morning with the sun beginning to shine through the well-worn drapes. Nicholas arose and began to dress. Alix sat up in bed, "You're getting up?"

"With our misfortune, surely they'll be bounding through the door with more instructions."

"Probably right about that. Where is Maria?"

"Making breakfast. She likes to do that. It helps her keep sane."

As predicted, the guard managed to barge in. "We will be taking you to Yekaterinburg, where we will await further instructions."

This was not what Nicholas wanted. In that particular city, there was no sentiment of respect for the Czars rule in the last decade. Probably never was and now with the uproar and killing around the area, there could be little chance of escaping. The city had been fed propaganda stating that in spite of the poor working conditions with the people on rations, the Czar and his family were living on caviar and imported wines having no concern about the citizens. The general public in that area, abhorred anyone in power and they would likely have enjoyed killing the Emperor and Empress in cold blood. That was a likely choice if the possibility of an escape was to be thwarted.

Nicholas, Alexandra and Maria were awaiting further news for when they should be leaving for Yekaterinburg, when Tyakovlev appeared. He turned to face all three of them while they sat at the table.

"You will come with me. I will be your transport. I can't promise a good ride but it is what it is and we must go. Just bring your essentials. That is all you will need."

Nicholas thought to himself, '*that doesn't sound too good. Does that give us only days? Surely this is the end.*' He said nothing.

The same crude wagons that brought them to Tyumen were waiting for them again. Was this to be the last journey of their lives? Nicholas was not the kind of Emperor who was accustomed to submitting to other people's authority much less abstaining from protecting his family. He had already lost all but one of his children and how was he to stand by and allow his wife and daughter to be murdered? Of course, they would kill him as well. When did a warrior ever just stand still and allow someone to lead them to the slaughter?

He was extremely concerned for Alix. She hadn't said anything and that worried him. She had to feel the same as he did. Still, she remained silent. Did she think this would be her last mile as well? He knew enough to know that God was the only one who could take control of their situation.

"How can anyone ask me to take just enough to hand carry? How can I do that?"

Nicholas looked down on her bags, "That'll be plenty."

No one was graceful anymore. Just commands, everyone gave commands. Commands to do this or to do that, and nothing more. They had no controls over anything. It was just the three of them. Was any of this worthwhile?

"What do you prefer, your Highness? Your wife and daughter travel in the other wagon or with you?"

"With us, please."

"You can put all but one piece of baggage in the other wagon."

"I need all of that stuff." Alix didn't want to let go of anything more.

Tyakovlev insisted, "It has to be done this way. Remind yourself, this is a life and death situation."

Nicholas could only put his arm around his wife. "Just think, Alix, we will make it. You Maria and I will make it."

Nothing more was said about the belongings that would go in their place and that was to Yekaterinburg. "We will be safer this way. We obviously are going another way with a different purpose in mind."

Nicholas asked, "Surely they will know if we haven't arrived at Yekaterinburg."

"Yes, they will. We hope they will be too late, though. We have made a dummy wagon that will arrive in Yekaterinburg. It will only have your baggage and a mattress like we had last time. It will appear that you are all huddled together. Those are stuffed dummies but because of your baggage they will be convinced you are there. We are planning that by the time they make the discovery we will be nowhere to be found."

Alexandra just had to say, "But I need my bags."

Nicholas ignored her, "Where are we going?'

"You will be given those instructions when we arrive at our destination."

They were stone silent for the next few miles as they drove on.

Tyakovlev finally broke the silence and continued to talk. "With propaganda, history will say that you have arrived in Yekaterinburg and then massacred."

So it was a planned massacre. No doubt about it anymore. Alix wanted to scream but her voice was but a whisper, "A massacre ..." her voice faded.

Nicholas added, "That means everyone will assume us

dead."

"That is correct. It is the only way to live."

Alexandra answered, "That means our children will also assume us dead. They will never come looking for us. We may never see them again."

"Please Alexandra." Nicholas didn't know how to console his wife. What could he say? Then he said, "How odd. We have to die to live."

Chapter 15

Disappearance

Dr. Botkin read to the girls and Alexei, as he traditionally had done many times while the guards appeared without being announced, coming and going into every room as they wished.

"You know, Burgess, you keep coming through to our room at will. I have a request."

In a guttural sounding voice, "Don't ask me not to inspect your rooms. We have been ordered to not let you out of our view at any time."

"I know that, but here's a request. You know the family is to be reunited when Alexei can be moved. You also know that none of the family will leave him behind. How would it be if the girls were to attend the live Opera Ball in town? Before you give us an answer, I am pleading with you. None of the girls have been permitted to leave the house in months, how would it hurt? In your mercy, could you make our request known? I believe the Opera is taking place this evening at seven. Could you grant this one last request?" Dr. Botkin, put the emphasis on the *one last request.* "I will be here but will send for a Monk to come in and watch over Alexei and then I will join the girls."

"Who is this Monk you seem to know well enough to come?"

"He is from the Chapel we attended."

He hesitated, "Well." He walked about the room for about five minutes, pacing back and forth clenching his fist, wringing his hands repeatedly. "I just don't know." He went over to the window and looked out into the street. Burgess saw people walking around ignoring the guards. Everyone went in and out, about his or her own business, almost as if nothing were happening. It seemed they had become numb to the events unfolding in history. On the other hand, maybe it was a way of survival. "Well, let me ask." He left.

Finally, Olga asked, "What if he never comes back?"

"He'll be back."

Dr. Botkin continued to read to all of them. It was easy to see that each of them hardly dared to dream of such an outing. Getting out of the home that had become their prison, would it even be a remote possibility?

Finally, Burgess came back. "Your request has been granted."

The girls stood up in anxious delight but dared not show their enthusiasm.

Then the ultimatum was leveled. "There are some conditions you need to know about. The Opera Ball is over at two in the morning. You will not be allowed to stay past twelve this evening. There will be a guard to escort all of you back to the Palace. You cannot stay one minute longer. It would be better if you were at the front entrance by eleven-thirty in the evening."

"The girls will plan on the escort being there for them."

"Tell me, where is the Monk you said will stay with Alexei and just who is he?"

"He will be here shortly. It is Rasputin's brother."

"God, pity you. When he comes, I'm sure we will

recognize him. We'll know him without ever having met him." He repeated, "God pity you."

"Then, if you will excuse us, the girls will need to dress appropriately. Give us some privacy while they dress."

"One more requirement. The girls will be escorted to the Opera."

Olga turned to Dr. Botkin, "Then what?"

"You will be fine. Follow their directions."

The girls dressed in their best clothes to attend the dinner dance. They fussed. Anastasia fumbled around in her belongings for a moment when Tatiana's curiosity was aroused. "What on earth are you doing, Anastasia?"

"Just a doll that Mother and Father gave me a long time ago. I've always kept it with me."

"You can't be taking that. There will be no room for stuff that isn't essential to life."

"I can't give that up. It will always remind me of our parents. I need to take it because it gives me comfort."

Dr. Botkin, spoke up, "Let her keep it. Sometimes things that mean nothing to anyone else can help us in hard times."

Soon their chaperones arrived.

Dr. Botkin called, "Come on, girls. Time for you to go."

"Like I told Burgess, I will come later attend the Opera."

Olga, Tatiana, and Anastasia began to follow their Chaperone with Jimmy in tow. They were about to climb into the back of the Van, when a public disturbance began. A gang of angry people appeared in their path pushing and shoving when Anastasia tripped and fell. She hung on to Jimmy's leash for all her worth. Olga helped her back on her feet. Unexpectedly someone ripped the dog from Anastasia's clutches.

"No, you can't take him, please, he's mine. Don't!"

"Anastasia, don't look. The girls grabbled their sister from the agony of witnessing her dog being torn apart. They couldn't avoid hearing the grueling howl and then the last screeches. It was over. The tears began to come.

"Not now, Anastasia. You can't cry. We have to ask God not to allow us to cry over the life of an animal. You know our very lives are at stake here. Please don't cry. Not now!" Tatiana wiped her tears away and whispered, "Don't shake, you will be okay. You know the plan. Think about the plan."

All she could do was nod in agreement.

The guard belted out in a loud voice, "If it is the Ball you are going to, get in the Van!"

Obediently they climbed in. Then the guard shoved Olga who was just behind her sisters, almost knocking all of them off their feet. They stumbled, as they made their way in to sit on the benches up against the sides of the van. Being herded like cattle was not what they were accustomed to, but they must now accept it as though they were on the way to the slaughterhouse. Their only hope was that they would be delivered to the Opera.

Anastasia couldn't talk. How was she to keep her emotions in check? She knew the plan. It had to be the plan. She would concentrate on the plan.

So the party began.

"Oh, there you are, Anastasia." It was Tina. "Haven't seen you for a long time. I've been looking for you."

"I'm here with Olga and Tatiana."

"Of course. Greetings."

Olga stated, "We have to remember to watch the clock. The guard said we needed to be at the door by eleven or we would be in trouble. Something has to give by then."

"For now, I'm going to have a blast!" Anastasia was

serious now, she would block out everything from her mind. She had already experienced enough difficulties.

They danced and sang with the band. It was a good evening but this time more than ever the girls were immersed with the people in the auditorium. It was apparent that Anastasia had been trained in ballet dancing. She had the grace of a swan moving freely in elegance like never before. Her thoughts had been removed from her murdered dog into the merriment of the moment.

"Anastasia, where did you learn to dance like that?"

"It came with all the tutors we had and didn't always appreciate. Sometimes when I wasn't well or when we all had the measles, Mother would teach yet another dance step. She was good at keeping us enjoying ourselves. She even did that for us when we were under house arrest." Anastasia winched as she thought of their total confinement. Not even a breath of fresh air without the guards surrounding the compound. It was no longer a front yard lawn or a backyard retreat. She shuddered as she shook her body into reality. "It was times like these that we were often taught to dance."

"Come see your *Uncle Jacob*. He's playing the violin over there."

"Yeah, my *Uncle*. How about that." It wasn't long before Anastasia was entertaining the crowd along with Jacob on the violin and she as a soloist. Her voice had the sound of an angel as she sang to the people. The singing and dancing continued for some time.

"You know we've been imprisoned in our home for some time now. I'm so glad to be able to get out. I was hoping the man of my dreams would be here and we'd ride off on a white stallion to live happily ever after. Isn't that how it is supposed to happen?"

"In your dreams, sweat heart. Only in your dreams could

that ever happen. However, you are a Princess, so who knows?"
Tina liked to humor Anastasia. "What kind of man were you
looking for anyhow?"

"Tall, blonde and blue eyed."

"I believe you're adamant about that."

"Well, that is a long story. Let's do some dancing before
the soldiers come around."

"There are some highly recognizable eligible bachelors
here."

Come on Tina, "Not for me, at least my first choice will be
a tall blue-eyed blonde man."

"Stop looking for the blonde men and you will find him
soon enough."

A handsome dark haired man slipped into place, half
bowing before Anastasia. "Please may I have this dance?"

"Of course."

So they danced together as the band played on. A few more
men and a few more dances were now beginning to tire Anastasia.
Taking leave to join up with Tina at their table, she said, "I
enjoyed singing while your Father played the fiddle. Where is he
now?"

Tina chuckled. "Come to think of it, I don't know. He'll be
around soon."

"There are many people, though, so who knows where he
might be."

"Let me get some drinks, I'll be back, just wait for me."

"Tina, look. There he is."

Chapter 16
Leaving

Dr. Botkin began the preparations. "Okay, Alexei. Let's get with it. We don't have much time."

"What if the guards come in before we are finished?"

"They really don't care about you. They think you can't walk anyhow. Let's keep it that way. You can help me with the boxes."

"What's in them, anyhow?"

"It's full of costumes, but really believable costumes."

"What were they for?"

"Masquerades. You remember those events that occurred every year your family attended, a party to dress up as some other fool. Your parents used to enjoy doing that."

Then came the knock.

"Dr. Botkin, I thought you said they didn't care about me." Alexei made a mad dash to his bed, moaning and groaning.

"It's okay, Alexei. It's Dmitri from the Chapel. You met him, Rasputin's brother?"

Dmitri didn't miss a beat. "Let's get the clothing dealt with, they won't wait too long before checking on us if they get suspicious."

Dr. Botkin began with the clothing. "Here put this on"

"What's that?"

"You're a servant girl. That should work."

"Where's your Monk outfit?"

"Here it is. Now I need to include in my bag enough for two Nuns clothing. How do I look now?"

"Very authentic if I have to say so myself." It seemed Dmitri approved, a monk should surely know what would pass inspection. "This could work."

Alexei was curious, "Why only two Nuns? Don't I have three sisters at the Opera?"

"We have to split up. We do have a plan. We have to make the bed authentic as well. Here, use some of this clothing to disguise the bed."

"Sorry, can't do that. We have to make it look like someone kidnapped us."

"Dmitri, won't that make them suspicious?"

"Don't want them to think it was us playing a joke on them. That could make them crazy and just go on a killing spree instead of just becoming suspicious of everyone. Make the bed to appear that someone was in it asleep, but no jokes."

It took Alexei just a few minutes to prepare the bed. After approval from Dmitri, they stood together preparing for the escape.

"I think, Dmitri, you and Alexei need to go out first. The hour is too soon for me to get the girls so I will follow later." Dr. Botkin hesitated, "Our plan is for you to take Alexei to France. You must go through Estonia not St. Petersburg. They'll be watching for you there. Here is the envelope from Nicholas to take care of everything you might need."

"I don't really need anything."

"Take it. You will find complete instructions. As a Monk,

you can go as his guardian."

The two of them began making their way out of the room, looking in every direction. "The coast is clear, Alexei. We have to remember if you hear your name or if someone is talking about you, don't answer. If we mess up ... "

"I know. We will all be dead."

They continued into the hallway when one of the guards met up with them and asked, "Are you not to stay with the boy?"

"Dr. Botkin is with him now. He sent us and my servant girl to get Medicine for him."

"I thought all you needed to do is pray. Not working this time? Couldn't make him walk?"

"I will return. He is in much pain."

"Why do you need the servant to go with you?"

"She is to help me remember all the stuff I will need for the time I'm to spend with the little heir."

"You are such a hypocrite. You claim you can pray for people to make them well but you still need the same things the rest of us need." He shook his head, "Continue." The guard left in a huff.

Silently, they pushed another set of big doors open, walking through the hallways. As Dmitri and Alexei passed by open doors, they could see other servants milling around doing house cleaning in rooms. One of the house cleaners noticed and shouted, "Hey, I need your help. Get in here and help me."

Dmitri answered, "Not now. We are on a mission that needs our immediate attention. She will be back shortly to assist you."

Turning to Alexei, "Great, I think we made it. I will saddle the horse."

"Dmitri, there is a guard at the gate. What do we do now?"

"Watch and listen. You could learn something."

"Stop! I order you to stop!" The soldier demanded. "State your business."

"We need to go to the Pharmacist just around the corner to get medicine for the Heir."

Scornfully the guard said, "Why is everyone so concerned for the Heir. He will die shortly anyhow. Just let him die in peace." He turned away for a moment, then answered, "Continue to your destination." The guard waved them on.

The Guards were mingling around, talking. "Now that the girls are at the Opera, are you going to look in on the heir?"

"Why waste the time. It was fun to disturb the women but they are gone for a few hours. When they return, our fun will continue again."

"I'd like to get one of them alone."

"There will be time. Just before we have to take them to the Emperor and Empress in Tyumen, we'll get at them."

"Come on, we have to get out of here. Alexi, think you can hang on. "

"I'm sure I can. Ride as hard as you can."

Though Dr. Botkin had instructed Dmitri to take Alexei through Estonia on a ship instead of St. Petersburg to keep from the continued surveillance of the Communist Army and they couldn't risk being followed. Dmitri, in his own mind, wanted the quickest route possible. He had been paid ample to escort Alexei to France and if he wished, return to Russia at his own convenience. Still, he preferred the St. Petersburg Ship, releasing him from the infamous plan of escape for Alexei.

Riding a pure-bred Arabian, made the journey an easy feat.

The Arabian stallion is one of the most easily recognizable horse breeds in the world. It is one of the oldest breeds and throughout history. Arabian horses were used to improve other breeds by adding speed, refinement, endurance, and strong bones. Even in biblical days' couriers often rode fast horses that were especially bred for the kings. Today, Arabian bloodlines are found in almost every modern breed of riding horses. A water stop for the horse was the best they could do. It was important to keep their only transportation in good health.

Alexei began thinking how it would be should he ever be able to come back to live in Russia. "Do you think, maybe someday, I'll be able to come back?"

"I wouldn't plan on it. Not worth the effort, there is always someone to turn on you. I wouldn't try it."

"I may be young but I wonder if that will ever be. I'll be fine, people in my position and younger than I have had to deal with harsh reality before. Obviously, I wished it could have been different. I always told myself, I would have been the leader for the people. I would have used the Duma to lead the people. Russia would have become a democratic state and we would have survived. I was just born too late for my time. It is what it is and none of us can change that."

"You are very mature for your age. Your Father did well for you. I've heard it said of him he would not leave his son ignorant as his Father had done to him. Your Grandfather left your Father unprepared. Who knows, Alexei, someone may well lead this country in a democratic way sometime in the future."

"Maybe then we can come home again."

"That would be good. For now, we have to survive."

Dmitri and Alexei on horseback were now nearing the pier. "The Pier isn't too far from here and I think we can make it if we hurry. Do you have a change of clothes with you?"

"Very little."

"That's okay. You will have to make do with what you have. How about money, do you have any?"

"Yes, I do. Plenty."

"Good. That should get you to your destination. We are close to saying goodbye now."

They had been riding in the early part of the evening when they finally arrived near the docks when Alexei noticed they weren't in the correct place.

"Dmitri, isn't this St. Petersburg? That's what the sign says. We were supposed to go through Estonia and then I thought you were coming with me."

"We'll see." On they rode toward the pier.

Dmitri hesitated. "Hang on Alexei. Look up ahead."

"The Red Army, four of them."

"Looks like they are questioning the Captain."

"What now, Dmitri? What are you going to do with me? Take me back to go with my sister's instead?"

"Not possible."

"You can't leave me here."

"Well I guess we have to go through Estonia."

"Don't look now, Dmitri, but those soldiers are heading our way."

"That's okay. Hang on. We're going to cross the border into Estonia to the train station. I have tickets for the train. We will to take it to the Estonian sea port."

"Are you sending me on the train alone? How will I know where to go?"

"No, we'll be together on the train. Estonia isn't interested in us. There's a Naval Ship that we will board for France. Just a slight detour but first, take off your peasant clothes and let's discard them."

"What a relief! Finally, I can breathe again."

"Your papers, do you have them?"

"I do. I've been wearing them. I'll be glad when I don't have to do that anymore."

They took the detour. "It would have been easier to send you on the ship out of St. Petersburg. That can't happen now but this will work better for you."

"I thought you were to escort me to France."

"I will, I will."

They approached the train station. "I'm just going to get the stable boy to take my horse." Dmitri disappeared and soon returned.

"Where from here?"

"Okay, I think you will be presentable."

"I probably shouldn't tell you, but I'm running with jewels attached to me I wished I didn't need to wear. At least if the Rubles are useless, I'll have the jewels to cash in for money. None of this is any fun, I wish I could stop being a fugitive."

"It won't be long now. Maybe the American troops will help you? When you get to your destination, you will be able to buy everything you need. There is an Estonian Ship you will sail on. You will be accompanied by United States troops on their way to France. By train it is only a few hours to the port."

"It won't be long then."

"Not at all. Again, you have all your papers available to present to them?"

"I do."

The trip was quiet but Alexei was determined to make the best of everything. It could be interesting to sail with the troops. He could learn a lot from them. Fighting wars had been his Dad's passion so this could be an awesome experience for him.

After the Russian Revolution, the Estonian ship came under

the control of the British Shipping Controller and was managed by the Willson Line and later, the Cunard Line. Under Cunard management in 1918 as HMT Czar, she was employed as a troopship carrying United States troops to France as part of the United States Navy Cruiser and Transport Force. After the end of World War I, the ship was returned to the East Asiatic Company, the parent company of the Russian American Line. Then she was placed with the Baltic American Line sailing in passenger service to New York under the name Estonia.

"That was a short train ride. Let's get you to the ship to France. You have an Aunt there, correct?"

"Aunt Olga. She would come to see us now and then."

"You have papers of introduction. I believe there is an address with some sort of directions."

"So you won't accompany me to France."

"No need, you will be just fine."

"It's about time for me to be on my own, especially for someone like me who should be right now the ruler of the great country, Russia."

"Good attitude. You are 15 years old. I wish I could be there for your next birthday. Who knows how everything will end? Take really good care of yourself and don't try any fancy acrobats. You can't afford another fall right about now. We thought you would never walk again."

"You knew about that?"

"The country didn't but your entire family knew that you and your sister Anastasia were never very well. The country knew nothing, but when the country figured out that you were not well, it was gossiped all around that you were dying of Leukemia. They never did know your sister had a heart problem. None of that could ever be shared with the country."

"Why do we have to live such a secret life all the time?"

"They always have to think that your family is in control and will continue to lead which means to them you shouldn't have any personal problems to be too concerned about. Sometimes I don't think people are aware that you too are human beings."

"Maybe if we had been more open to the people, they would have been more merciful with us? You think?

"You know, you could be right about that. For now, none of that matters."

Both Dmitri and Alexei stood before the customs officers to present the paperwork. "Looks good to me. You are cleared to board."

"Okay, Alexei. They've accepted your papers, so I'll be off. Take care, God speed."

Chapter 17

The Escape

Dr. Botkin in his disguise knew he must be quick and get out sooner than later should there be any difficulties that he hadn't expected. Checking again to be sure he had the Nun clothing for the girls, he walked through the halls when he was stopped.

"You just left with the servant girl. You are leaving again?"

"I left Dr. Botkin with Alexei for now. If you like, you could go and check on them."

"Not interested. Proceed."

He would have to go into the stalls where the horses were kept. This time he needed two horses and an open wagon. A Monk using a wagon would be a good disguise and he certainly was on a mission. Dr. Botkin hadn't expected anyone to be in the stable but now he saw a light. Who could be there? He approached the open barn doors seeing a young girl brushing the horses main. "Are you taking care of the horses?"

"My little brother was supposed to but he hurt himself so I'm doing it."

"Would you please harness two of your Arabian horses to one of the wagons for me?"

"Yes, Sir."

Within a few minutes the young girl had the horses harnessed and ready to go. "Take these Rubles and if someone should ask you, tell them the Monk said he needed them but you can't be sure of the direction he went."

"For that much, I will never remember where you went and if you were even here, Mister."

Dr. Botkin was now on his way to the Opera. This was how it had to be. He was hoping his outfit would get him admittance. Surely, they couldn't refuse a Monk. Hopefully people would think he was an authentic Monk. That was the plan but he had to appear realistic and then a Monk with an excuse to find the girls in the Opera house. That could be dangerous.

The old clock on the corner had always been faithful as he caught sight of the time. He knew he didn't have any time to spare. Somehow he had to make an entrance. That was what he had to do, but how?

He rode around to the rear of the Opera House where he found a stable boy to take the reins. "Would you please take my horses and wagon to the back? Here," he gave the boy a few rubbles. "I will need both the horses and wagon in just a few minutes. I will pay you more when we come to get them. Wait for me. Would you do that for me?"

"Yes, Sir! I will be pleased to do that." The boy happily accepted the money as he held them at the back of the theatre. If he was able to get extra money, he could be relied on. All Dr. Botkin could do was hope that what he paid for would happen.

"Sir, there is no admittance without a ticket."

"I must escort two of your beautiful girls. They have sent for me."

"Do you wish us to announce their names and have them come to you?"

"That will never do, it would embarrass them. Please, I'll not make an issue or a scene. I know who they are and I am expected." There was obvious hesitation. "I'll just be a moment, please have mercy?" Coming from a Priest, *mercy* seemed to be the key.

"Oh, all right, Father, go ahead in. Do be aware that the moment it becomes evident that you have caused people to stop and take notice of you, they will escort you out regardless of how important your plea is. Do you understand that?"

"I do. I'll only be a moment. You have my word on that."

Who could deny a priest? Wasn't he a man of God?

Tina made her way through the crowded dance floor to the bar. She was about to ask for drinks when someone nudged her. Their eyes joined, when Tina realized this must be her contact. He had the French cap and a pipe in his mouth. This had to be the man. "Tina?"

"I've been expecting you."

"I have a message. Your Father and a Monk are at the entrance door trying to make their way to the back of the auditorium. Rally up the girls."

Tina pushed through the crowd toward Anastasia in a panic. "We need to grab your sisters, now."

From nowhere came a voice, and then someone grabbed her arm, "Anastasia, let me have this dance with you?"

"You frightened me. I thought for a minute you might be someone else." She hesitated, looking at him, "Why don't you wait just a bit, I'm trying to find my sisters." he continued to talk but Anastasia ignored him, pushing her way toward Olga and Tatiana.

Without any notice there was a sudden crackling sound as though something might have fallen from the ceiling, when disorder ensued. She looked everywhere. Instantaneously, her eyes caught the light pouring through the front entrance of the auditorium. Jacob's voice came through loud and clear as he spoke to Tina, "You know what we must do."

"I do."

Standing next to Tina, Anastasia froze immediately. Tina turned to face Anastasia, "We must go but where are Olga and Tatiana? We have to go out the back way. The guards are waiting at the front. They are here early, but we have no more time." Tina pulled Anastasia by the arm.

Dr. Botkin grabbed both Olga and Tatiana by the arms "Come with me. Don't say anything."

"Who are you?"

Dr. Botkin repeated, "Don't say anything."

Olga recognized the voice, "Okay Father."

They hurriedly began making their way through the crowds, "There is the fire door, let's go through it, I don't believe it's alarmed. Our horses and wagons should be waiting with the stable boy."

"You know that for certain?"

"For money, he should be there for me. Don't look now. The guards are not far behind us already. They are pushing through in a panic. Somebody is screaming now." Dr. Botkin grabbed both girls by the hands, pushed them through the giant doors.

The stable boy was standing there with a smile on his face and horses ready to go.

"Here's the rest of the money. Please tell them you don't know which direction any of us went."

"Thank you. I will tell them I saw nothing. Don't know anything."

With one swoop, Dr. Botkin pulled the two girls into the wagon. Olga and Tatiana quickly threw on the robes with the Nun

hobbits. "We're off." He looked over at Anastasia as she
scrambled onto the wagon with Tina and Jacob. "Go with God.
Until we meet again."

Jacob waved Dr. Botkin on as he started his horses up. "I
don't think they've spotted us yet, Anastasia, there are too many
other wagons lined up and waiting for the Opera to be over."

Grief entered through Anastasia's entire body as she sat in
the wagon stunned, unable to comprehend anything. Totally
frozen, she was saying nothing. They were well on their way when
she finally whispered, "I may never see my family again, where is
Alexei? How will he get out?"

"Don't know exactly. We can't go back. We have to go on.
I promised to keep you safe. That means we all have to work
together so that we can make it out of the country."

"How about my Mother and Father. My sister Maria?"

"Given it is war time, we can't go back to see anything."

No one talked any more. First it was her dog, now her
family. How would she handle this difficult situation?

The sun began to set in the West, as Anastasia's somber,
still mood could not be lifted. She was immobile sitting there.
Could her weak, aching heart withstand the torment now fixated in
her mind? Would she succumb or survive?

"Come, Anastasia. We must go home to our house and get
some rest. Tomorrow will be a better day, you'll see."

For Anastasia there was no vocabulary that could give the
right words to express her feelings. All she had now was her large
handbag that had tucked inside the little rag doll. Nothing more.

Chapter 18
The Mission

"Girls, they are after us, I thought we had lost them."

"Will they know it is us or just want to question us? What do we do now? Surrender?"

"No, Olga. There is a mission just a few miles from here. We will find refuge there."

The wagon bobbed along the way. "Isn't this wagon slowing us down, Dr. Botkin?"

"That it is, indeed, Tatiana."

"We have two horses on this wagon. What about undoing them and then we can ride the horses."

"Problem is we'd all have to ride bare back. You'd have to be an experienced rider to do that. We can't risk wasting time by stopping. I know the Mission would appreciate having another Wagon." Dr. Botkin hesitated for a moment, "I do think we can make it."

They rode on as hard as they could. The Mission was just barely coming into sight, "There it is, just over those hills. See, the top of the roof just over there?"

"You're right Dr. Botkin. I can see it. Don't you think the

soldiers are gaining on us, though?" It didn't take long for them to approach the outside of the Mission.

"We are there. We made it! Hang on!" Dr. Botkin jumped off running to the side entrance of the large enclosed compound. "Good, there is a bell." He rang it repeatedly. "I just hope they answer before those guys reach us." He waited. And he waited. It felt like time was running out and would not be on their side. Then, finally a someone answered.

"My, where did you people come from?"

"Sister …?"

"Sister Mary"

"Sister Mary, we have come for refuge. The Red Army is chasing us, they are just a few yards away."

"Come in."

"Shall we bring the wagon through?"

"Yes, of course. Help me open the gate."

"Girls, come in with me while I do that."

Sister Mary spoke quickly, pointing the way, "Go into the chapel girls, we'll be there shortly. I don't want them to see you."

Dr. Botkin and Sister Mary opened the gate and led the horses and wagon through. "I don't think we made it. Here they are."

"Leave it to me. I can handle this."

"Stop! I order you to stop."

Sister Mary approached the soldiers, "How may we help you? Do you wish us to feed you?"

"We chased this wagon from the Opera house. There were three people in it. Where are the others?"

Sister Mary answered, "It is just Monsignor and myself. Are you hungry? We have food we would gladly share with you."

The courtyard was quiet, nothing stirring. "We have many other Priests here that you may want to ask about your concern.

For now, we are the only two out here as you can very well see."

"You said food?"

"I did. Please then, come with me and we will see to your supplies. Come."

Dr. Botkin knew his cue. Sister Mary turned to walk with the soldiers. She motioned with her arm from behind, pointing him to get the girls into the opposite direction. He knew they would have to be prepared to hide.

A boy from the orphanage approached Dr. Botkin. "May I please see to the care of the horses and wagon?"

"If you like, please." He then, proceeded to find the girls in the entrance of the Chapel.

"Dr. Botkin, what are they doing here? What do we do, now?" Olga had to know what was next.

"Mix with the other Sisters. They won't give you away. If they ask, just tell them the Soldiers must not recognize you, they'll understand. You aren't the first people to seek refuge in a convent."

After much fussing over the soldiers, satisfying their hunger, Sister Mary offered to have them stay overnight.

The girls were within hearing distance, standing with the kitchen staff. Tatiana whispered, "Oh God, forbid that they would accept that invitation. They'll be all over this convent to find us."

"We haven't had time to be introduced, but I'm Sister Mary. They won't find you here. Men stay in an entirely different building and we lock this one securely. It won't be very comfortable for them. They'll have to sleep on cement."

Tatiana laughed, "Good. How cruel though. If that sends them on their way, thank God!"

The soldiers looked around trying to see if there was anyone suspicious around the compound. They were still convinced others had been riding in the wagon. They hadn't given up even though they were being told only a priest was in the wagon returning from doing chores. They checked out the accommodations offered them but saw the cement beds. Sitting on them, they looked at one another when the soldier in charge said, "Well, I don't know. We aren't that far from town. I think we better hurry back. Just maybe, there is another wagon we need to find out there."

"You know, the stable boy at the Opera said he thought one of the wagons went toward St. Petersburg. Maybe he was right."

"Let's go there. If they do come by seeking refuge, be advised you must let us know immediately. We are here to arrest them. They are to be in our custody."

"What are they guilty of?"

"Treason. They are guilty of death. Anyone hiding them will experience the same." The soldier turned to face Dr. Botkin being dressed as a Monk. "You know, Father, we could arrest you and tell Moscow we found you and not the girls."

Sister Mary interrupted, "You have the wrong man, he just arrived back with the wagon. He was sent on an errand for the mission. You obviously have the wrong man."

Dr. Botkin assured them, "I will keep an eye open for them. Who knows, they may still be on the run."

The soldiers rode off back toward the city. "That was a very close call. What do we do now? I'm truly sorry, I am Dr. Botkin and my two girls are Olga and Tatiana."

Looking shocked, "You don't mean, the Romanov's? They are here with us?"

"I do mean, yes, two of the girls are here with you."

"I thought...?"

"We are on the run of our lives."

"Come. You can stay with us until the time comes for it to be safe to leave. You'll see, God will find a way for all of you."

They sat together at dinner, a bit somber, having just escaped with their lives.

"Tell me, sister Mary, what do you people do besides pray? I've never had the privilege of knowing anything besides my practice in the medical field and I know the girls haven't either."

"You must remember, Dr. Botkin, all of us used to all help Mother with the wounded soldiers. It was her passion to aid them so she set up a hospital just for that reason. We have some experience on that account."

Olga answered, "We did enjoy helping. It certainly was better than doing nothing."

"Our Sister's and the other Sisters do more than just stay inside these premises. Often, they do charitable work to raise funds for our orphanage. We have an orphanage on the premises and maybe you could keep yourselves busy by helping us?"

"We'd be delighted to."

"You, Dr. Botkin, being a Doctor, could help us medically before you have to leave."

"Very pleased to do that. I would love to help in any way I can."

Olga and Tatiana were excited about the prospect of being engaged with children.

"Sister Mary, I found this calendar on this shelf, not being used. Can we please use it to count the days?"

"Well, of course."

The days were marked one by one as they busied themselves with the Orphanage. It wasn't long before a few months working in the Convent had gone by.

Chapter 19
On the Sea to the Unknown

The Military Soldiers of the United States Army now surrounded Alexei as he boarded the ship. They had seen his paperwork. He was boarding as a refugee from Russia. There were just a few scattered civilians among the people boarding the same ship. The atmosphere didn't seem given to jubilation or excitement in traveling, they were here because they needed protection all the way to France. Alexei was fortunate that he not only spoke Russian well but also had been tutored to be fluent in both French and English. As a result he could speak well with the crew. The heir to the Throne had been given the most elitist education available for the time.

'*Here goes nothing. Where to? Let's see, they've already accepted my papers and boarding documents. Everything should be in order.*' He continued up the gangplank with the other passengers. Alexei glanced at his papers noticing a difference in name. '*Am I ever glad I looked. That's my picture on the Passport and it says Heino Tammet. Thanks Dad and I understand. Okay, that must be who I am.*' He waited in line until it was his turn.

"Your Passport please." Alexei handed the passport to the military Captain for inspection.

"It's already been checked, Sir."

"We have to check again just to make sure no one else finds a way in without proper documentation. Okay, yes. Let me check my roster. You're Mr. Tammet. Do you go by Heino?"

"Just call me Henry. It's easier. A good translation, don't you agree?"

"Here's your key, and the Log for today. Those are our plans but if there is any action in the ocean, we could be diverted. Your room is located next to the mine on the upper deck."

Alexei began to settle in for the evening. Before he knew it, he was sound asleep on his bed. He awoke abruptly when he heard the ship's whistle blow. Dazed for the moment, he checked his watch to find he'd been sleeping for a couple of hours.

He freshened up, touching the softness of the towels, '*Wow, I haven't had such luxury since yesterday and then I didn't enjoy it because I was afraid for my life. Am I safe or what? I must find Dmitri ... oh, I forgot, it is just me now. For the first time in my life, I am independent. That means I have to know what to do and see what's happening.*'

Alexei checked for his pocket key, made sure his papers were on his person and was about to open his door, when he heard a knock.

It was a crewmember, to be sure. "You must be Henry?"

"I am."

"I'm here to take you and introduce you to other crew members. I will be your 'go-to' person until we dock in the south of France."

"Who set me up with you?"

"Actually, Dr. Botkin, your family physician. He had telegraphed ahead. I am Alvin Elbreth. Please, you can call me Alvin, your Highness."

"Oh, please don't address me as Your Highness. How

would you even know who I am? I would prefer you to call me Henry, like my passport says. I wish no one would know my identity. Being a fugitive is no fun."

"I am so sorry. You do know the Captain does know who you are and so will the military. The other civilians might be a different matter. If it is of any solace, you are not a fugitive with us and especially on this Ship."

"Well, it has been a while. I'm free? Free from what? Free from my family? Free from a country that hated us and preferred to kill us? Don't even have a clue whether any of my sisters or parents escaped. My youngest sister is probably still in Russia trying to get out." Alexei was hanging onto the rail of the ship as looked out over the ocean.

"Then it is right. The papers said there were two children that might have gone missing which would mean you and your sister, Anastasia?"

"Alvin, what did they say of my other sisters?"

"There are some reports that they escaped through the mountains or maybe a tunnel. Moscow denies any such statement."

"Exactly what are the reports?"

"I don't rightly know, Henry. Let's go and get you taken care of."

For a young lad to be kept busy was no easy task. Henry found his way into the staff kitchen. "Please, sir, can I help?"

"We don't need help. Everything has been taken care of. You are to enjoy your time with us. Just make yourself comfortable."

"I know, but I want you to train me to cook, be a chef."

"Why would you need to be trained?"

"I need to be useful. My mind needs to be occupied."

"Go read. We have a library. There are plenty of books to read. Plenty of Historical facts to occupy you."

"I want to learn to cook. Please? I'll do anything you want of me."

"Alberto, please teach me to be a chef? I need to learn."

"Okay, if Alvin says you can." It wasn't long before Alexei had become everyone's favorite lad on board.

Alexei tried to keep busy but now and again, he could hear whispers from crewmembers until he came near earshot. Then the gossip would stop. Finally, he decided to ask what the talk was about.

"I'm sorry, Henry. We didn't know you hadn't heard."

"Heard what? What are you talking about?"

"Your family was massacred. They said all the bodies were burned beyond recognition."

"What did you say? That can't be, I'm here. There was a plan for all of us to escape. That has to be propaganda." Alexei took another look at the paper, "See, look. They say that I had leukemia. They don't know what they are talking about. Yeah, I have a blood disease but that is not what it is."

"Well, I'm sorry," one of the waiters, continued, "at least that's the report from Moscow. I wouldn't believe anything they say. Propaganda, like you say. You already know that. That's what they want people to believe. You are here and well. Why wouldn't your family be?"

Alexei suddenly felt sick to the stomach. "Do any of you really mind if I go to my room for a few hours?"

"Of course not, Henry. You need to do that and take your time."

It was all Alexei could do to make it to his cabin. He unlocked his door, closing it behind him, making a dive onto his bed and wept. It wasn't long before he was asleep. It was evening before he began to stir when a knock at the door brought him to his senses.

'*Where am I?*' Hesitating, then asked, "Who is it?"

"It's Alvin. I need to know that you are okay."

Alexei opened the door. "I'm fine and I will be okay."

"It's dinner time and the Captain would like the privilege of your company if I may accompany you to his table."

"You may."

Alexei enjoyed his time with the Captain while they made conversation about the world situation as well as how Russia would fare in the future. They discussed how France was now viewed in the eyes of the world and what direction they were headed.

"I guess, Henry, you will be disembarking soon. What are your plans from here?"

"I'm not sure except that I have an address to my Aunt. A woman I have not met very often. Father assured me that I would be fine with her. I have a letter of introduction and I'm sure she will think I'm just a figment of her imagination with all the reports coming out of Russia by now."

"When you disembark, there is a police station just about five short blocks down from the pier. They will be glad to show you the way to wherever it is your Aunt lives. Just so you know, it is not uncommon for the police to escort a lost traveler to his destination. You will do fine. I don't suppose you have much luggage but if you think you can't walk, you can always take a cab. Here's a stupid question for me to ask the son of the Czar, but do you have any money on you?"

"I do. I have plenty. How much for transportation?"

"A ride on a mashrutka costs exactly 13 Rur regardless of the length of the trip. The city revolves around Lyubinsky prospect. It is easy to walk the distance for an able body person such as yourself. This town is best experienced and explored on foot"

"Good, I should be okay then. I just have to find my Aunt and then with her help, I'll be good to go."

"Good for you. A man with your *like ability*, you will do well."

It would only be a few days before he would be looking for his Aunt. An Aunt whom he had only met occasionally before and it would be up to him to tell her the news of his family. How was he to do that with what he knew?"

Chapter 20
Hungry and Waiting 1918

Alexei disembarked with the other passengers just before daybreak. It appeared most of the people were being met by family or friends. He was one of the last few stragglers carrying baggage. Everyone seemed to be going somewhere, no doubt. A few hailed the nearest taxi. Finally, there was no one left but Alexei. It reminded him of his childhood when dignitaries were entertained by his father the Czar. He often felt as though he would rather be in other places than where he found himself. This was his situation for the moment. He knew that as long as there were people, he'd always know what to do next, except for now. There was no one, not even so much as dog to wag his tail in friendliness.

It seemed to him he was standing in the middle of nowhere. Surely, he could find his way to the Police station just as the shipmaster had advised, to get directions for his Aunt. That was all good and well for someone who was confident with whom they were. Yes, identifications he had and a letter of reference was in his possession. A letter of reference. If he showed that to the police he would definitely have a major problem. It was introducing him as Alexei.

Alexei now realized it might not be okay to continue with

the information he had been given from the Ship Captain. It occurred to him, if his entire family had to stay in hiding, it might not be the wisest idea to announce to any official that he had arrived from Russia. Giving everyone his specific location in France didn't seem to be the wisest decision for him to make. Even though he was using an alias, it wouldn't be uncommon for the Police to unravel his identity. This could very easily put his Aunt in jeopardy, to say the least. It certainly would make for good news in the local newspaper's headlines, "The Son of The Missing Czar has been spotted in France going by the name of an alias, Henry Tammet." Possibly, if anyone in France wanted to earn a bounty, even if there wasn't one out for the present, why not make one now?

Alexei continued standing on the spot stupefied, feeling frozen as he stood at the edge of the water just a few feet from the docks, trying to gather his comportment. He had never been here before. He gazed at the red tiled roofs of the old Riviera town and then looked north to the gray-green hills. He turned to face the South at the open sea. It was now early morning as he watched the dark fishing boats put out to a broad, gloomy sea overlooking the gray horizon. As day break began to lighten gradually he could begin to see the softer, silver lights far out over the water, to where Corsica lay assuming the appearance of a fairy island with its purple hue.

There were soldiers milling about. It was obvious some were from Africa, the East and then even possibly from Russia. Russia! That was the whole reason he needed to find his own way. He unfolded the map on his lap as he now sat alone on the shore. Maybe he could make sense of it all now. Alexei studied the map intently. Surely, if he could see on the map the location where he was sitting, he just might be able find his own way. He seemed confident he could find his Aunt's house. There was only one problem, by now he was hungry. Perhaps they fed him too well aboard the ship. With no food on hand, he would have to make his way first to his Aunt's, and then maybe she would have pity on him. He stood up, stretching just a bit before he grabbed for his small bag. Making his way through the branching palms that barely stirred in the warm and fragrant breeze. The air was clear, almost like a tasteful liquid. That made Alexei even hungrier.

Alexei had been walking for a good while when he felt he was near the right neighborhood. He had walked by the Cathedral. It was huge, massive, and very majestic. Many large mansions lined the roadway. They were each spread apart with huge green bushes trimmed as a fence along the way. It appeared to be more about privacy rather than a friendly neighborhood. This was indeed the French Riviera. He looked at each number on the gates as he passed by them. To his amazement, he spotted the address. Was this to be the place? Should he walk through the gate and knock at the door? If he did try to make connections, and she was no longer to be there, what would he do next? Would the only option be to find someone in authority after all?

Alexei could open the Iron Gate or just stand there and look but that would get him nowhere. He was here and he needed to face his fate that was about to be dealt him. He needed to make a decision. Try, he must and if it were to be his lot to be turned away, then he would walk that path. For the moment he needed to know.

He opened the gate, continuing down the walkway to the large double doors. Using the doorknocker, he made his presence known. Knock he did.

A tall man formally dressed in a white shirt, black bow tie and black suit answered the door. "How may I help you, Son?"

"I'm presuming this to be the address on this paper?" Alexei had scribbled the number on a scrap piece of paper.

"Just whom do you wish to visit with?"

"Would you please tell me, Sir, am I at the correct address?"

"I must insist on knowing whom it is you wish to see?"

"I have a letter of introduction."

"Do come in, Sir. Please be seated. If you will, I'll take the letter."

"Sorry, I can't do that."

The Butler disappeared. Now Alexei was worried. What if this wasn't the correct home? If the wrong people recognized him this could very well not be the outcome he had hoped for. If his Aunt were to come, would she recognize him? Then, that was why the letter of introduction. What of the rest of the family? Surely there would be other decisions to make if they even were to believe that he was who he claimed to be.

He could do nothing but look around at his immediate surroundings, waiting for the Butler to return. The marbled floors shone with inlaid specks of gold. The rose-colored drapes picked up on the sheen with neatly placed ornaments all around in what appeared to be the reception room. To amuse himself, Alexei wondered around the room as if to inspect each object. It reminded him of home. Everything adorned to perfection. This had to be his Aunt's home. He was sure of it.

Taking Alexei by surprise, the Butler reappeared with a slender looking woman with blonde long curls that rested on her shoulders and down her back.

Alexei looked for a moment, startled. This woman was certainly not his Aunt. He had seen his Aunt from time to time and even had seen recent pictures of her but this woman was not the same person.

She looked Alexei over for a moment. Then spoke, "Where do I know you from?"

"You are not Aunt Olga."

"No, but I'm sure I can help you if you tell me about yourself."

"Then where would Ms. Olga be, exactly?"

She insisted, "Tell me who you are, and maybe I can help you."

"Then, if you'll excuse me, I'll take my leave. Thank you and sorry for having inconvenienced you." Alexei turned to the door.

"Son, you can't leave until you tell us just who you are."

"I must. The patrol car is just outside waiting. I didn't know whom I would find here so they wanted to wait for me. If I don't report back, I could have a problem." Alexei hoped that they would take the bluff. He couldn't think of what else he might do.

Reluctantly, the butler opened the door, Alexei ducked under the Butler's arm, ran down the stairs through the iron gate, then from the walk way, into the road until he was out of sight. From a distance he could hear the Butler say, "But where is the Patrol Car? "

That wasn't good. Where to go from here and what should he do next? Perhaps he could enquire about directions from someone in a local store. He remembered the local grocery store on the corner of this very street so he decided to find it. Money, he had but it was Russian. He needed to find the nearest exchange location to take care of his currency. What if his money had no value now?

Chapter 21
Stopping at the Bar

He quickly walked into the first open bar and sat at the counter.

"How can I help you, Son?" The bar tender hesitated, "Are you not one of the people from the ship? Didn't I see you at the docks earlier this morning?"

Alexei had to catch his breath. "You did indeed."

"You sound winded. Where from?"

Alexei knew he spoke excellent French without an accent so he ignored the question but instead asked about the address he had been given.

"Well, son, that location is some ways up the road. It could be a mile or two. I might add it is rather an exclusive upper class location."

"I just came from there. It seemed weird."

"Why, so?"

"I asked to see Ms. Olga. First they pretended the address was hers but then suddenly it didn't seem as though they even knew her."

"Ms. Olga who?"

"Would you know a Mrs. Nikolai Kulikovsky?"

"You mean the Grand Duchess Olga of Russia? Of course, everyone knows her. Do you know her?"

"It has been a bit but I have a letter I must deliver personally. I need to know where she might be living."

"Well, you must know the right people. She is a wonderful woman and has a great reputation. She is very active in helping the poor and needy in our town and might I add, she is quite the artist. Look here, we have a painting on the wall that she did herself."

"Wow, I like that."

"It's too bad her brother's entire family was massacred. However, if you want to see her, she is about to board the next ship to Denmark. I do think she and her husband are staying at the Hotel next to the docks until their ship comes in. They have house sitters staying at their estate. The address you showed us is correct. Here, you can read all about it." He handed Alexei the local newspaper.

"You said her brother's family was massacred."

"That was what was reported. They killed every one of them."

"Even the heir to the thrown?"

"They said Nicholas II and his entire family. First, they said they were killed. Then they couldn't produce the bodies so they claimed they all had been burned."

"All of them?"

The bar tender insisted, "That's what the papers said."

"You are saying, the house sitters are friends of the Grand Duchess Olga from St. Petersburg?"

"Don't tell me you know them as well?"

"No, no. I don't. Would you know how long they've been in town?"

"They arrived on the last luxury ship that docked here. You came in that Navy ship with the American troops. I remember you from there."

Another man behind the bar interrupted. "No, you have that wrong. I met one of the family members in town. They've been here longer than that. They arrived on a previous ship to this one. They have been here, maybe two months."

Alexei went back to looking at the painting for a few minutes. "Then I have another question, where is the nearest exchange office."

"That's easy, just a few blocks north of here. It's called the World Exchange Bank. You can't miss it. Obviously, you are you from out of town, then?"

"I suppose you could say that. You have been very helpful. I appreciate your help."

Fortunately, his passport had his alias, and he would use that but should his family try to find him they couldn't, accept for his father. He would be the only one that would know. This was now a dilemma for Alexei, yet he had to use that name. It had to be Henry for now.

With his Aunt about to leave town, it would mean he had to make connections quickly. He would find work locally or just relocate. '*I think I'm about to have a panic attack.*'

Before his mind would allow him to wrap his thoughts around finding Aunt Olga, locating the exchange office would be paramount. He would need to make his own way before too long and how would he know if his money still had value. His plight would be to make several deposits over several days to avoid suspicion.

Alexei found his way to the exchange office. Standing before the teller, "Rubles. Okay, you want to open an account or just do the exchange, Sir?"

"Deposit, please."

"New to town?"

"I am, but my family has always been in and out of Nice because it's your port city in Southeastern France and might I say on the beautiful shores of the Mediterranean Sea."

"Welcome. You speak excellent French."

"Merci, merci à vous. How about the name of a good restaurant and hotel?"

"Why not stay where the Grand Duchess is staying? L'hôtel. Who knows, you might just get to meet her. We are going to miss her. She does good charity work."

"So I've been told."

"If you were recommending a flat to rent, what would your choice be?"

"You'd do better if you could afford L'hôtel. There are plenty of rooming houses. Just depends if you want people to visit with and be in your business. Up to you."

"Thanks for the advice."

The next stop for Alexei would be the Hotel, indeed. He needed to find his Aunt now for sure. He couldn't bear the thought of missing her.

He stood at the desk to make his inquiry for a room.

"Please sign your name here." The clerk showed him the cost of rooms according to what he wanted.

"This is good." He laid his Francs on the counter. I understand the Grand Duchess is also staying here. I have a letter I need to deliver to her personally."

"I can't give you the room number, against hotel policy. She and her husband will be down in a moment. If you just have a seat momentarily here."

"It has been a very long time since I saw them last. If you could just give me a sign or call me to the desk, I'd appreciate it."

"Can't promise but I will attempt that. You seem like a good young lad."

"Merci. May I read your local newspaper while I wait?"

"Certainly. On the house."

Alexei prayed as he sat there. This would be his only chance to connect. If they boarded the ship without making that connection, he would have no way of making contact. Never again would he be able to connect with family.

Chapter 22
Grand Duchess Olga

Alexei waited for what seemed to be hours and he was hungry. He hadn't gotten the chance to eat all day. If he dared to leave now, he might miss them losing his chance. He just couldn't risk that.

Finally, a couple appeared that could possibly be them. The clerk at the counter made no motion whether he was correct or not. Alexei decided he must approach them on his own. It would be worth a try. If he were to make a fool of himself, so be it. He made his way attempting to face them. Olga looked shocked.

"Please don't say anything, Aunt Olga. Surely you recognize me?"

"You can't be ... you were ..."

"Please don't say anything. I am here now. Can I please visit with you before you leave for Denmark?"

"Come with us. We are going to the dining Restaurant for dinner. You must be our guest."

"I didn't think I'd ever dare say to anyone that I am hungry. I haven't eaten since the ship docked this morning." Alexei pulled his map and letter from his belongings. "Here, just so you can be sure."

"Oh, I don't need that, I know who you are. Don't remember if you made my husband's acquaintance?"

With a few introductions, they sat together at dinner quietly talking. "Please call me Henry, my alias is Heino Tammet so I chose the name Henry. Apparently, my name is Dad's choice. I do hope I can get away with that." Alexei hesitated and then asked, "Why to Denmark?"

"Your Grandmother, Maria, lives there. Maybe we can be of help to her and when Russia opens up again, we can return. Getting back to you, yes, we'll be glad to call you Henry."

"You have better suggestions?"

That sounds good to us, Henry. Tell us about your Parents and Sisters."

"As far as I know, there was a plan in place but no one dared share the details. Probably afraid if one of us would be apprehended it would've meant the end of us all. I do know Anastasia, Olga and Tatiana were to go to an Opera Ball. They sent Maria, Mother, and Dad to Tyumen. The rest of us were supposed to go with them but I couldn't walk."

"What happened to you? Did you get into trouble again?"

"I did. It wasn't as bad as the first time but we had to come up with a plan. The soldier in charge of watching our every move apparently wired Moscow. Moscow decided that Olga, Tatiana, Anastasia, and I were to join them later when I would be able to walk. Well, that's when we made a brake for it. Dr. Botken begged the soldiers to allow the girls to go to the Opera, as a last request. They did but I don't know what happened to them from there. Rasputin's brother helped me come through Estonia on a Navy ship sailing to France. So, here I am. The whereabouts of the rest of my family I know nothing."

"You know why your family wanted to come to France, don't you? Not because France gives us any favors but because we are all very fluent in French and we have our family home here. That makes it easy for us."

"We have been waiting for you to come. We thought you would have come a lot sooner so we almost gave up hope that the plan had not worked. We left our house sitter in charge, just in case you would come by."

Olga continued, 'Here's the deal, Henry. If they could, each of your family was supposed meet here in France. You can all live in our home. That was the plan when we left Russia. We're all praying that they make it. They could be joining you if they make it through. You are the first."

"What about Anastasia? Why couldn't she have come with me?"

"Possibly because Jacob was willing, it was safer for her to join up with him and he did need to get out of Russia as well. He had already been threatened. We don't know, but it is possible that Nicholas may have had to pay a ransom for him. It was said that Jacob would have no part of it. The better way was for him to take Anastasia with him along with his girls. I think he was to be sponsored by a religious group. As I remember the times I met him, he had always been a very God fearing man."

"He was that all right. He taught us everything we know about God. Surely, we've been taught in our Orthodoxy but he taught us about a personal God. So that was good."

"Nicholas told me he liked him so well he made him to be in charge of the Vineyard in the Crimea, correct? I heard he was able to produce the best crop in all of Europe. Not only that, his Father before him was the first to be hired on to work in the Vineyard. If I remember, his name was Jacob Sr., also. That being said, Anastasia was to sail to Canada with Jacob. If we ever get to see her again, I don't know. They had wanted Jacob to send her to meet us here in France. However, if Jacob had to give up his gold, that wouldn't have been possible."

"Didn't know any of that information."

"The plans were to be divided, not shared with any of you so that no one could go back to change anything. Surely, if that happened, none of you would have gotten out."

"Your parents and Maria were to escape through a tunnel but where, I'm not sure. We made one attempt to free them when they were on their way to Tyumen the plan was thwarted before we were able to start it. Again, I just don't know if we will ever see them."

After much talking and catching up on the family, Olga asked, "Where are you staying?"

"I'm staying here at this Hotel. I'm in room 115."

"Very good. We are in 116. Just across from you. I have some thinking to do but our house sitter is aware that you might come. You can stay at our house. We will introduce you to them."

"I went to the house that was written on this paper. The people there seemed strange and didn't want to let me go. I felt they wanted to trap me or restrain me. I made the excuse that the cops were waiting for me outside. When they opened the door I ran through and down the street."

"At our house? Hmm. Olga turned to Nikolai. That's odd. Tell me what they looked like."

"The one that wanted to keep me was the blonde woman."

"Blonde? That's her all right. We had told her some of the family might be coming but she wouldn't know what you looked like. That might have been the hesitation. We will investigate, we'll figure it out but you can stay at our house. Like I said, they are aware that you could be arriving soon. The one thing I want to do for you is to give you a good education. We will see that you get it."

"Don't worry Aunt Olga, I have plenty of money."

"Sometimes it takes more than money. Tomorrow we will get together, meet us here for breakfast and we will get the ball rolling before we sail for Denmark.

Alexei wasn't sure he would appreciate this arrangement. He was already 15, almost 16. A babysitter he didn't need. Why, some people were planning to be married at that age. He was ascending the marble stairs to his room, being careful not to lose his footing on the highly-polished marble steps in the hotel, the rails appeared glazed, smooth and shinning. The temptation of the banister was still there. In his younger life it would have been his delight. Besides, he was on his way up not down. It hadn't been that unusual for him to make up time coming down from the upper floor. He needed to be an adult now and was that so impossible? He didn't need another accident to cripple him for the rest of his life. He unlocked his door and threw himself on the bed. He needed to unravel his mind.

He had fallen asleep. When he finally awoke, he looked at his watch to find it was already 4 am. 'Wow, I slept a long time. I wonder if the Bar is open. I could get a soda there and get my head settled before I have to meet with Aunt Olga.'

He did the usual as he prepared for the day. The shower, 'ah ... I need to get a shaving kit. It appears I could at least begin. Man, I have much shopping to do. Maybe I can skip out right after breakfast and get myself together before I have to meet these strange people.'

It was time to do the meeting. He met up with his Aunt and Uncle at the doorway to the restaurant. "Good morning, Aunt Olga."

There they were, seated at breakfast. "I've asked our house sitters to meet us here. Her name is Emily and her husband is Ernie."

"No, you don't mean the blonde woman?"

"The people you said you saw yesterday, yes."

"Please, don't say it is her. I can't let them know who I am. I will disappear. So tell me where I can meet with you alone and I will come back."

"Henry, you can't be serious."

"I am. Please don't tell them which room I'm in. I'll be there until you reach me. I've escaped from them once but I can't have to do that again."

There was no convincing Alexei. He had decided he wasn't about to meet these strange people. "We'll meet you here tomorrow at breakfast, alone."

"I will." Alexei disappeared immediately. He was out the door and walked down the road to where the stores where located. The shopping he had wanted to do and it seemed that now would be a good time. He was quite proud of his decisions he had made in clothing. He hoped that he could disguise himself enough not to be noticed as separate from the French young men. He made his way to the bar he had been at the day before.

"Hey, hey, I would have never recognized you from yesterday. Don't you look sharp? Where did you decide to live?"

"Haven't yet. I was supposed to meet some people but I reneged."

"Can't be that bad?"

"Probably not. Better to be careful than not."

"Did you get to meet Grand Duchess Olga?"

"Yes, I did. Quite a remarkable woman, she is. Sadly enough they will be leaving soon for Denmark, just as you said. Glad I was able to get in before they left, thanks to you since I had no idea they were leaving."

"You must live a charmed life to be able to visit with a woman like that. Do you plan to find yourself a flat?"

"I took your advice, I'm in the hotel."

"May cost a little more but it may be more to your liking. I know it would be my choice."

Alexei's sat at the bar for a while. It felt as though his head was still swimming. He decided he needed to follow his instincts and figure this one out. So far, he had protected his identity, he could have it lost so easily. Settling his affairs in the bank, staying at least a month in the Hotel, and then see what he could do from there.

He went back to the bank to make another deposit in the Bank. "Your name, please." The bank manager was glad to take the deposit.

"Henry Tammet." He had decided he would make deposits weekly to avoid any suspicion. It would appear that he was making deposits weekly from earnings.

Alexei was beginning to feel more comfortable and maybe just a bit more in control of his circumstances. He had a good night of sleep finally.

Finding a job would be another thing he needed to do. This wouldn't be too hard since he had already learned the job of a cook on board the Estonia. This would work to his advantage. He proved it wasn't hard for him to find work at the local restaurant.

"Fancy meeting you here, kid. You found a job? Good for you. Better than working on the boats."

Now he had a job, which gave him a sense of confidence. Meeting at breakfast with his Aunt again, would not be so awful. He could now state his needs and get out of the scenario of having people always taking care of him. He felt it was just about time that he made life to be what it should for himself. He needed to handle his own life.

His Aunt and Uncle wanted to discuss what was next for Alexei to do.

"I didn't quite get what you were saying, what happened?"

Olga inquired.

"I felt they wanted to trap me. Keep me in their home and I didn't know what that meant to them."

"Well, let me tell you what this is all about." Olga explained. "These people are the care takers of our home. We already talked about Nicholas and Alexandra who are supposed to all come out of Russia eventually. When they do, they will come to this very house and live here. Your sisters are all supposed to do the same. It just happens that you came first."

"Let me tell you what I have done. I found a job and am to start work tomorrow. Like I said, I do have enough money but I want to get acclimated with my surroundings so I felt I needed to work and just become one of the people in this community."

"That's all fine and good. However, we want an education for you. Keep doing what you want but please live in the house. I still believe your family is coming and if you are already there, it will give them some amount of peace."

"Let me do some thinking. An education wouldn't hurt. I think I could be a good attorney, maybe an international Attorney. What do you think about that?"

"Whatever, that would please us. You choose the University when you are ready. We will be leaving for Denmark, as you already know. We still feel that Russia will open up again and then we would return."

——————————

Working at the Orphanage had many rewards but Dr. Botkin and the girls were getting anxious. Until they could leave Russia behind they would always be on the run.

"What do you think, girls? Should we head for the coast soon?" asked Dr. Botkin.

"Sail for France?" Tatiana's continence changed.

"I think it is just about time that we make a run for it. Now is as good a time as any. I just wish I knew when the Ship for France docks at the pier."

Sister Mary, joined in the conversation, "I believe it should be there now."

"I'd be sad to say goodbye to the children. It has been so refreshing to work with them. I've enjoyed our time with them. Maybe when we get back to France, I'll be able to find an Orphanage to work in. By the time we get there, it won't matter who we are or even who we were. We won't want anyone to know, anyway."

"You and me both, Tatiana. I'd be all for that."

"Tomorrow we pack up and leave. This time we will take both horses and see if we can get to the dock that way."

Sister Mary didn't like that. "I have a better idea. No one is looking for me. We will pack up the wagon as though we are on a mission, and we will be. We will take Jack from the orphanage. He always wants to help, to ride along with us. Then we won't seem so much like the ones they are looking for. I have to get supplies from town anyhow. They are not looking for five people. We will go to town and if no one follows, we will go to the pier as though I'm about to buy fresh fish. Since the Ship has already docked they will accept passengers when we arrive. I will go off buying fish and you will board the Ship."

The morning came and the loading of the wagon began. They harnessed the horses and were about to jump on to start the short journey when they heard the excited chatter of children as they came running toward them.

Out of breath, one of the little children shouted, "We have something for you. We want you to take this." They held up embroidered crosses, "One for each of you."

"What a pleasant surprise. When could you have made them? We were with you every day."

"When you all left to retire, we made them. Sister Mary helped us because we wanted to surprise you. We prayed over them and want you to take them with you. We prayed that God would protect you until you get to where you are going. Not only that, but that God would be pleased to keep you in whatever you do."

They said their thanks and goodbyes and then Dr. Botkin said, "We will need to wear these garments until we get to the fish market. When we are about to board, we will take them off, give them to Sister Mary, but not until then."

Finally they were on their way. It felt as though they hand been riding for a long time. The girls were almost afraid to talk for fear that all their dreams of leaving would vanish causing them to hide out again. They enjoyed Sister Mary's incessant talking to carry them away from the fear they dreaded to face. Would they make it all the way to the ship? Would they be followed and captured in spite of the care they had taken?

Finally, arriving at the fish market, Sister Mary was the first to spot the Ship. "Here we go. I'll go with you to the Ship. Come with me."

Chapter 23
Learning the Ropes 1918

Anastasia slept out of pure exhaustion and awoke with a slight headache and a heavy heart but morning came anyhow. Had yesterday been all a nightmare? She wished that would've been the case. How would she fit in but more importantly, where was she to go? In the past it had been the place to come visiting, but to live? In earlier years, it was to play with Cornelius and Alexei when tutoring lessons were finished or any one of them had a sick day. Then, quite suddenly in May 1911 Jacob's wife Heather died in childbirth, then just a few years later Heather's son Cornelius died. In spite of his circumstances, Jacob had always held strong to his faith, never wavering. He, so admirably stated, God would see him and his family through everything. Jacob continued to serve as the church elder, always available to help the people of the congregation through trying times. His home was like grand central station with people coming and going.

Remembering how pleasant it had been to come into this brick home with walls that were a foot thick, Jacob had often said that the cold would stay out though the temperature often plummeted to subzero degrees but in summer it would stay cool. The thickness of the walls made all the difference. The front entrance led to the living room that had soft couches and chairs strategically located everywhere. A fireplace that heated the entire space graced itself in the center of the living room. It could be viewed from all the surrounding rooms with its vast stone surface. Stone upon stone built to be the true centerpiece. Visiting with neighbors was very common. Jacob's advice was always wise and he would never demean anyone. His habit was to pray with everyone for he felt that with God's help, any problem could be resolved when it was bathed in prayer. Could his praying solve this problem of an angry world?

It had a large kitchen, stocked to the hilt. Anastasia enjoyed the times she was invited to accompany Jacob when he needed to restock his cupboard. She was delighted when he told her the list of items he needed. He refused to write it down, so it was her job to remember. He hated writing notes and his excuse was he would lose them anyhow. He relied heavily on Anastasia for what he needed to buy. Her memory was such that there was no need for notes anyway. As Jacob went from store to store, Anastasia would remind him of his needs and then skip off with Alexei to do the window-shopping. Alexei and Anastasia had no *needs* as such, so walking through town and seeing the sights, as ordinary people would, gave them delight to no end. Now, it wasn't as much fun without Alexei and the thought at this very moment made her feel sick to the stomach. How would she handle this difficult situation?

From the kitchen was a huge hallway that led to separate bedrooms, and the bathrooms, not a common commodity in the countryside. Then there was a very large covered entranceway that gave way to the connected horse stalls from the house. With foot thick walls at this point, there was neither animal odors nor noises that could carry through into any part of the main house. Though the *whiteouts* were a common winter occurrence, the animals couldn't survive without the shelter. If any of the horses should ever be needed for emergency travel, it was easy access.

Every time Nicholas brought the family down to the vineyard, Anastasia remembered the times she played with Sparky, Jacob's horse. It had soon become her favorite, a horse she could teach any trick. Often, she tossed him a hat to twirl with his nose. Uncle Jacob didn't always appreciate his hat being snatched up by the horse's nose, but it was fun to watch and even he would laugh and then beg Sparky to give it up. That wasn't all that Sparky could do. Of all the many horses Jacob had, he was the leader of the herd. He would be the one to bring that family safely home even in the most severe storm in the winter. Yet, Anastasia often said, she would never ride him, just play with him.

Everyone had grown up, wanting to look forward to the future but now everything appeared to be in a mere shadowy form of fog on the horizon. On the streets people did nothing. They could do nothing. Factories were closed and stores had little or nothing to sell. Food was rationed causing lineups everywhere for what share was available. The unrest in the streets was astounding, with people looting at any opportunity if there was anything left to take.

It was inevitable that Anastasia would now remember she had just lost her entire family. She might never again see any of them and never know if they were even alive. Everything she knew was now in the past. All she had was a grieving heart. Anastasia scratched her head, now what?

Tina approached, "Let's have breakfast and then we must work hard."

"What kind of work? You mean work for my keep?"

"No, no. We have to give you lessons on your identity. We have to hide you from reality. You can no longer remember that part of your life. You have a new life and that is to be our sister."

"How will I do that? Can't I even try to contact my family?"

"Dad just said, unfortunately, they probably all are dead."

"I suppose everything I had is really in the past but I can't understand that I'm not to remember it all."

"Someday this may be all over, but you'll still be around if you forget who you were."

"I don't know enough about your family. Oh sure, I know each of you by name and stuff but there has to be more to you guys than just that."

"There is but we will learn all that. You will be our sister and Jacob is now your Father. You not only have to think that but you have to believe that. I made up a list of our entire family history last night while you were asleep. You must memorize this so that if anyone would ask, it is what you will say. There is no room for error."

"I guess tears won't even help. I have no one to turn to."

"You do have God and all of us. Again I'm emphasizing, we are your family. Learn all of this and then I will quiz you. I know you have a brilliant mind for remembering so that part shouldn't be too hard."

"I suppose, Tina, if I believe it means death not to do this, then I must. I don't want to die. Then, when I come to think of it, I don't think I will die."

"How did you come up with that conclusion?"

"Maybe you don't like me saying this, but I went to see Gypsy Wanda and she says I will meet a tall blonde blue-eyed man in another country."

"So that's what you were saying at the Opera. That's where it came from. Anastasia, you know you weren't supposed to go see her! She will tell you anything for a kopek. All she wants is money and then play both sides to get her needs met."

"What do you mean both sides? She didn't even want money, as a matter-of-fact she didn't want me there for fear of getting killed. She wanted me out of there."

"Well, there you go. She knew only too well, they wanted you and your family dead. So learn this stuff for your life's sake."

"Okay, okay, already. I will learn that for the sake of living. I want to live and somehow I will."

"By the way, your name is no longer Anastasia, it is now Ana.

"I know what I can tell everyone. I will tell everyone who asks, Gypsies kidnapped me. They picked me up at the Palace when I was a baby. They realized they were going to get caught and the easiest way out was to bring me back to you. So, who am I? I only know you guys."

"Sorry, Ana, that's a far stretch, that won't fly. They know who you are and they have pictures of your entire family. We have to do better than that. I have a much better idea. Susana and Johnny's adoption was just approved so they are adopting a little girl, Maya. She will be with them. Just as soon as they get their baby, when we need a baby for you to carry, you'll do that. It will help."

"One other thing, you will no longer be able to talk Russian, only Friesland Dutch and a little proper German. You have to plead ignorance when you are questioned."

"Let's now get to work Anastasia. It's important that we get this done. I made up a list of all *your* relatives. You must memorize them and they have to become a part of your life. You must make yourself believe it, your life does depend on it."

"No more excuses Ana, just learn the stuff." Tina began going over the paperwork she had laid out on the kitchen table. "You must say that Russian was always a problem for you."

"I will tell people that I was always too ill to be educated and that I only have a fourth-grade education. Then no one will expect anything more of me."

"That might work. Go for it."

Anastasia had a memory that would not lighten up but this was a matter of living through horrendous circumstances. It meant *fearing for your life* to help you do what life demanded.

"I really know I have to do this, but you want me to be *that* young. I was born five years later? Who will ever believe it?"

"Let me deviate a little on a lighter touch for us. Lena is getting married soon so we what you to be one of our witnesses." For Ana, this would get her mind off of current events. Party time for a teenager was good news.

"But, let me remind you, must know all this family history of ours by heart. No excuses."

"I will. You have my word. I just have to memorize this stuff, right?"

"You do. You are going to be quizzed until you feel like going mad. You have to know this backwards and forwards."

Chapter 24
The Firing Squad 1918

The room was full of warriors on a hunt to kill. They had
been given strict orders. This was the firing squad and they were
about to get the job done and bring back all the plunder. Who
wouldn't shoot to kill when unpaid soldiers were going hungry?
Now they were assigned to the killing of the Emperor and his
family. They could argue that they had suffered far too long under
Nicholas's II command. He had not met one of the people's
demands for more wages and better conditions. This assignment
would pay for all the suffering they had been through. Only the
most brutal men were especially selected to carry out the orders to
kill.

The Bolsheviks chose a house belonging to Ipatiev, a
military engineer, for the escapade. Ipatiev had acquired the home
in 1908. The mansion had been built on the slopes of a prominent
hill in Yekaterinburg, a mining town. He conducted his mining
business in the bottom floor that he had turned into his offices. A
mining friend, Voikov, supplied Moscow with information about
the mansion and as a result Ipatiev was summoned to the office of
the Ural Soviet at which time his house was seized for the
Romanov family.

Voikov was chosen and given the specific task to burn and dispose of the Romanov's remains. He is said to have obtained 150 gallons of gasoline and 400 pounds of sulfuric acid from the pharmacy in Yekaterinburg for the burning of the bodies. He was to declare to the world that no one should ever know what was done to the Romanov family. This proved to be an easier task than he had anticipated.

"Where are they?" The Military General, demanded to know.

"They disappeared."

"Who lost them?"

"Tyakovlev was commissioned to bring them but he disappeared as well."

The General paced the floor. His body was bent over as he went back and forth until his dark hair was all you could see of the man. "Fetch us a family of seven. Bring them in!"

"You can't kill innocent people!"

"The barrels are burning. We have to burn somebody. It was too much work and very costly to purchase the gasoline and sulfuric acid. We have to burn somebody." Voikov wouldn't let it go.

"I command you do what I say. It is too late for anything else." The General needed seven people.

A family of seven was ushered in to make up for the loss. They had them dress in clothes obtained to disguise the possibility of them being peasants.

The man pleaded, "We are not even worthy to be the Emperor and his family. How can you do this to us? You are falsely accusing us. We are faithful to our new government. We have not betrayed our loyalty. How can you do this to us?"

"Shut your mouths. We need a family and you have been chosen. It should be a great honor."

"So that you can murder us too? Is that all you do? Is your party not to be for the people?"

"Do you want us to shoot you now?"

"If you shoot us now, you will not have a family to display for murder. I say you are the traitors, or you would let us go. We are innocent of any wrong doing."

The General paced the floor, twisty his long boney hands. He could not come to peace with himself. He must do something soon or he would have innocent blood on his hands and that was not his intention. Maybe not having the Romanov family would mean he did not have to accomplish this death sentence after all. Maybe, he could figure a way out.

There were plenty of people roaming about the house knowing that soon the Romanov's family would reach their designated time of execution. Final preparations were being made with many eyewitnesses, as the executioners were about to determine the final hours.

The General realized that among the crowd were many reporters.

"Where's your identification?"

"My passport?"

"State your business."

"News Reporter."

"Your nothing but a spy. We need to herd you down with the others."

Another official heard the commotion. "Get him out of here. There will be enough claims of how we deal with our people. Get him out of here! Get everyone out of here."

The captured family began to disburse. One of the military man shouted, "Stop! I demand you to stop at once!"

The General shouted again, "Get everyone out of here, now!"

Some of them protested, not knowing the Romanov's were not there. Suddenly, several shots could be heard from outside the building.

"Who shot the guard? He had just been shot in the stomach and the throat, now lying on the floor. "There is blood spattered everywhere." The soldiers were shaking the rest of his life out of him, asking, "Where is the Emperor? Where is all the jewelry?" The guard, lying in a pool of blood, in a raspy voice, whispered, "They are ... gone." There was one other witness but he too, was already dead. The Soviet leader shouted, "Who shot these men?" No one answered.

Suddenly, the Red Army surrounded the entire building. They were not only looking for the Imperial Family but primarily for the jewels.

"Who took the jewels?" At this point, they would be willing to kill one another for any kind of money. They had gone hungry far too long. It was time to be rewarded.

"Where is Boris?" Even he could not be found. More Soviet soldiers arrived, having been ordered to arrest all the people who had been with the family. They began searching each of them for jewels.

Some said, "Don't you know, they all left in trucks?"

Another said, "Impossible, the trucks are all still in place."

Struggling for answers, another shouted, "A detachment sent by the Soviets took them out secretly."

"Yeah, in a Hurst. It left while we were in the house looking for them. That's the story we'll tell Moscow!"

"You'll do no such thing. They were all killed and burned in the barrels." Voikov insisted.

"In that way we don't need the bodies to bring back to Moscow. We'll have accomplished our mission and still be alive."

"With no jewels to bring back with us, you think they will

believe our story?"

"If you keep your mouth shut, they'll want to believe us. They need a story to tell the world."

Under his breath their leader could barely be heard to say, "We'll all be dead. No jewels to show, we'll all be dead."

"Idiot, just don't return to Moscow. Go another way. Disappear. This is a vast country and if you've already lost the Imperial family, why couldn't you get lost?"

"That's your story?"

"Don't ask."

Though they knew their information was obviously wrong, they needed a story and so it was wired to Moscow.

Voikov, with all the plans he had prepared now had no one to burn. He was assassinated a short time later in Warsaw in October for his so-called part in the Romanov's murders.

Chapter 26
The Manhole

Yekaterinburg had one of the largest Russian iron producing plants that was started on the banks of its river. It was a young city when the iron plant was constructed near Bolshoi, a Siberian Road. It became a key city to a rich Siberia and a window overlooking Asia. Yet, there were no workers because of the lack of food. No one was being paid for work causing extreme disorder throughout the town. The factories were empty with unemployment high. Food was rationed with long lineups to buy the few remaining edibles available. As a result the people hated any mention of the Czar and wanted them dead.

Tyakovlev and Nicholas settled the wagons in an empty neglected stable at the end of the deserted street. They all quietly walked the gravel road to the center of town. All that could be seen was broken windows and streets littered with debris in all directions. It was already evening and with a curfew in place, there wasn't any activity to be seen.

"At least the streets are empty but where are we going?" asked Nicholas, "and where's Boris? I thought he was going to be here already. He was supposed to show us the way."

Tyakovlev was ignoring the Czar, being more concerned with his plans but he was beginning to show emotional panic in not being very sure what he should be looking for as of yet but didn't want to be perceived as not knowing.

"What's that I hear? Could that be him?" Tyakovlev looked relieved.

"I hear someone coming. What do we do if it is the wrong person?" inquired Nicholas. Alexandra and Maria kept silent.

"Stand in the shadows, your Highness. Stand in the shadows, all of you. I will go out to see, first."

Tyakovlev walked into the lamplight. He could hear but he still couldn't see. There was no movement as he walked out into the open. The sound became louder as he moved into the center of the street. It seemed something was bobbing, making loud bangs. His eyes began to cover the street surface. Then suddenly, he could just slightly see movement. Then he heard a voice. Could that be... it sounded like ... Boris?

He motioned to Nicholas, "Your Highness, take a look."

Nicholas moved forward trying to see what Tyakovlev was pointing at. "That's just ..."

"No, I think this is it. Come quickly." The manhole now lifted.

Nicholas, Alexandra and Maria were anxious.

Maria asked, "Must we go in there?"

"Hold off. I'm still hoping Dr. Botkin will make it." Alexandra wanted the comfort of their Doctor being with them.

"He was much too busy. No, but Boris will be with you. It will be the four of you. I will take the wagon and hopefully disappear."

"Tyakovlev, they know you. You will never make it."

"Not in this disguise." He was busily putting on a peasant robe.

"Just so you know, this is a spy tunnel and it goes all the way to the Ural Mountains. Take this map." Tyakovlev opened the map, "Be sure to follow the red line and you will come out at or near a hospital. If you continue in any other direction and then discover you're lost, you need to turn back to the red line or you may miss your contact at the other end. Do not stray from it. That is the key, you must stay on track."

"Are you ready to go? Do you have a lantern? Here are two and a bottle of oil. I also have some matches. If you can, use one at a time. It should not take you long since it is a short distance. Whatever you do, remember you must follow that red line on the map. Like I said, there are other exits but don't take those. Only the red line will lead you to the hospital where you will meet your contact."

Nicholas asked, "You were in that tunnel. What did you find? Was it safe?'

"I only went in a short distance to wait for the three of you. There was some debris further up but I'm sure we can get through it." Boris interjected, "I can see soldiers in the distance coming our way now. Let's get down in here. You will make it. We just have to follow that map."

Nicholas descended first with Alexandra and Maria to follow. Boris closed the manhole cover behind him. Not any too soon as some of the Red Army rode up to Tyakovlev.

"Listen, can you hear that?" Nicholas whispered. They stood still for a moment just under the manhole cover.

"Halt! What is your reason for being here?"

"Sorry, Sir. I was in the neighborhood?"

"Are you not aware of the curfew?"

"I'm just headed to the barn."

"You appeared to be talking to someone. We saw other people with you in the distance."

"Look around. Do you see anyone?"

"You are obviously a peasant. Where do you live?"

"Like I said, I'm going to that deserted barn, over there."

"He's insane. That's probably why he talks to himself. Leave him alone, there are plenty more like him around here."

"He's just saying that to throw us off track."

"What track are you referring to, Sir?"

One of the soldiers inquired, "Want us to cuff him?"

"Let him go. He'll be more of a nuisance than value to us."

He was left standing over the manhole.

Chapter 26
The Deadly Tunnel

There was nothing but heavy breathing by now. Nicholas looked up to see that the manhole cover was closed. Each of them could easily hear what they feared the most for themselves but they determined to ignore everything for the moment, the thoughts of the past and attempting to live in the moment. Nicholas turned to his family, "We should be safe." Desperately trying to reassure them he said, "I have the map, we have Boris with us, and so we should be able to make it."

Maria spoke up, "You know Dad, it's musty and damp down here but we don't plan on being here forever."

"You are right." Then Nicholas continued, "This might be a Revolution we are trying to escape but as of yet, we aren't facing any firing squad."

Alexandra couldn't help herself, "At least not now. I'm glad you are with us, Boris. That gives us some comfort. Are you familiar with the Tunnel?"

"Sorry, not at all. I know nothing about it, just as I said there seems to be some debris ahead but we should be able to work our way through it."

That didn't help settle Alexandra.

"I have the map. We just need to follow the directions. So let's just do it."

Maria asked, "Did anyone think to bring food."

"No food, but we do have water. We need to ration it, but we do have it."

"I have food." Boris had a pack on his shoulder where he kept all his belongings. He pulled out cheese. "Let's eat first, we'll think clearer."

Maria took the lead, "See if I get this right. Now that they know we are nowhere to be found, they could be on the lookout no matter where we are."

"Maria, the plan is to board a ship for France. We just can't come back to Russia until it settles down. Who knows, someday we might be able to. It just can't be our family leading it anymore."

Boris answered, "Well you know, just maybe it will satisfy them to use the propaganda to tell the world that they've done what they set out to do and leave it at that. When you think about it, they really don't care about any of us. They want the country controlled by them, no matter what." Boris began chuckling.

Nicholas asked, "And why are you so jovial?"

"I'm not. The people wanted to have some say in how things were done in Russia and now they get just the opposite. The people have no say in Communism. If they think that you, Nicholas, as an autocratic leader, controlled the country, now if they dare complain too loudly they just get shot. Go figure. Now the law stands so you must keep your mouth shut. No freedom to come and go. You do what you are told to do. You can't even as much as question anything."

"You will see, they will relent eventually and maybe there still will be a chance."

"Don't count on it Alexandra. We do have a way out even

if we didn't get the exile we wanted." Nicholas stated.

Boris asked, "You wanted?"

"Britain. We could have stayed with relatives but they didn't answer soon enough. It had a lot to do with who would support our family. They didn't want to pay the bill to have us live as Royalty but you have to remember they are in the middle of a war as well and I had committed Russia to help. Instead, here we are."

"So then, are you saying you are as poor as a peasant?"

"No, not at all. However, we certainly couldn't afford the Royalty life style. They would expect us to throw parties and the like. That would have to come from them and I don't think they were prepared for having us live in Britain as Commoners. First, they would be ashamed of what everyone would think of them. You know how the English are. They have to keep up appearances. With the English that is important. So here we are. We get to take care of ourselves."

Maria responded, "I rather like the idea of just being ourselves. I never did like being pretentious. Mother was always good about allowing us do things out of the ordinary. We even helped our servants do their jobs. For us it was fun."

"I always tried. I wanted each of you to be capable in your own right." Alexandra was indeed a good Mother in a Royal situation.

"It wouldn't be long before they would be looking for us anyhow. If we finally get out of this tunnel alive, they'll still be hunting us down." Maria was right.

Nicholas continued, "I'm hoping they believe our bodies were buried or burned, whatever suits their propaganda. My thinking is that after a while their unreasonableness with the country will be rejected and the people will know they must stand up and say they've had enough."

"You keep saying that Dad. I don't care anymore. I want none of it. I just want to get out of here."

"Our family has been the Royal Family of our Country for centuries, at least 300 years. Suddenly the wind blows and here we are hiding in a god-forbidden tunnel. We have our lives Honey, and we can't change any of what has happened. Just maybe, if possible, they believe they shot us so when we reach the other end of the tunnel with these clothes on, we not only won't be recognized but more than that, we won't be hunted anymore."

"Dad, where are we to go even if we get out of here and even if no one recognizes us?"

"We do have directions for your Aunt Olga. She has a house we often used when we vacationed in France. We do know the language fluently."

Alexandra asked, "Does France care about us?"

"I'm afraid not. However, we will be able to be ourselves. Since we are supposedly all dead, we won't want to admit our identity. We must remain anonymous."

"What we are going to do in the future? We are never getting out of here. Look at the piles of dirt everywhere and who knows if this tunnel will not collapse on us? There is water seeping down the sides everywhere. Can you smell the mill dew? Anastasia and Alexei are the only ones that might survive but for what? Our lives are over, you know that!" Maria was getting to the end of herself.

Earlier, Maria was encouraging now she was complaining, "No way would they have let Dr. Botkin escape with Alexei. How could he have accomplished that? Everyone knows he is a doctor. They would've been shot on the spot. They already killed Rasputin. They had planned to get him for years just as much as they planned to get rid of us."

"Easy, daughter. We all have to realize this was our only

option."

"But we all know we could die in this tunnel."

"Think of it this way, everyone believes that Alexei will never make it anyhow, so they won't be looking for him. He'll be able to make it out of the country and probably the first of us to get out. Anastasia should be fine with Jacob." Alexandra continued, "However, we will be fortunate if we ever get out of here."

"Stop the whining, both of you. How do you expect us to get out alive if we don't even have the will to survive?" Nicholas was insistent.

The Empress and Maria were silent. They both knew they needed to be stronger than they were. Indeed, it was a blow to their ruling empire. A major shock mentally and psychologically not to mention the physical toll it was beginning to play on the entire family.

Maria could no longer hold it, "God knows very well that we will not make it either, we are going to die in here. Don't be surprised if you see a dead body on our way through here and if you do, I don't want to know about it."

Nicholas said because of all the complaining, "The stench will be so bad you won't miss it. You have to go through everything we have to go through. Let's just work to get out of here." Nicholas was very sure they would make it.

"Best of luck to them and to us!"

"Come on, people. I don't want to die in here either. We will make it, believe me. Spies went in and out of this tunnel more times than any of us realize. Even with all this mud and debris. Look over there. That's probably what we should be looking for. You can see someone dug himself out before. Let's get with the digging." Boris used a pocketknife and began stabbing the dirt.

The Empress added, "You need to be encouraged. It is our understanding that the Bolsheviks have guards at the other end waiting for us."

Boris said, "Oh God, I hope the Bolsheviks aren't waiting for us. They've betrayed you all the way. That's not what we want."

Alexandra asked, "If not them, who will we meet?"

"There is a Doctor but it won't be Dr. Botkin." Boris was intently studying the map. "It looks as if we need to take this route to the left. Then, here, see this?" Showing it to Nicholas, "There is a hospital. Look, it says, "Doctor." There's a star next to his name."

"Name? What is his name?"

"No, we don't have a name. It just says Doctor. That would mean there still is a Doctor at the hospital. We should be able to find him there."

"It is wet in here. How are we going to make it?" Alexandra was getting concerned.

Nicholas added, "The River runs by not far from where we come out. Someone, assumedly the Doctor, will escort us to the ship at the pier. Somehow, we will sail for France from there."

Maria had no intention to give it up. "What if we come out at the wrong exit? How will they find us then?"

"Maria, enough. How do you expect us to get out alive if we don't keep digging our way through this gravel?"

"Mother, Father, look!"

"Are my eyes playing tricks or is that a glimmer of light?"

"I can see that." They now stood, staring at the flicker of light.

"If we stand still, it's a steady light. How do we get to it? We can't squeeze past the rocks and mud and who's to say everything won't collapse before we get there."

"Dear Maria. Just help us dig our way through here."

"With what do we dig, with my bare hands?"

"You got it."

"You have to be kidding."

"No, I'm not. There is no fairy godmother to help us. Use a stone to push through."

"We are never getting out of here with all the piles of dirt everywhere and who knows if this tunnel won't collapse on us. There is water seeping down the sides everywhere. Can you smell the mud?"

Boris and Nicholas were using whatever they had. Pocketknives, stones, and rocks, it just had to work. "Come, help us."

Maria, in her realistic manner, grumbled under her breath. "I would just as soon have been shot in the palace as die here!"

Alexandra was beginning to feel desperate as she listened to her daughter complain. Her arguments were legitimate but not helpful. To keep her sanity she deemed it a necessary thing to do would be mark the date on the sides of the tunnel with rocks. "At least if ever they were to find our bodies, everyone knows how long we had survived."

"Let's rest a bit, Maria."

"We could lay our coats down."

"That will make them filthy. You want to be seen wearing them after that?"

"That's a switch, Maria. I'm with you, we are going to make it, you'll see. Here, I've found a dry spot. Let's rest, at least for a short time. Let's share some of our food that should settle us down. Remember, we have that speck of light. When daylight comes we will see it again and then we can start digging our way out."

"I'm willing to dig by lamp light. I have to get it done. I'm feeling a little claustrophobic." Nicholas kept digging while everyone rested. Hours passed by when he found himself leaning against the sidewalls of the tunnel, dozing.

Even when it felt as though no one could go any further, rest seemed impossible. The mere smells kept them awake, not to mention the fear of what was underfoot. Rats in a damp tunnel? The few items they brought would not be enough to sooth their tired aching bodies. Snacks had to be shared and rationed not knowing how long this journey would take for survival.

Every inch of Alexandra's body ached, as she feared what might become death in the tunnel. She knew in her heart that they were running and more than eager to find the way out. They must try with every fiber left in them to get out of this horrible mess. If ever there was a proud moment for their position in Royalty, this was truly the end of that. On the outside, they were to be killed and in the tunnel, wealth had no importance. Death would come either way. Hope to see daylight was all they could wish for now.

Boris said, "I heard rumors of spies and tunnels so when Tyakovlev came up with this plan we just knew it should work."

"It's hard to believe that I was so involved in the War that I didn't have a clue this was here, Boris."

"Probably a good thing, Nicholas, or this wouldn't be here now for your escape."

They knew undoubtedly that they must believe in their hearts that this passage was the solution to their dilemma. Their very survival depended on that.

"We are all going to make it." Insisted Boris, "I'm certainly not giving up."

"Mother, Father, look!"

"What is it, Maria?" The Empress was afraid. Had they discovered bodies? Were there other skeletons in there?

"Are my eyes playing tricks or is that light getting brighter? Is the hole getting larger?"

"I can see that." Everyone now stared at the light.

"How do we get to it? We can't squeeze past the rocks and mud without causing the tunnel to collapse before we get there."

"Use our bare hands, let's do it."

"Do you think we can do it Mother?"

"Maria, you know we will."

"The mud and rocks doesn't make this easy work."

"Do what you can and I'll clear all the rubbish away." Nicholas used his military knife to stab at the rocks. "Grab a sharp stone. It will help break apart the mound of dirt and rubble. Remember, we have that glimmer of light ahead of us. Keep looking at it while we work, it'll make our hard work easier."

"Sorry, Dad. This is still very hard work. Considering we never worked a day in our lives before, this is hard! I have too much weight to carry."

Alexandra spoke up just in case Maria would divulge too much. "You know what is the smartest thing to do. Just go with it, we will be out of here soon."

Boris asked, "You are such a slim woman, you can't be carrying any weight that amounts to anything."

"You are right. I'm just a complainer, you know that." Maria caught the cue from her mother. She couldn't mention the jewels no matter how heavy they were.

"Any paper money you carry can't be that bad. I'll take it for you." Boris was sincere.

"I'm fine, I'll be all right. I can manage."

At this point, Nicholas had to butt in. "If you have paper money, by the time we get out of here, much less out of the country it could be worthless. If you want to unload anything, it would have to be the paper money and that isn't heavy but that will just get us out of the country if we make it before it becomes useless."

"You may be tired for now but when we get to France,

you'll appreciate the little you have."

"I get it, Dad."

Empress Alexandra continued Nicholas' advise. "You know your Dad is right. When we get to the exit, we will be dirty and grimy to say the least so you need to be very careful. Don't even begin to trust anyone or even let anyone know you have anything on you. We must realize that everyone will have gone through the Palace for the Jewels and won't have found anything."

Boris asked, "You are talking jewels now. What did you do with them? That's all the Red Army wants from you. They don't care what Moscow says, they just want the jewels."

Nicholas thought quickly, "I took the time to bury them. They are all in the back of the Palace at the very edge. Not too easy to find but it is by the supply gate and no one will know that. The Red Army gets nothing if I have anything to do with it."

Alexandra added, "If we were to have taken them, our lives would be worthless. We'd be killed for them. So why would we want them? We love life more than jewels."

"Imagine a good looking young man finds you have something of value. He'll offer you the world and then likely rape you taking your valuables, also. That would be if you were lucky. We don't want that to happen to any of us. Let Dad take the lead."

"Sometimes I think maybe if we had all been killed we wouldn't be worrying about getting out of here. We are going to be poor and no one will even care whether we are dead or alive." Maria was getting a little depressed from all the darkness and smell of mold everywhere.

"I have never heard you say anything like that. Are you not well? This is so unlike you. Let me feel your forehead." Alexandra was convinced, "You are running a fever. Take my jacket. Take it easy while the rest of us do the work. You will see that you will be okay. We are all getting out of here."

Each one of them continued to pick at the rocks and rubble as the dust crumbled beneath them. It seemed something should open up by now because water began seeping in and down the sides of the wall with much more intense.

"Are we going to be under water in this tunnel?" Maria asked, "Are we going the right way?"

"According to the map, we had to go this way. See this Nicholas?"

"You are right, Boris. This is correct and it should get us directly to the entrance of the Hospital"

"If it still is recognizable, with all the fighting around here."

"They still need a hospital, even the bad guys."

"That's our salvation. I know we are veering to the left. We saw that glimmer of light. We have to be close." It was as though Nicholas was thinking more than talking. "We are getting through."

"We sure are, your Highness. I know we can get through there."

Maria was right there to examine what her Dad had been talking about. "That's just a hole. It's so dark in here that any light coming through seems brilliant."

"Thank God for that. Let's chisel through that. It's coming, it's coming!"

Nicholas soon realized he needed to get his wife and daughter into the fresh air quickly. Maria was beginning to have a difficult time to breathe. "We should be able to squeeze out of here. Look, there it is. At last!"

"Dad, isn't the opening too small? Here let me work on widening it."

Both Boris and Nicholas began chiseling through to the light. Stone and dust sprayed everywhere. There it was, a hole in the ceiling of the tunnel.

"Okay, let's be careful, we don't want a collapse on our hands. I think we need you, Alix, on the surface first, then Maria. I'll stay to the last. Let's get pushing."

"I'll be the last. I know how not to panic and get you all out of here. That's my job." Boris knew he could do it.

"Don't push so hard!" The rumbling began to echo in the background. "What was that?"

"It sounds like the Tunnel is beginning to collapse—up and out. Come on let's move it right now!" That was the distress sound from Nicholas. Alix was now on the outside, carefully, looking about. He could see nothing in any direction. How were they to find help for Maria? There wasn't a soul around. On the other hand it would be better not to have to meet anyone until they were all safely out. They were much too vulnerable to be met at this point. "I don't see anyone. I need your hand, Maria. Come, help me pull you out." They struggled and finally she was free. "Just sit there until we are all out and together."

Alexandra's voice was now shaking, "Nicholas, the rumbling is getting louder now."

"I need to try to open the hole a little more. There, I think I can do it." His head popped out but he was struggling. "Help me, Alix. My foot is stuck and I don't want to break it." He continued to struggle while Boris pushed, then his foot seemed to dislodge from the stones. "I made it!" Nicholas hesitated. "Come on Boris, you are next!"

Out popped Boris, "Thank God, we made it. Now, where are we? Do you know your Highness?"

"Stop with the Highness stuff. Just call me Nicholas. Let's move away from here in case it caves.

"Can you hear the rumbling now? It is getting loud. Indeed, God has been with us. We didn't need Rasputin to pray for us!"

"Don't say that, Nicholas. He was a man of God and if it wasn't for his praying, Alexei would never have lived as long as he did."

"Mother, are you saying he is dead, now?"

Boris answered, "None of us know the outcome but there was a plan in place. All I can say is that we have to find our contact to get out of here. Remember, it will be the three of you leaving and I will stay back."

"What will you do? If you are caught, they will kill you."

"Not so. This country is far too vast for them to look in every geographical area. I could even hide in your vineyard and enjoy the fruits of your labor. How about that Nicholas?"

Nicholas didn't respond. "How are you Maria? Still have that fever?"

Chapter 27
Running

"I don't think I can go another step. It's just too hard. The perspiration is pouring off me."

"You will be okay, Maria. Just get far enough away from the entrance, the tunnel is collapsing."

"Where are we? What now? Who comes to get us and where are we going? Do you know, Boris?"

"I don't know any more than you do."

Nicholas poised himself. "Well, let me see. I haven't looked at the instructions for a while especially since I didn't really think it would ultimately come to this."

"You didn't think, what?"

"Until I stand at the end of the conflict, I think of nothing but getting there. I don't know anything until I am finally there and then I go for it with gusto."

"Here, let's look. The hospital has to be here."

"Are you telling me, Boris, we are going to be abandoned here? What about Maria? She needs medical attention. You don't know what to do now?"

"Settle down, Alix. Let me open this note." It had been severely torn. Would they even be able to read the words and then know whom they were to find? Who and where is that someone to be for us?"

"Okay, I'm reading it. Here's a map with a route that we are to follow. First, we have to take our outer peasant garments off. We'll bury those among the rocks and then we have to make this walk through to the dock."

"Don't look now, people, but the entrance we came out of? It just collapsed. Thank you, God, we even made it through. Please God, show us the way."

"Good Alix, they will now be convinced that we are dead if they had any idea that we escaped in this tunnel."

"That should mean the Red Army might never even try to find us." Boris was delighted. I'm sure if the Communists know about this tunnel, the newspapers will say that even our possible escape route ended in tragedy. Now, Nicholas, that is a good thing."

"Good as all that is, we have to find our way to the dock and who knows where that might be and will we find it in the daylight? In the night anything can happen to us but right now we need a doctor for Maria."

Maria was now begging. "Please let me just sit here while you all go and find your way. I'll be okay, really. I just can't keep walking with you. I don't want anything to happen to the rest of you. I probably have a contagious disease and none of you need that. I just might die, take this money, you might need it."

Alexandra whispered, "No, please don't do that. Not now."

Boris tried to intervene, "We won't need your money. You will be all right. Nicholas and I will see to that. Just hang in there."

"Keep what you have Maria, if we can't help you come with us, I'm staying with you." Alexandra wasn't going to leave her daughter who may have just become her only living child.

"You are being foolish. You can easily make it. Just not

me."

"Sorry, no, go. Either you let us help you get to the dock where I know we will find help or I stay with you."

Suddenly everyone fell silent, listening.

"Listen … I hear something. Be quite for a minute." Nicholas had been trained to hear what usually would be dismissed as nothing. He could hear the sound of horses in the distance. "I'll be right back." He sprinted back into the trees that surrounding the pathway before them.

Alexandra sat on a nearby rock with Maria. Boris just stood near the path that Nicholas had disappeared into. He wanted to wait for Nicholas to return but he wanted to head back to the Palace as quickly as he could. Was it to find the hidden jewels? If Nicholas had heard the sound of horses, he could make it out of there. A horse is all he would need.

"I'm just going to check on Nicholas, see where he went. I'll be back."

Before anyone could say anything, he was gone.

Alexandra knew in her mind that Nicholas would know his way around the forest having led his army in every predicament possible, clearing brush, making paths where it was impassable. She knew he could do it. Would he and Boris just go and abandon them? Nicholas couldn't do that. He would never do that.

It seemed like hours had gone by. Maria was resting now up against Alexandra. Sometimes her breathing was heavy but at the moment she appeared quiet and peaceful.

Nicholas remembered the area and knew there had been a clinic nearby. As he turned the corner the front entrance came into view. For a moment he stared at the deteriorated state that was now

merely a ghost town. What was left of the clinic would still be
accepting and treating the injured soldiers or people caught in cross
fire. Maybe, since it was still early in the day, he could find
someone who could help Maria.

"That's it, the entrance!" He turned the knob to the door. It
wouldn't open. Looking through the dirt stained glass, he saw what
seemed to be a person. He knocked on the door as loudly as he
could, praying someone would answer.

The voice was faint but it was there, he sighed in relief
when the voice came through, "What do you want?"

"I have a sick daughter who is running a fever. I'm afraid it
might be typhoid. Please help me."

It took a minute and the man in the white jacket opened the
door. Nicholas knew he was taking a chance, should someone
recognize him. "Where is your daughter?"

"Just where the tunnel used to be on the other side."

"Let me load up my horse and wagon. I'll come around to
where you are." With that the door was again latched tight.
Nicholas thought again, what if he'd been recognized. Either this
man would be for him or against him. There were no other choices.
He waited.

Suddenly, Nicholas saw the horse and the man in the white
coat coming his way. He quickly looked to see if anyone was
following. He saw no one. This had to be good news. It had to be
the Doctor.

"Hop on Sir. Point to where we should go."

Within minutes, they came to where Alexandra and Maria
were resting. "Your contact, the doctor?"

"Yes." He introduced them and then asked, "Where's
Boris?" Nicholas didn't expect him not to stay with his family.

"He said he was going to find you but I don't think he's
coming back after you told him where you hid the jewels."

"If that's so, I wish him luck. May it be his reward if he manages to live through finding them."

The doctor paid particular attention to Maria. He examined her closely and then continued to treat her. "I'm guessing that you went through some damp digging from what I see with your clothes. Where were you hiding?"

No one dared to answer why they looked so distressed. They were surviving, trying to get through the musty smelling tunnel. Dust, dirt and water were their dreadful enemy, but they were fortunate to have survived thus far. Thankfully Boris had the food that kept them but that was inconsequential, they merely wanted to survive.

"I think I understand." Then he hesitated, "I have some medicine that will help your daughter. Here is enough for each of you. You may very well need it and do take it if your symptoms become anything like hers. Where did you come from to get here?" When no one answered, "Don't tell me, I'm just glad to know you are here. God go with you."

"We just have to walk to the docks. Is it far from here? I don't know that Maria can walk there."

"My wagon isn't very big," turning to Nicholas, "but your Highness, the women can sit in the back and you can ride with me."

"Are we going to be safe with you?" The Empress wasn't sure any more about anything.

"I believe I am your contact. I just didn't know when you were coming and how many of you there would be. Did the others not make it?"

"We don't know."

Dismissing the questions, "You need to be well when you board your ship. It is here already and stays in dock for a week to load cargo, supplies and of course, the passengers. I think it is getting ready to leave tomorrow but you can board already. You need to be well enough to endure the trip across the water. When you get to France, do you have any plans?"

"My sister has a home there. If anyone has been able to escape successfully, that's where we will all meet."

The Doctor then suggested, "You might want to check with the Captain if any of your other family members had made it before you. He could check the rosters of the previous passenger lists. At least there might be some encouragement for you. That might put your mind at ease. About now, you do need all the encouragement you can get."

"I appreciate your information and I will do that."

"Once you are on board, you are out of Russian jurisdiction. Take the medicine I gave you and you will be fine. I think Maria's illness is only due to the dampness from the tunnel. By the way, I heard the rumble from inside the hospital, I'm sure this arm of it collapsed. How did you make it out? I've expected it to collapse for years already."

"Did you know about the tunnel?"

"I did, Moscow didn't, I'm sure, or it would have been destroyed years ago. We just don't talk about it, but how did you make it out?"

"With our trying to open the passageway and without reinforcing it, we weakened the structure."

"That was a spy tunnel and has more than one exit so I'm sure only one crumbled. I did hear from propaganda coming out of Moscow that your entire family was massacred and then burned but other rumors came out that you might have escaped. No one knew how or where. Thank God that you made it through. My wife and I have been praying that you would escape. We just didn't believe you needed to be murdered. Indeed, God is with you. Stay safe."

"Climb on the wagon and let's be on our way."

Just as the doctor was headed toward the pier, he turned to Nicholas, "Let's take a detour."

A detour at this point was not what Nicholas wanted to hear. They had been making detours through this entire process in attempting their escape. Nicholas was about to jump off the moving carriage. The Doctor saw his intent, "Don't do that Nicholas. You are safe with me. I'm thinking we have clothes that could better mask who you people really are. We were told that you could have been disguised as peasants. In addition, you need to get rid of all that grime and mud. I also, heard people rumor that you would have to work for a living now so you could be spotted should anyone be looking for you. The Red Army is wicked to say the least. You should see the wounded I've been treating. If you are seen, immediately you will have someone spreading unneeded information. You must come with me."

Worried or not, the Doctor was correct but was this now for real? "We need to be quick. Like you said, the ship leaves soon."

"You'll be okay. I know you can board now but they aren't scheduled to leave for hours at the earliest but I thought it should be tomorrow."

"If we miss this connection we have to stay in hiding for another month or so. That wouldn't be good news."

"You can't be recognizable to the majority of people and as it stands, you'll never even get on board in those clothes. You know that Nicholas."

"Then let's all go quickly and change."

Chapter 28
The Whistle Is Blowing

"Honey, I need you to gather up clothing for three people to wear, two being women. With what they have on now, surely anyone could determine they are on the run even as they board the ship. We must help them and make it more comfortable while they travel to France." Turning to Nicholas, "Come with me."

Nicholas, Alexandra and Maria entered a darkened room that had obviously been a small hospital room to treat patients. The curtains were tattered, allowing little light into the room.

"I know it is dark in here, but take these clothes I have given you. Do the best you can and I will return."

They did as they were asked and soon were wearing clothing suitable for travel. Then waited for further instructions.

Finally, the Doctor appeared, "Okay, if you will follow me to the outside entrance, I'll bring the carriage around for you."

Outside the building they stood in the alcove waiting when Maria asked, "We must hurry, there isn't much time. How do we look? Will we really get there on time?" Feeling very anxious she was trying to be sure to look as well kept as possible.

"He'll be here soon, I'm sure." Nicholas appeared

confident that all would be well, whether he believed it or not.

Shivering more from fear than from the cool breeze that swept through the passageway, they stood silently waiting for what seemed like an hour as time ticked on.

"Dad, he isn't coming?" Alix feared the worst.

No one answered as they continued waiting. Yet, they could see the ocean in the far distance as though it was miles away. "Oh God, please make the Doctor come."

Nicholas tried the encouraging method. "He said he would be here, so he will come."

"What if he was detained? Then we miss our ship and what then?"

"Honey, we can't do that. Do you know the price we pay if you save them?"

"I know. As a doctor I have made a vow to save whomever, whenever possible. I will do this until my dying day."

"It isn't only you. You are jeopardizing your entire family. If at least you hadn't given them our clothing."

"Ask for God's forgiveness. Please stay with me on this. Trust me, God will take care of us just as we are taking care of them. I'm leaving now."

Just as he was about to leave, he quickly glanced back and down the path. There must have been a posse of at least ten men. That would not be unusual, but if they were bringing someone to be treated, he had to get the Emperor and Empress out of his courtyard immediately.

"He yelled to his servant, take this carriage to the waiting family. Have them tie it up at the dock and I'll be back to pick it up later. Surely that will work."

_____

"Here comes the carriage, Dad. Who is the driver now?" Maria was frightened.

The man climbed off and urged Nicholas to take the reins.

"Take this carriage with your family to the pier. Tie it up there and we will come by to pick it up later, an emergency just came up. Everything you might need, like medicine to keep you well for your time on the ship, is in that package." With that the man left running back into the stables to mount up another carriage.

Nicholas immediately jumped into action, as was his custom. "Climb on! We need to be quick about all this!"

Alexandra shouted, "Quickly, Maria, get on the carriage. We must hurry,"

No one made a sound, until, "Hey, I found combs and look at all this? Even make-up! How wonderful is that?" Maria was impressed.

Quickly they made the few miles back to the pier, tied up the carriage on a pole at a nearby stable. Alexandra and Maria tried straightening their clothes and then hurriedly, almost in a run they approached the pier.

"Dad, look! They are about to pull away from the dock!" Maria was exhausted. "Surely, that means we will die here."

"Please, God, don't let them leave us behind now!" Maria was in earnest now.

Alexandra gasped as she turned to look at Nicholas.

They stood in silence as the Whistle blew.

The ocean slapped its waves against the pier. A lone sea gull flew by them. If only they could grab a wing and fly to safety.

Maria could only whisper, "We're doomed. Our plight is

sealed." Again, she prayed, "Please, God. This cannot be!"

The blue water was all that lay between them and their passage out, with no ship to rescue them, even a raft could never do that job.

A Crew member shouted, "Captain, there's another family standing at the dock. They obviously planned to come on board."

"We've started the engines. We are already late in leaving."

"Sir, there are three of them."

"It doesn't matter."

"I don't know why I'm saying this, but surely we can make an exception. There are not too many people allowed to even leave Russia and God only knows we have room and could use the fare."

"That's exactly my point. We allow them on only to have to refuse passage."

"Sir, what if?"

"What if what?"

"The word on land is that the Romanov family is trying to escape. What if these people are a part of that family?"

"Couldn't be, surely that couldn't be. There are only three of them and there should be seven."

"You know as well as I, that some of the newspapers reported that two of them were missing. I'm sure they had to separate even to get out."

"How could the Emperor leave any of his children behind? You and I couldn't do that even if it meant death."

"They would have made provisions for them to be sure. The Emperor certainly had the means to pull that off. Then, you will never know if you refuse these people passage. Should these people be the Romanov's and you refuse passage, they will all surely die just as the Russian authorities would have it. If they couldn't get them before, they certainly will now. I'm won't usurp you, Captain. It will have to be your decision whether you can show mercy."

The Captain hesitated. "Reverse the engines!" He shouted, "Put out the plank. Let them come and we will see what they have. If it isn't them, we will at least leave without blood on our hands, as you say, they surely will be slaughtered now if we leave them behind. In my heart, I would do anything to defeat those ugly Communists. Having said that, we still must follow orders. They must also have the correct paperwork or they would be stowaways and I can't let that happen on my watch."

The plank was lowered and just as quickly, the Romanov family began the boarding.

Upon recognition, "Come with me. My cabin and office is on the upper deck." Nothing more was said as the family followed the Captain to his quarters.

"I need to see your paperwork."

Nicholas handed him what he had on his person. Soiled and wrinkled from the climb out of the tunnel. "I'm sorry everything isn't in pristine condition but you must know that all didn't go as easily as we would have desired."

"I'm amazed!"

The Captain carefully examined every piece of paperwork, going over it more than once. "Where are the others? Please don't tell me they are already dead."

"It is to be hoped, my son left with Rasputin's brother who would connect him with my sister. I don't know how that went. Dr. Botkin was to take Olga and Tatiana to the ship but how soon we wouldn't know. Supposedly, they were to be disguised as a Priest and Nuns.

"Your youngest daughter?"

"She was to leave with Jacob for Canada. Jacob, being a Jew would have been under suspicion anyhow, so he volunteered to take her with his daughter. They have the necessary paperwork but who knows how that would've gone. With us, neither of them would have been able to endure what we just went through."

"You are on a foreign vessel so this should be okay. It will certainly take a few days to reach your destination but you are no longer under Russian authority." The Captain hesitated, "Your paperwork is in order but we must be vigilant. Though we are in international waters and no longer under Russian jurisdiction, nonetheless, you will need to not make it known who you are. I don't need any violence on my watch."

"I'm interested to know if you have a roster of passengers from previous voyages."

"I do." The Captain pulled a stack of paper from his desk. "Here, let me check." Thumbing through names, "But would they go by their formal names at a time like this?"

"You are right. Alexei had a passport with the name Hieni Tammet. Are you finding that name?"

"No, not anywhere."

"Knowing Alexei he would have gone by Henry."

"Not that either. Sorry. However, I only have the logs of this particular ship. There is another ship we alternate with. When you reach France you might check with the other ship Captain."

This wasn't the news they wanted but for now they could only hope. Was this finally reality? Had they finally made it safely onto the ship? Had they reached the end of their journey?

"My head is swimming. It is so hard to comprehend that finally we are away from the rioting, the threats and the killing. It is behind us." Maria looked at her Dad in earnest. "What now? We've never been on this side of life. What do we do and where to now, Dad, Mother?" Maria couldn't get her thinking around any of their surroundings. Surely, though it was good to be free from the threat annihilation.

"Come on, people. The crew will wait on us. Enjoy that for what it is. We will worry about tomorrow later."

"I guess we will need to learn how to do things for ourselves? That could be fun, don't you think?"

Nicholas and Alexandra made no more responses. The cabins were there, finally the place they could relax. For the first time in months they were free from being terrorized, running every step of the way, not knowing what lay ahead.

Maria asked, "I wonder where Anastasia is, where Alexei is? Is he going to be okay? Will we ever see them again?"

"I don't know Maria. I just don't know."

"How will we ever know? Alexei just might contact us by way of our Aunt, don't you think?"

"How unfortunate for us. Here we are running for our lives and never again can we reveal our identity. No more than Alexei or for that matter, Anastasia."

"Do you think either of them will ever talk?"

"You know what we just went through. Would we talk? If we can't talk, how will we ever find them?"

"It hurts to think of that. Sometimes I think death is easier to get through than continually being on the run and if not on the run, under cover. Is this really worth it all?"

Chapter 29
Soldiers on the Move 1919

"Let's get working on what you have to know, Ana. There has to be a lot to prepare for."

"It won't be anything big but we want to do it now. Eventually you will be leaving for Canada but I won't be going with you there. We think we still can make a life here."

"Just what I need to lift my spirits."

It was a year after Tina and David were married when Lena and Herman made plans to marry. Herman's wife had died in giving birth to a baby girl. As Herman struggled to work on the farm and care for his baby, he met Lena. It wasn't long before Lena was active in all parts of Herman's life from doing his house cleaning, cooking and caring for his baby.

"So, you really are going to marry Herman. You will make a wonderful couple." Jacob was pleased that his daughter had made such a wise choice.

"Herman's daughter is the sunshine of our lives and who knows, if I have my way, we will have a few more children."

"Then there is Susana."

"Yes, Johnny and I want to marry but he has to make himself invisible until we can have children or he will surely be drafted."

"Nobody really knows the census anyhow, just keep him in hiding for a while."

"That's not so simple. Both David and Johnny have to disappear when the soldiers come around and they are due to come again soon."

Jacob knew he had made a promise to the Emperor he planned to keep. Anastasia must get out of the country, but the timing he still didn't know. It would have to happen soon. He knew what to do when they would get to St. Petersburg but until they could make that trek, they would have to watch every step.

He knew the troops would come by as predicted. Their habit had been every four days. Jacob invariably gave them a bite to eat knowing soldier's rations were few which was giving them excuses for pillage and harming whomever might be in their paths. Jacob offered them good homemade food and often transported them to the next town. As a result they established an amicable relationship. Consequently, he and his family were always treated with respect. He told his girls, no harm would come if he continued to do their bidding.

As always, when the soldiers arrived, David, Johnny and Anastasia stayed in their rooms, hoping no one would think to check for hidden people. Anastasia knew she could lose herself in the large wardrobe closet.

It was a bright sunny morning when all of them sat at the dining room table at breakfast. Everyone one was in pleasant conversation when they heard the sound of horses. "I'm out of here." Anastasia went to her favorite hiding place, followed by Johnny. David hesitated.

Jacob went out to meet the soldier as always had been his custom inviting them to join his family at the breakfast table. Walking over to the horses, making small talk, hoping his family members would have found their hiding places by now.

However, the soldiers paid no attention to Jacob and barged into the house, just as David was trying to walk away. "Stop, young man. What is your name?" Ordered the Captain.

"David. I'm married to this lady, Jacob's daughter, Tina."

The Captain began to question Jacob's family. He turned to David, "Do you and your wife have any children?"

"Not as of yet. We are planning for a family."

"Since you have no children, you will have to come with us. The Army needs you and I have been commissioned to draft all the young men I can find on this run. Prepare your things you want to take with you. You will come with us."

Tina was too stunned. She couldn't say anything. It was hard to eat breakfast knowing her husband was to be snatched from her. It wasn't long before they said their goodbyes and David was gone. Gone to War, a War he had never wanted to join. He had no choice, no children, which to the Army meant he had no obligations. He was drafted and swept away into a War he vehemently objected to.

Before they left the house, they hadn't given up in their hunt for draftees. "And you, you said your name is Herman?"

"Yes, it is."

"How many children do you have?"

"This little girl, playing in the corner of the room but my wife is also pregnant and due any day now."

"For now we are not taking any men with children. You can stay with your family."

The troops left with David. They would not now know his whereabouts for some time. David was a man who believed in nonviolence as a way of life. Could he survive a war that was not accountable to anyone?

The soldiers were gone and so was David. Tina was devastated. She didn't know what she would do. Jacob tried to console her, "You will hear from him soon, and when he comes back for a visit we will make our break and leave with both of you. Just as soon as we hear from him we will begin our trek out of the country." He reinforced his decision for his daughter's comfort.

Ana was concerned, "Susana, you've been seeing Johnny. You need to be careful or they'll grab him before you guys have a chance to tie the knot and then with no children."

"We know. It is really easy right now to adopt. Just as soon as the adoption agency finds a baby for us we will marry. We wanted to do that anyhow. This will be a good time as any."

The day came, and everyone was sitting around when suddenly the soldiers were back again. He would give them dinner, as always and then he would gladly transport the troops to the next town should they need that. He had done this for months and had no trouble.

Until today.

After the soldiers, had been given food, the much-needed nourishment, Jacob accompanied the soldiers to his carriage with the intent of taking one of the soldiers to the next town while the other would ride in another direction, just as in the past. Standing outside of the house, the soldiers turned, staring at Jacob for a moment. Jacob ignored the stare while continuing making the preparations to ride. Nothing was said. They finally climbed on the carriage while the Captain rode with Jacob as he guided the horse down the road.

Then the Captain replied, "Sir, we are not entirely sure you are being honest with us."

"Why are you asking? What have we done? Haven't I always fed you and done exactly what you ask of me?"

"It isn't what you have done, but what you are keeping from us. There are rumors that you know where we can find the Czar's youngest two children if not the entire family."

"I'm sorry, but I have no idea what you are talking about. How would you even come to that conclusion? The Newspapers say that they were massacred and even all the rumors confirmed that. How should I know anything more? Obviously, I had hoped that wasn't true. Now you tell me you are looking for them? How is that possible? Are they all alive?"

"You know very well, Jacob, that the Newspapers are censored and regulated to control public behavior. You aren't that naive. Orders have been to bring them back alive for questioning. We feel confident that what you just said is true but there is also hearsay floating around that they might have escaped. If anyone would know, you should."

Jacob, being an Elder in his church tried desperately to keep things very cool. He had agonized over this dilemma praying God would protect him from this very situation. Since he had made his decision for Jesus and to serve Him for the rest of his life, he was now pleading with God to intervene. He knew very well he and God had to work this out. "I'm sorry. I have absolutely no confirmation that anyone escaped. Most of the news is what the towns people tell us and the newspaper."

"We questioned Martin, Marta and their son Marty. Martin told me you were acquainted with the Czar's family. He said there was no truth to knowing Anastasia and Alexei's whereabouts but Marta disappeared in a hurry. We questioned him more intensely, offered concessions. He insisted he knew nothing, we decided he was lying so one of my soldiers shot him."

"Oh, my God! You shot him and yet you just said, you wanted the Czar's children alive for questioning!" Jacob knew that meant *dead on sight*. What have you done? How will Marta care for her farm and Marty? How can she care for herself?"

"If you defy us and don't tell the truth, that's the result. We told her son if she talks and gives us the information we would see to her needs. This means her survival will require our assistance. Now tell us, do you know where the Czar's family disappeared to?"

"All I ever knew was that the Bolsheviks wanted to help them escape but then you conquered the country so now Communism is in power. I still don't get it. Everyone knows that the assassins already buried the bodies. What other proof do you want? According to the journalists report in our local newspapers the bodies were found thrown into a makeshift grave. Why would you even question this now? How would I or anyone else know anything different? I'm not sure I understand."

"You're just an old man. Their bodies were supposed to have been burned. You being the Elder of a church, I thought you would know the talk of the Town. Take us to the next town! We'll get our answer there. We'll shoot the answer out of someone."

There was no small talk on this journey. The deafening sense of fury was now hanging over Jacob's head. The only sound that could be heard on this trek was the hooves of his horse as they continued on.

Jacob finally broke the silence on their arrival to the destined town. "Here we are. What else can I do for you? I'm sure I'll see you on your way back."

"Give us your coat."

"Why do you need my coat? You have your own. It's very cold out here, probably close to zero."

The Romanov Dynasty ... What if

"Good, so give us your coat. You hear me, give it to us, old man!"

To avoid a struggle, Jacob handed them his coat. He knew he could just as easily be the next victim.

"Maybe now you'll know how serious we are. If you find anything out, you can have your coat back."

Without another word, Jacob exposed to the elements of zero-degree weather with no coat on his back, beckoned Sparky to move ahead. It was freezing cold as he sat there hanging on to the reins of his horse until he was out of gunfire range. Jacob slowed Sparky down, fumbling behind his seat where he kept a bag filled with emergency items. Fortunately, he never left anywhere without an extra blanket or two, just in case he would find someone in need along the way. He tugged at the blankets, grabbing onto one, nudging it out, pulling it over his shoulders. Stopping to do this was now not an option, he needed to get back quickly. He clung to the reigns praying Sparky would hurry as fast as he could. He felt the bitter cold temperature biting at his body.

Jacob knew now he had his work cut out for him. The decisions of what he needed to do had been made for him.

Chapter 30
The Plan

"Why don't we call it a night, Ana? Dad will be home soon. Somehow God keeps him safe even when he has to deliver the troops to the other town. I know I'd be too afraid but he says as long as we feed them they'll leave us alone."

"Sometimes, Tina, I'm just not so trusting."

Johnny and Susana had finally had the adoption finalized. They were now feeling much more comfortable when the soldiers would come by. "Susana and I had better be getting Maya and ourselves to bed. Tomorrow comes early enough as it is and we don't need a crying baby when knowing all we need is the sleep." Johnny knew what was best for his wife and baby.

"You are right, Johnny. Maybe that's why I married you. Are you going to call it a night Tina?"

"I'm going to wait awhile. Personally, I think Dad should have been home by now. I'm sure he'll be home soon. Then I'll see if he needs anything."

Anastasia, who was now going to be called Ana, was off to retire, too overcome by her circumstances. "Thanks and I too, have to give it up. I'm totally exhausted. Had enough for one day."

It was dark and cold outside so the very best place to be

was under down comforters to keep the cold out. Tina was still up brewing tea when Jacob finally arrived. He had barely opened the door when he heard, "Dad, why so late?" Noticing that he had only a blanket over his shoulders. Tina asked, "Why no coat? You look really cold. If you would've been out there much longer, you might have frozen to death! What happened?"

"Can't talk about any of this now but I'll get some sleep and in the morning, I'll have to be off with a responsibility I still have to accomplish."

"Drink this Dad. I'll get your other coat for you. In the morning, I'll have breakfast ready."

"Tina, you don't have to do that. I'm leaving really early. I have to leave before anyone stirs. I can't risk Anastasia's safety."

"No matter the time you plan to leave, something is going on and I want to be here for you."

"Tell me, how is Anastasia doing with all the changes she has to comply with?"

"You knew she has a photographic memory. Every bit of information about our family including years they were born, days they died down to their individual names, she has memorized it already. She knows everything just as though it was always a part of her life from birth. I can't remember birthdates and death dates like she does. It's unreal."

"The memory part could work against her. She won't easily forget who she is. I'm praying that God will enable each one of us in all of these situations to keep our saneness. None of our choices that are about to happen are any good but we have to do them."

"I don't understand Dad?"

"I need one more thing from you, without telling you the details. I must ask you to accept what is about to happen. Be aware, our lives are now in perilous danger. We will have to pack up and leave after I get back tomorrow. First I have to do something you and your sisters may not approve of but it is what it is."

Tina hesitated. Then asked, "Okay, okay. I get it. This had something to do with the ride to the other town and losing of your overcoat, right? Where are we leaving for and what may I not approve of? Since when did you need my approval and then when did you ever have to ask for it?"

"Sorry, I still can't reveal anything. I always had a plan but leaving here was going to occur later than sooner. I thought we had the time but now everything has changed and there is much more we have to do."

The two of them just sat there drinking hot tea. The plate of cookies stayed untouched while both of them tried to relax, and that was no easy task.

"Well, Dad, the least we can do is get some rest. Let's do it."

The duration of the night wasn't long enough to sleep under these distressed conditions. Tena's mind kept spinning. She was very aware that there was no security and being on the move would make an abundant amount of sense yet where were they going? Would the distance make them more secure? She knew only too well the whole country was in a total upheaval. Would they all just run and hide somewhere in the mountains and maybe someday there would be peace? Tina was not so naive as to believe such a scenario. Tina needed to cut the thinking and start the sleeping. How could anyone ever accomplish that?

Some sleep had come to both Jacob and Tina but both were up way before daybreak as not to awaken anyone and especially the baby. That's when each of them appreciated the foot-thick walls.

Daylight hadn't come yet but Tina was up, true to her word, making breakfast. Jacob came and sat at the table in total silence. Not even a good morning was uttered to his daughter as she waited on him. Finally, he broke the silence. "Tina, you need to trust me even when you don't understand. I need you to stand by me when my whole family thinks I'm crazy. Will you be able to do that for me?

Tina didn't say anything. Jacob prayed over breakfast asking for safety to be theirs. Slowly, they ate. The cloud hung over Jacob's head as he tried to eat what had been set before him. Would he be able to keep his family and Anastasia alive if Tina wouldn't be willing to work with him? Surely, they would all die if they couldn't work together on this matter.

It took Tina at least thirty minutes sitting and eating in silence. Finally, Tina spoke, "I can't know what you are talking about but it sounds like a life and death situation. Yes, I'm sure I won't understand but I will do as you ask. I will always do as you ask, no matter what. We only have each other. You still haven't told me where we are going but it will work, you will see. God is with us and He is definitely with you. I also know, though you are not able to tell me what you have to do, our dependence will have to be on God and then each other."

"Tina, this is the only way. God has shown me. We have to walk in it. Sometimes I have to sacrifice to enable all of us to live. Tina, I am not afraid of death but I could never live with having sat idle and then losing everything because I wasn't obedient to my God. Together we can do this." Jacob hesitated, "Thank you, Tina."

"I know Dad. Life will get a lot worse but we will follow God's leading and He has already won our battle for us. Go now! Be safe!"

Chapter 31
The Old Farm

Marty was on his knees as he filled the troughs with grain for the few cattle they had. Then he went over to fill the troughs with hay for the horses. He prayed, something his Dad never did, at least in his presence. He pleaded with God because the soldiers had threatened to return. Marty knew it meant he and his mother would be shot just like his Dad had been. Assassinated, was more like it. No one cared anymore. It was just no use in caring for anyone. The grieving in his heart would continue to bleed for his Dad. He didn't know what would happen but he assured his mother that he would take care of her. "It's just you and me Mother, we can and will do it."

Marta Klaassen couldn't be comforted as she sobbed, "I could have saved your Dad's life but instead I hid!"

"What do you mean?"

"If I would only have told them what they wanted to know."

"I'm not sure I even follow what you are saying, but had you done that, you know very well, we'd all be dead now."

"They promised ..."

Marty interrupted her, "And when do the *Commies* keep

their promises? This is a civil war, Mother."

"We are going to die!"

Neither of them knew what their next step should be. Martin and Marta had been farming the land since the day they married. Martin had always promised that once the fields would be productive enough they would rebuild the shack into a dream home. Then little Marty was born and it seemed as though all they could do was scrape by with the little they had. From time to time, the village would send food over to make up the slack and at Christmas time, the elders of the church would visit with gifts for the family and extra food for their dinner. Yet, Martin never entered the church door since the birth of his son.

Both Marty and Marta just stood in the tiny kitchen looking at one another in despair. "Mother, I can rebuild this house and make it to be what you want. I will do it for you."

"Marty, you are a good son. I believe you want to but we have no money."

"I'll make the farm productive and pull in the profits and you'll see, we can do it."

"Son, the country isn't stable enough even to get a job. The Communists came and killed your Father, do you think for a moment they won't be back? They said as much because they believe I know something."

Startled by the noise of horse's hooves, Marty turned his head, looking directly at his Mother, "I can hear a horse in the distance. Someone's coming ..."

"That'll be them again and this time ..."

"Oh, Mother, you're going to get us both killed. Please, I beg you not to say anything. I will answer them for you, please I beg you!"

Looking through the small window in their meager kitchen, Marty realized, "Look, I don't think it's them ... Wait...It's Jacob.

What does he want with us? He has to know we didn't say anything!" Marty went to meet him.

Jacob's wagon stopped at the house. It didn't take a minute to jump to the ground from the buggy. "Where's your Mother, Marty?"

"What do you want from her? Haven't you done enough? She's inside crying. She thinks it's your fault that Dad was killed."

"I just heard about that. That's why I'm here."

"Why don't you just leave her alone? Haven't we suffered enough? Just leave us alone! You can't fix anything!" Marty was in tears and began shouting, "Death is death. Dad is dead, did you hear me?"

Jacob ignored Marty's comments. "Is your Mother in the house?" Without waiting for an answer, he bolted in the front door. Seeing Marta with her head in her hands, sobbing, "Marta, I'm here to help you. You may hate me right now but there is a solution to all of this. I can't change what happened but maybe we can work this out and protect ourselves and make it a little easier for you."

"Marty and I will surely be killed."

"That's just not so. Let me share my plan with you. Since my wife died a couple of years ago I have been a lonely man with just my daughters around to encourage me. If you marry me, I will have a companion and you and Marty will be protected. I have the means to do this so you don't need to worry about anything. When the soldiers come back to do the terrorizing, you and Marty will be with us."

Marta sat there thinking for a moment and in her grief, she looked at Marty as he stood in the doorway. "What do you think I should do, Marty?"

"Mother, you don't have to do this. We can pull out of here by ourselves. I will take care of you. I'll go into the city and get some work, earn money so we can eat. The Farm isn't doing well for us anyhow, it never has."

As if ignoring her son, Marta looked at Jacob, "Who's going to marry us?"

"Pastor Nelson would do that for us. It has to be immediate. After that we will all be leaving our homestead."

"Where are you taking us?"

"I don't want to say just in case we could be followed. We will be safe. I do have a plan."

"I certainly can't say I'm sorry to be getting out of this pigpen. Martin never did anything around here. He always said it didn't matter and maybe some other day he would get to it. Now his excuse was that everything would be taken away anyhow. That good for nothing bum! I loved him! Can you believe that? I loved him. I didn't want him to die. We can't even have a funeral, there is no closure to any of this."

"Where did they bury him, Marta?"

"They didn't bury him, they just pushed him in the ditch over there. They threw dirt over his body, and then left with a threat for me. They said they would be back, expecting me to talk. I hid, but that's what they said to Marty."

"Let's go over there and as an Elder, I will perform the last rites. Come Marta."

Turning to Marty, "Come Marty, let's do the honorable thing."

Together Marty and Jacob dug a grave. "This is tough work Jacob. The ground is so hard from all the cold weather we've had."

"You are right but we can do it. We're almost finished." After the grave was dug they took a sheet and wrapped the body and placed it in the make shift grave, covering him with the dirt. They placed stones around it to show that a grave was there. "Let's make a cross, Jacob. Here, it's simple but I'll write his name on it.

There, that even feels better."

At the graveside, Jacob began the short, brief ceremony, "We thank you, Lord for what you have given us. I know we are in terrible times, but be merciful to us. May Martin be home with you as a sinner saved by grace because of your Son, Jesus Christ, who died on that Cross for our sins. Now, ashes to ashes and dust to dust, Amen." Together the three of them walked back to the house.

Get what you can, put it all in the buggy and we need to be out of here."

Marta sobbed as they drove away. Her heart had been broken by a very cruel mob. Surely, the soldiers would get their just rewards eventually. "There isn't a person I can trust anymore." She wept some more. Marta had to grieve or she could never be accepting of her circumstances.

Finally Marta broke the silence as they rode along in the buggy, "When and where is the wedding to be?"

"It has to be quickly before the troops are back to see us."

"They'll hunt us down, you'll see."

"Marty will be one of our witnesses but we need to see Rev. Nelson quickly and that means today, this moment, right now."

"You know Jacob, I still hate you and your daughters. Somehow you will pay for this."

"Mother, can't you be nicer than that? It's because of Jacob we could get to live."

"Let me finish Marty. I did want to say thank you for saving the life of my son and me. It is my opinion that you should never have taken Anastasia with you. They got what they deserved."

Jacob ignored her, "If you are ready, let's detour to the chapel. As far as I know, it should still be there."

The Chapel was small but shepherded by Pastor Nelson in

spite of the scattering of his entire flock. He knew, those who stayed behind would need encouragement and he would be there for them. He wanted to keep everything together for his people. All he had was his hidden Bible not yet discovered by the Communists. God was the only hope anyone had in these Revolutionary days. For years, he had taught the people to persevere and care for those around them. It was now his opportunity to prove, he with God's help could do it. Share what they had with the hungry but most of all to evangelize the lost. It almost seemed to be too late. What had been done for Christ would last but anything else would be worthless. Wealth was of no value. It couldn't buy anything because there was nothing to buy. Escaping with their lives would be their only goal. Eventually the soldiers would come to the Chapel and destroy the Bibles as they had done in most of the churches already. Now it was time to perform one more honorable duty and that was for Jacob and Marta to marry.

The Wedding was as unceremonious as it could possibly be. No formalities, just the vows they needed. Then they would be off to gather with the rest of the family and then be on the run.

Jacob thanked the pastor, "I appreciate everything. May God be with you and keep you. "It won't be too long when we shall all meet again but then it will be in the presence of Jesus, to be sure."

"Let's get your things together and get going. All I ask from both of you, Marta and Marty is, my daughters are special to me. Leave them alone."

"To be sure, the Princess isn't yours. Just so you know, I refuse to treat her special, no favors coming from me, not on your life. She is going to have to live like ordinary people, like the rest of us. I have been poor all of my life and she will have a taste of real life. I will make her tough."

Jacob made no comment. All he could ask is that she would say nothing of Anastasia's identity. The horse's hooves continued to hit the ground repeatedly as they rode on.

Chapter 32
Unwanted News

"I think I hear Uncle, I mean … sorry, Dad is coming."

"You're right. Let's go see what's up with him." Tina knew something was to happen on his return. He had said as much, not to think he was crazy, he had a reason.

"Are you coming, Lena?"

"I wanted to start dinner for everyone but first help Susana take care of the baby. You go ahead"

Anastasia and Tina stood in the doorway on the way to meet the carriage, "Tina, isn't that Marta and Marty? Where's Martin, her husband?"

"Don't know Ana."

Jacob and Marty climbed off the wagon and then helped Marta get down. "Now I want you to meet your knew Mother. Treat her well, and things will be fine."

Anastasia wanted to speak, Tina nudged her whispering, "and it will work out."

"Marty will take the stuff from the wagon and then let's have our first dinner together."

"Welcome, Marta." Tina smiled, only because she had promised her Dad that she would be accepting of his decision.

"You must call me Mother," demanded Marta.

"Mother," Tina complied.

"As for you, young woman, you are not a Princess around me. Just remember, no favors from me."

"I hear we have extra people for dinner." Lena didn't know the reasons but she wouldn't question anything she wasn't able to think through first. That was her style. "It's not a problem. In this household, we always make enough food to feed whomever wishes to join us."

"Come with me, Ana."

Marta immediately responding to hearing the name change, "You are now going by Ana instead of Anastasia? You think a name change will help you disappear into the woodwork? Everybody recognizes you. It'll take more than that to protect your identity."

Anastasia said nothing.

Tina said, "Work with me, Ana, we have to do some preparing for our new family members." Both of them, Tina and Ana began the preparations for the living quarters.

"Let's get the guest room ready for Marty and put Marta's stuff into Dad's room. It should be as he would want it, I'm sure."

"Tina, how will I ever learn to like Marta?" Whispered Anastasia. "She surely isn't making that very easy. I'm beginning to think she will shout it out on the rooftop. What am I to do? She's bent on telling everyone who I am."

"Don't even begin to worry about that. She won't do that on her life. Her husband was killed for that exact reason. There is no way she'll do that because she is afraid for her own life."

"Is that why Uncle Jacob married her?"

"If I think about this logically, there would have been more than one reason. First to shut her up or we would all have been killed just because there was suspicion whether they found any proof or not. Probably the major reason, it would be the decent

think to do for him to save them from starvation and torture. We all
know the Communists are not very trustworthy with the killing
going on, even as we speak. They might just kill for the sake of
killing. Then, if there should be a third reason, it would be to save
you. Please don't worry about any of this, we will make it, God is
with us. This is what He wants for us, I know it, Ana."

"I guess I have to submit to this unbearable, hateful woman
and all her venom she has for me. All of us would rather be alive
than dead. I know I want to live. Hey, I know I'm getting out of
this alive. After all, that's how Gypsy Wanda saw it too."

"Ana, you need to stop that nonsense. God is not pleased to
have you trust in soothsayers."

"My mother always did that so why shouldn't I. Oh, I know
I was told to never do such a thing, but that coming from Rasputin?
Give me a break. He thought he was God's gift to women."

"You don't just do things for spite. You should know
better. God will always show us the next step. We don't have to
guess at the future when we follow the Lord. After all, God knows
the future."

"Well, Gypsy Wanda told me I would meet a blonde, blue
eyed man in another country. I'm just going to hold on to that."

"You really do need to stop that Wanda stuff. You must
simply follow Jesus. Wanda can't protect you and keep you safe.
God can and He will."

"Why is there so much taboo toward Soothsayers,
anyhow?"

"God protects you and wants you to trust Him and only
Him. He doesn't share His power with anyone. He is a jealous God
and He wants all of us to follow Him only. Every part of our being
has to belong to Him and really, that is how He will protect us. If
you start putting your trust in Soothsayers, then Satan gains a
stronghold and you'll find yourself doing things that are not right

and eventually you will be where you don't want to be. Who knows that this so called tall blonde man is the man you should marry? He could easily lead you away from God. You don't want to do that, do you? The other choice is follow the Lord totally and completely, like *Love the Lord your God with all your heart and with all your soul and with all your strength*, and God will honor that. Then you'll live the life God has planned for you."

"I definitely do love God. Somehow, though I would like to know the things that God doesn't reveal as quickly as I'd like Him to. I guess I have to give that up and just trust in Jesus."

"Let's do that, you'll be better for it. That doesn't mean everything goes easy for you or me, but it is the only way."

Tina remembered only too well her Dad's comments just before he left this morning when he said this was not an option. "Don't know any answers."

Lena finally entered the room, "Are you guys done? Dinner is on the table, come. Let's get acquainted with everyone."

"Before we all sit down to eat, Marta and Marty, follow me and I will show you your rooms. Now, Mother, this is where Dad sleeps, so it is now prepared for you to share it with him."

"I need my own bed and my own room!"

"Okay, I'll get Marty to help me prepare another guest room for you."

"No, Anastasia can help you. Marty needs to stay with me." Both Marty and his Mother, Marta dismissed themselves to enter the living room and settle on the Sofa.

"Is everything to your liking?" Jacob questioned.

"It will be when Anastasia prepares another bedroom for me."

"Extra bed, extra room?"

"Yes, Jacob. What do you expect of me? Martin is not dead more than a few days and you expect me to sleep with you?"

"Couldn't Marty help Tina with the bed?"

"I told you I am going to make Anastasia a survivor. If she thinks she's special, I will remove all doubt."

Marty answered, "I'm sure you will."

Ana would spend her teenage years mourning the loss of her family while at the same time it became apparent, hatred would be laced into the very family that was there to protect her while she was traveling as a fugitive. Would this be her legacy to live by and for how long? Even the ordinary citizens hated the sight of her family. The time had come to leave the country her father had made an oath to protect until his death. She had heard of wicked stepmothers before but she never dreamed it would become her lot to suffer. Now she had a stepmother that hated her very existence. *But then, she's not really my step-mother.*

Tina spoke, "Mother, Ana and I need to get back to studying so we will absence ourselves for a bit."

"Just be sure Anastasia is available when I want her!"

"Please, Mother, do not call her Anastasia. She is to be known as Ana. We must be consistent with our facts. It's life or death for all of us."

"You know very well, Tina, you are teaching the woman you call Ana a pack of lies. Do you think you can get away with that?"

"Only if you will help us and help you must. Your life depends on it as well. You might want to think about that."

Normally, Jacob would have run interference but he didn't. He knew he had taken on an unthinkable task but had to accomplish this no matter what. Nicholas hadn't prepared papers for Marta so in the end she could not travel to the Americas with them. He was totally prepared to send Anastasia on the ship alone. She could make it alone. She had what it would take. Maybe Jacob wouldn't survive to the end but at least he would have completed his promise. However, this he must keep to himself and not discuss with any of them.

It was a relatively silent dinner since any conversation had become extremely awkward. Jacob tried to talk about the uncertain plans of the future. Don't settle in too well but we have to be gone before the next round of soldiers come through."

Marta wasn't done with Ana. "I'm not finished with your Princess. There is a broken chair in the kitchen. I want your precious Ana to go into the garage and get the tools to fix it. It must be she who is to repair the chair. It is dark out there but she must do it by herself."

While Tina and Lena continued to clean the kitchen after dinner, Marta kept after Ana to do as she had ordered.

It was, as Marta had said, already dark out. Ana could barely see the walkway that led to the tool shed. She walked a few steps when she realized someone was following her. *'Please not that wicked woman,'* turning to look behind, she saw Marty. "How come? That's your mother in there. You heard what she said."

"She's being totally unreasonable. It isn't called for so I thought I would go with you."

"She said she will punish me if anyone would dare to help."

"Mother is just all talk. She is still very angry because the Red Army killed my Father. The Soldier's had no reason to shoot him but it was my mother's fault."

"You said what? Her fault?"

"When the soldiers started asking Dad questions, Mother ran into the house making it look like we were aware of your whereabouts. That made them suspicious so in killing him they figured Mother would break down, they would find you anyhow."

"What's to stop her even though she married Uncle Jacob?"

"She'll never do that. Your Uncle is rich but my family has always been very poor. Poor mostly because Dad didn't want to work the farm."

"Maybe he wasn't well enough to do the hard work."

"I don't think so, he just didn't care. He didn't even care if I got an education. We didn't even always have enough food on the table so I would go and see what I could get from the neighboring farms and if I could work for food. When I brought food home he wanted to know where I stole it and if I had any money. It wasn't long before Dad and I just quit talking to each other, seemed to be easier that way."

"How did the education go for you?"

"I managed to sneak out. There was a school close to our farm. Mother knew about it but Dad didn't so I just kept going. It kept me from going mad. There was nothing else to do but work so I grabbed all the learning I could. I managed to learn a little Latin, English and Russian. I can take care of myself if I have to."

"Tougher than what I'm going through, huh, Marty?"

"Hardly."

"Anymore, none of us know what safe is."

"That's right, Ana. I don't think there is such a place of refuge. We just have to be vigilant. Maybe if we get out of here, and find a more desolate place, they won't come looking for us."

"They'll never give up looking. Somehow, they think I'm alive. Oh, how I wish my family did make it out alive. That might be wishful thinking. That's all I have for now Marty."

"I guess."

"You know, Marty, I think I could do this just by remembering where Uncle Jacob kept his, oh, sorry, *Dad* kept his tools. Here it is. Do you think this is what I need?' Can you believe this? I'm supposed to repair the chair? I've never had to fix anything in my entire life."

"Here, let's take both these tools. I don't even know what she expects. Look, we'll take this glue. She'll think it's fixed and when she sits on it we'll know you passed the test."

"You're mean, Marty."

"That would be hilarious. Want to try?"

"When she complains, I'll tell her she should've hired a carpenter." Marty thought his mother was completely out of her mind.

"She could hurt herself."

"Think of how she hurts you and how the rest of us feel about that."

"You are right Marty. It isn't enough that she orders me around every hour of every day but I had a stuffed rag doll I couldn't find anymore. I kept it with me when we knew we were going to be on the run. Dolls aren't important in times like these, I know that. It doesn't even mean anything accept that it was given to me by my Father on one of my sick times. I just wanted it to remind me of my parents should I never see them again. I happened to be straightening clothes in her room and there it was. I Asked Uncle Jacob to get Marta to give it back to me."

"Then what?"

"He said it was better that way. If it was found, the Soldiers would know it was mine."

"You know he is right but with all you've been through, I'll find it and sneak it out for you. Trust me."

"Why are you so good to me?"

"I know we are to forgive people, even if my mother is hateful, but you have been through enough."

Chapter 33
Typhoid Breakout 1920

"Ana, bring me a wet towel. Marta is coming down with a fever. Grab some of those gloves. Remember the ones Dr. Botkin gave us before we left. Get them now!"

"Where are the gloves? Okay, I see them." Ana grabbed the box. It was only because they were leaving the city that Dr. Botkin insisted they take first aid supplies. There would be no Doctors to assist anyone if they were in a remote area and especially if they didn't want to be discovered. Rubber gloves were rare but Dr. Botkin knew that Jacob would never hesitate to help and assist anyone in need even if it would be a dangerous feat.

The first known gloves were made from sheep's intestines and intended to protect the surgeon from getting infections. A German physician used these in 1758 to perform a gynecological operation. Surgeons then often wore only a simple apron over their regular clothing. By the eighteen forties, pathologists began using rubber gloves.

"We need fresh water to help keep the fever down."

Everyone was running now, Typhus seemed to be the after throw from Typhoid. Conditions had been deteriorating rapidly and very few people were careful with cleanliness and eating habits. Homes and stores had been destroyed and looted resulting in the extreme hunger.

Supplies for the Army was sparse also. When the troops came through the Cities they seized everything they could. Rape was not unheard of in the rural areas either. Should anyone object, the soldiers would kill at will as they stole from Adults and children alike.

"Tina, I have the water, here. The cups are slightly broken but it holds water."

People everywhere, around the compound could be heard crying out of pain and desperation wanting relief. Just a cup of water was all Ana could do to help at least some of them. They had done the little that was possible to help the dying people get through the severe situation. Night finally came when Tina said, "I don't know about the other people but I think Marta will rest now. Maybe she is able to get through all of this."

"You know Tina, as much as she hates me, I'm praying she will make it and maybe all of us will get out of this country and have a life of at least some kind of freedom."

"It seems as though all the countries are at war most of the time. Governments are determined to expend their borders, no matter what the collateral cost. Why can't we be in peace in our own countries?"

"You're right, Tina. I always thought we were protected from most of that. They could do all the fighting they wanted but I believed we would be safe. How mistaken I've been. Here we are running for our lives and it isn't over yet."

"Come with me, I think it is over for Marta though. She won't have to worry any more about anything."

"I feel so badly for Marta. She lost everything and Dad rescued her for a time. Now all that is over. I'm really sad."

"I'll find Marty and Dad."

Another day and another death, it wasn't getting any easier.

Not even Jacob's family was now immune to any of this War. They just had to be on the run.

Survivors were few but the epidemic for the present was over. Jacob spoke, "We need to clean up and then get ready to travel to the train depot. From there it will be a long train ride."

Marty was preparing to take his leave of the family. His mother had just been buried and he would be off to care for himself. Find a job somewhere and do what he could. "Here's where I get out on my own."

"Are you definite about that?"

"I am. I don't need to be running. No one is looking for me. I will find property out in the middle of nowhere and make my own life. Maybe, I'll find myself a wife. Who knows, but I want to take my leave of you. I don't need to be running from soldiers that are bent on drafting every man they can find. Thank you, Jacob, for what you did for my Mother and myself. You saved our lives."

"Why don't you take Sparky with you. I'm sure you will need him."

Sparky had been like a family member to Anastasia. He was Ana's personal buddy she had trained and cared for him during her many opportunities she had when she spent time with Jacob's family. Now she had to give him up. He had stood by her and now that tormented Ana. First it was Jimmy and now it would be Sparky. Just possibly, if Marty had him, he would be taken care of.

"That would be wonderful. I would like that. Then I can get away and really be on my own. Thank you."

"Go with God. Never forsake your God, He will be faithful to you."

———————

It was now 1921 Lena and Herman were married with four

children. Susana and Johnny had already adopted their first child.

There just had to be one more surprise visit from the troops before they had time to begin the move to points yet unknown. Again Anastasia disappeared, staying out of sight. Jacob offered food and rest as he did before. When they were about to make their departure, they hesitated. Jacob didn't want another experience like before when they had him under suspicion of knowing where Anastasia might have gone to escape. What did they want of him now? Did they know she had always been here? Had he delayed too long the leave for St. Petersburg?

Jacob decided he needed to inquire of them if there had been any word from David. Waiting for what they would want just wasn't now in the plan.

"Have you heard where David might have been stationed and when it might be time for his leave?"

"With all your good will to us, I almost forgot. Here's a telegram for your daughter." They handed the letter to him. "Our condolences." They left.

Tina heard what had just been said, and there was no consoling her. It would take time for her to deal with the death of her husband.

The next day, Jacob had made the decision. "Come, all of you." They gathered in their living room to listen. "There cannot be any delaying our time to leave. Pack up your belongings and we will begin our trek out of the country. I wanted to hear from David first, now we know he isn't returning so it is time to leave. I just need to know which of you wish to come with us."

Herman made the first suggestion, "Lena and I have talked much about this day and we will stay and rear our family in the family home. Should any of you wish to come for a visit in the future, we will be here with the lamp on. For us, we think it is the thing to do."

"Johnny and I, with our baby Maya, will come with you until Anastasia boards the ship to sail for Canada, with any of you who want to accompany her. It may be a good thing for us to do. We have Maya and she might just be our salvation when we are traveling. If Anastasia is followed, she can have the baby with her."

Jacob then said, "That means Tina will come with us and we have exit papers for all three of us. We've wrapped up all our loose ends here. What do you say? Let's get out of here."

Packing and farewells were done and now they were preparing for the trek to the train ride for St. Petersburg. It was only a few hours' journey so Herman took one of the other horses to pull the carriage to the train station.

Ana's determination to survive was ingrained in her mind. Everything she needed to know should she be interrogated was clear for her. The drive to live in freedom, would there ever be such a place, was her only goal.

Jacob sat with Johnny and Herman driving the wagon with the women and baby in the coach. Before they had gone very far he searched his jacket pocket to find if he still had his papers. He held the envelope up, just slightly, "This tells us where to go and has our fares to get to St. Petersburg and Canada. The Emperor gave me instructions and an address. We have somewhere to go. We just don't know the conditions we will find ourselves under."

"I still don't understand, Dad. When you get there," Herman asked, "what then?"

"I have our papers to be dropped off at the Consulate to be stamped so that we can travel abroad."

"How much money are you going to need for that? Do you have enough for everyone? I know, Jacob, God will see you through this journey to the end but are you really prepared?"

"I still have the gold bar given to me by my father and

some money from Nicholas. We will be just fine." They stopped in the city, just short of the train station. It would only be a few blocks to walk.

Herman headed back to be with his wife Lena and their children. He was trusting all would go well for them. Leaving some of the family would always leave a whole in his heart but he knew God would be in control.

Chapter 34
Like Nomads 1922

The journey, thus far, had left everyone feeling lost, forsaken and with an uncertain future. Jacob knew he must get Ana away from suspicion. They would have to keep going.

Susana, in earnest looked at Jacob, whispering, "I think we are being watched. Quickly, Ana take my baby, play mother." That wasn't a difficulty for Ana. She enjoyed fussing over the baby.

"We're still being followed. Here, let's go through the train yard. Make sure the trains don't start moving when we go through."

"Tina, I'm going between the trains. See you people on the other side. They are coming our way."

"Go! Go all the way through with the baby. She'll be fine with you and when you are seen, make sure you have your shawl over your face. Go!"

"I've got it. I'm gone." Ana quickly walked between the motionless trains, from one to the other. "Maya, please don't cry. Don't be scared, I'm right here, rest in my arms." Ana knew she was whispering words, desperately trying to comfort herself. Maya would be just fine.

"The trains are moving, be still Maya. If we don't move,

stand still between the tracks, they'll pass us by. Oh, God, we need you now!" The minutes felt like hours. Anastasia attempted to gain her composure. Looking around but feeling dazed, she held Maya tight.

"Ana, Ana, behind you, we're here," whispered Tina.

Anastasia jumped! Turning around to see who was next to her, "You scared me. I am glad to see you, Tina. Things are beginning to be dangerously close and everything is starting to close in on me. I have to get out of here."

"We should be okay now."

"Did they stop you guys?"

"No, but they came close enough to get a look at us. We kept our heads down and pretended not to notice. I saw them nod to one another and then they continued on their way. We made it this time."

"That means they were looking for me."

"Let's get to the train station now. We have to figure out which train goes to St. Petersburg." Jacob wanted just get to where they were going with no more delays but before he had a chance to move, a short man in Chinese garb stopped him to inquire of him where they were going.

Jacob answered, "St. Petersburg."

"Follow me. You want out of Russia. I take you through China. Pay me gold. I insure you and your family get to China. Then you go anywhere. You be free."

"Why would I pay you in gold? Where would I get gold? I have no gold with me."

"Sir. We know you have gold. Come with us." The Chinese man walked just a little closer, "See over there? It is not far. We get you across border."

"What about that Jacob? Could we make it?" Johnny questioned.

Jacob stepped back with his family, and spoke, "How would he think I had gold? How would he even know? Are you sure that man is Chinese?"

"He talks broken English like he might be Chinese."

"Take a good look. Then look all around. There are dead bodies scattered around and you think we will get through? He'll take gold all right but we will be dead as they are."

"Then who is following us? Is this now about the Czar or about gold?"

Jacob wasn't sure but he was going to make a safe gamble, "At the moment, we have to believe it is about both."

Johnny said, "If we were to give the gold to this Chinese man and we crossed over with them, we'd lose the Red Army."

"Look more closely, all of you." Tena, and Susana joined them. "Look at that man. He is no more Chinese than any of us. I just don't understand how he thought I would be carrying gold."

Johnny answered, "Let me get this straight. We are being followed because of gold as well as the Red Army."

"The good thing about the Red Army is that they aren't exactly sure if they need to follow us. However, that so-called Chinese man is sure of why he is following us. That isn't good." Jacob was visibly shaken.

Tina, joined in. "There are other ways, Dad. We can go through the mountains and work our way into Peru. Then we would be totally free, become citizens there and then eventually go to Canada. Canada is our destination, isn't it?"

"I don't think I could survive taking Anastasia and Tina with me alone through the mountains into Peru. I can't be sure I can keep everyone safe. For me, it'll be safer on the train."

Johnny hadn't given up. "It'll be dangerous on the train as well. None of us will be able to rest. We will need to be alert all the time."

"You are right, Johnny, but we have all our legal immigration papers. We should be fine all the way to St. Petersburg. It shouldn't be that hard."

"You might be right, but it's a couple of days on the train. If anyone gets suspicious, we are all dead. You know that?"

"I'm willing to take the risk. Are the rest of you with me?"

Ana wasn't usually so obedient but she stood with confidence, "I know we will make it to Canada. That's where I'm supposed to find my husband. So how can we lose?"

Uncle Jacob turned to look at Ana. "Since when did you come to that conclusion?"

Tina responded, "Ana didn't tell you because she knew you and the rest of the family would never approve of her talking with a Soothsayer."

"You what? Are you out of your mind?" Jacob was clearly disturbed. "Do you know how easy it is for Satan to deceive you when you mess in his territory?"

"It's okay, Uncle Jacob. Sorry, Dad. I know better. I can honestly tell you Satan will never deceive me. I know the difference. They can say what they will but I know my God is the only one who really knows. Just the same, playing with the future can't be that bad."

"Mark my words, Ana, that is not what you need right now. God can only help you if your trust is entirely in Him. He does not share himself with Satan's innovations. God and I are working hard to get you out of here alive but I need your cooperation."

"I promise, I'll behave. I will only do as you say from now on."

"It won't be because of God or me you don't make it."

"Dad. You know my own mother used to go see Gypsy Wanda all the time. So I thought, well maybe I could learn something. I'm always willing to learn. Mother said she went to see Gypsy Wanda to listen to the *word on the street* so she could tell Dad and in turn he could protect the people."

"Think about it, Ana. It didn't work, did it? Follow God and we will all make it out of this country alive."

Tena started talking, "You know, our people have been moving from one place to for centuries. We should be called Nomads. First, we had to run from the Priests because we were following Martin Luther who translated the Bible so that everyone could read it. We were being persecuted for that. Now we are running again because the Communists want to assassinate us. Well, not so much us, but you, Ana and your entire family."

Jacob responded, "Maybe if a few more good Christians would have been willing to stand up for what is truly right, our Country wouldn't have been taken over by Communism. Just letting things happen wasn't exactly the right thing to do either. God certainly didn't want our Country to go in the direction it did. If we weren't free to worship before we came to Russia, now we can't worship either. So, what is the answer? We need to be obedient to God first. We do have to be willing to stand for what is right. I guess, I don't anymore think that we shouldn't bear arms. Sometimes God requires it of us."

"When it comes to protecting our Country from forces that would destroy the very principles of God, we have to defend our freedoms. Freedom is far from free. The cost is more than any of us care to admit."

Johnny joined in, "I agree with tolerance but we do need to have the free will to accept or reject God. We also have to know what the result is going to be if we do or don't choose to believe. That's why we have preachers and teachers. Yet, I have a very strong opinion when it comes to standing strong to protect the people of a nation, we have to be willing to fight for our freedom."

"I, for one, agree with you Johnny. Even I have to admit

that learning all this stuff about our country, Russia, and then not being willing to take up arms is making our country weak enough for any group of people to take it over. Dictate what they want and now where is our freedom? Isn't that what is happening now? For me, I have to believe that our people must protect themselves. My Father was the Czar, surely, I have to agree that he tried to protect this great country." Anastasia was sure of herself.

"Too many wars to fight. It's impossible to continue doing that without neglecting the people. When the people get neglected too long, this is what we have. I agree we have to bear arms for our freedom but then I don't believe for a minute that not bearing arms was the sole reason for the downfall of Russia. The civil unrest was more likely caused by not listening to the needs of ordinary people and when they were promised, by turning from the Romanov rule, it will become nothing but good, well, here is what you get. Apparently, the people don't care about principles anymore."

Tina spoke, "But if everyone would lay down their arms, people wouldn't die senselessly anymore."

"Tina, in an ideal world that might work but with evil running rampant, how can that be?" Jacob continued, "Right or wrong, being armed now in this instance might save our lives or get us killed. We just need to get where we are going to get out of here."

"So the train it is. Where do we board?"

"Let's stay together and Ana, the baby is yours for now."

Chapter 35
Train Interruption

The family was finally boarded on the train to St. Petersburg.

"I hate the squeakiness of the wheels on the tracks. It seems to give me a headache."

"I'm sorry Ana. Is that the only thing you hate?"

"Good Tina, I hate running scared. This wasn't supposed to happen to any of us. For me, all I ever wanted was peace. What has happened?"

Jacob spoke, "That might be your only desire, and I don't believe in an *eye for an eye* and a *tooth for a tooth*. I believe in forgiveness and if we can, turn the other check, but you know what, that won't stop the violence. There will always be evil in this world until the coming again of Jesus Christ. No matter our intentions, Satan thinks he can succeed by attacking us all. Suppose we have to trust God like Job did. No matter what, follow the Lord, He will take care of us in the end whether He chooses to take us home or allows us the privilege of living through all of this."

"Yeah, I guess this is supposed to be a privilege. Life is a gift so we should treat it as such and treasure it." Tina was right.

Waxing philosophical was all good and well, but they were

on their way to an unknown place where they would await further direction. Anastasia thought about it. Until now, nothing had been easy. People said her parents and sisters were dead. They even said Alexei had been killed. In her heart, she could feel their presence every now and then. Maybe God might have spared them. Seeing them again would never happen, dead or alive so what did it really matter? Well, she had her own life to be concerned about now and if they would get to sail for Canada, the future prediction that Gypsy Wanda had given her, might just come true. She still would have the rest of her life to live and maybe even have children of her own. Would she want the past now that it had been taken away? Could her new life ever be a good life?

Finally, they had boarded the train, found their seats. They sat, looking out the window as the train started to move. First, it was the bell and whistle of the train that verified it was on the move. The feel of the ground vibrated under them. With the window pulled down and open, the smell of hot steam and oil was all too prevalent. Then there was the chuff-chuff of the smokestack. Ana thought to herself, this is all just temporary and only until they would arrive at their destination.

A middle-aged man and woman approached them, "May we sit next to your family?"

Now everyone sat silent. This isn't what Jacob wanted for his family. They needed to be discrete and not draw attention to themselves.

The couple pursued, "Where are you people from and where are you going?"

Johnny thought for a moment and immediately realized how vulnerable they could be. They couldn't just ignore everyone or it would cause suspicion. "We are from the countryside. Where are the two of you from?"

"Like you, from a small town just a few cities down. We

are merely sightseeing." For a moment, they were quiet. Soon they spoke again, "We just came from the Diner Coach and the food is incredible. If you want to go try the food, you can leave your stuff here and we'll take care of it."

"No," Jacob insisted, "we are okay. There are enough of us to take care of our things. We'll be fine. Don't fret about us. By the way, how's that baby of yours Ana?"

"Just fine, Grandpa. My baby is just fine."

At first thought, Jacob was afraid they might be looking for Anastasia.

The couple interrupted again, "We didn't introduce ourselves, my name is Charles and this is my wife Betty." He waited for a moment hoping someone would offer a name but when no one identified himself he continued, "I have a really good deal for you, Jacob. We are looking for investors."

Johnny realized that without introductions, these people knew Jacobs' name? He wasn't the kind of person to say much but now he asked, "Investing in what?"

"We have discovered a mine just outside the city of St. Petersburg that is producing diamonds from a greenish-colored dirt. We want to offer you a portion for your investment. I have a certificate that I would sell you for gold."

Jacob remained stoic. He made no sign or acknowledgment.

Johnny continued, "Can I see the deed to your mine?"

"These certificates prove everything you need to know."

"Do they? Do you have a map for location?"

"I think we left that stuff at our office. When we arrive in St. Petersburg, come with us and we'll sell it to you. We've already had several investors so we only have about three certificates left. I wouldn't want you to miss out on a good deal."

Jacob spoke now, "At the moment, we wouldn't be able to.

Maybe in another year we would be better prepared."

"We won't give up on you. We'll go to the dining car for now while you think about it."

"The answer will still be no." They left walking back through the cars behind them. Jacob gathered the family closely to himself. "Be careful. Don't talk about anything important. I detect a problem."

Johnny said, "Here's part of the problem. He knows your name, Jacob. Has no certificates with him and wants only gold?"

"He isn't selling anything but paper."

It wasn't a moment more when the man in the seat ahead of them peered back and said, "I don't know if you noticed, but we heard them. They are out to rob whomever they can. Do be careful."

"Thanks Sir, that's exactly what I told my family. Thanks. You be careful too."

Sitting back in their seats, Tina asked, "Why the warning, Dad?"

Jacob turned to Anastasia, "I don't know, but we could be in a bit of trouble, maybe not personally. We have to watch. Be very aware."

"Usually, you are assigned to specific seats. They didn't seem to have that. Something is wrong." Johnny knew how it worked.

Nicholas in his preparations had managed to procure a sleeper for the entire family. At least they could sleep and not be too tired in the morning when they would need to have their wits about themselves. Anything he could give his daughters and Anastasia would still be his best even if it might have been the last thing he could do for them.

Jacob made the first move. Let's see if we can get some rest."

Try, as they might, going forward into the unknown, would not be an easy task. Everyone lay quietly trying to sleep while Anastasia's thoughts kept racing through her mind.

Jacob knew God was in control so whatever would be, had to be in God's plan and it had to be God's best.

"Dad, can you hear me?"

"I can, Tina."

"It's noisy out there, what's going on?"

"Tina, Ana, Johnny? Do you hear me?"

Like it was in unison, "We do."

"It sounds like all out pandemonium has hit." Johnny volunteered to check it out. "Stay put everyone. I'll look around."

In an instant, Johnny had dressed and was out in the isles to see what the ruckus was about. He saw the Porter next to him. "Sir, what is going on?"

"Someone has snatched another's belongings. We think he might still be on the train." Within moments, there were officials everywhere. The Conductor was now checking identifications from all who stood before him. Every coach had to be checked.

Johnny made his way back to his compartment. "Everyone, there has been a train robbery. The conductors are coming around to check identifications."

"We all have been over everything a hundred times if once. Tell them what they need to know. No more, no less. Be very vigilant and don't draw attention to us."

Anastasia whispered, "What would the robbers want anyhow?"

Jacob answered softly, "This is a mail train going to St. Petersburg. It has been robbed before but this time the *good-guys* are armed. So there might be a fight. Be still, but get dressed in case we have to jump off."

"What about our stuff?"

"We don't have much anymore. Sit still, the mail car is all the way in the back. We just have to be careful should we get derailed. That would be dangerous. The last heist they did, the mail wagon was blown apart."

Now Tina was disgusted. "Not some more dead bodies! We need to get out of here."

"Tina, stop that right now. We need to stay together and not make any rash decisions. I'm sure they will have this under control in minutes if not already." Johnny was insistent. He didn't need a sister-in-law to jump before necessary and then even at all. Not only that, they had a schedule to keep. This could mean everything would go awry, even their ability to get Anastasia out of the country.

"Oh, good, the train is running again. We're going, that's a good thing. I don't hear any blasts." Jacob looked relieved. "They may still come around for more information. Be careful."

Johnny answered, "Well, I'm glad that was nothing like the Great Robbery of 1903. That time they blasted their way in to get the money. That's why we have armed officers on board. It certainly is a good thing when the *bad-guys* want to kill people. None of us want to read about our obituaries in the Newspapers."

Chapter 36
Locked in the Train Station

Johnny couldn't help himself. "We made it! We are here in St. Petersburg!" They all stood in the lobby of the train station having collected their baggage.

"I need to wet my face with water. Anyone with me to use the facilities?"

"I'm right with you, Ana, a splash of water on me and my baby and me. We still have a way to go so freshening up will certainly be helpful." Susana was anxious as anyone else. "Dad, I guess you are going to get a wagon for the rest of our trek?"

"I am. Let me go make the arrangements."

The three women began looking around the facilities when Tina said, "Oh, I'm glad at least the window is open. Can you imagine how stuffy it would get in here if they didn't open that up?" Looking around the room, Tina said, "Can you see that, Ana?"

"I can feel the breeze."

"No, Tina and Ana, in the corner. Like a bug, maybe? It flickers." Susana was sure of what she saw.

"Well, let's just do what we need to quickly. I feel a little uneasy. Probably just eager to get going and get this behind us."

"I don't know, Tina. I'm just glad I can feel the air coming

in from outside. It was enough that the train ride was stuffy."
Susana looked around, "I need to get the baby fed. Here, this
should help her. So how did you like the train ride, Maya? I'll bet
if you could talk you would tell us how foolish we are. We should
have stayed where we were so that you could learn to crawl. Oh,
well, it won't be long. Just hang in there, honey. You know Ana,
Maya said, *Momma* yesterday."

"She did? Where was I? I wish I could have heard her."

"Isn't she precious? I'm hoping she'll never remember all
this and that it will all be over soon."

"You know my Dad said, 'Just wait and see. It will all settle
down like it always does."

Throwing water on their faces just to freshen up was what
they needed. While you are finishing up, Ana, I'll check on our
transportation. See you just out the door, okay?"

"It shouldn't take me long. How's the baby doing?"

"She's a good baby. A little crying doesn't hurt, does it?
I'll be outside the door with her and check to see how Dad is
making out."

Just as Susana and Tina stepped out, a security guard
walked over to the door with a key in his hand. Susana watched as
he put it in the door. "What are you doing, Sir? There are people in
the bathroom."

"According to our surveillance, there is only one person in
that room."

"Then why are you locking the doors?"

"That was my instructions. Orders are to secure this room.
We will be securing this entire building, shortly. You might want
to hurry and get out of here."

"Sir, please, my sister is in there. Please, open that door!"
Susana was now pleading with the officer.

"Sorry, ma'am. I don't know who you are but for security

purposes we have to keep that person in there until the Soldiers get here."

"What do you want with my sister? She hasn't done anything. She's been with me and the baby."

"Sorry, I don't want anything from your sister, I'm just told what to do and when to do it. I was ordered to lock this door. If you had stayed in there much longer, you would be in there with her."

"When can she come out? When are you going to unlock that door?"

"I haven't been given those instructions. My job is just to lock up and keep that person in there."

"Sir, you have the wrong person in there. This is her baby. How will she feed her baby if you keep her locked up?"

"I don't know that answer. The baby seems very happy with you. Keep her. It will be better that way. Besides, it could be a day or so."

"How is she to survive in there without anything?"

"That's not my call. I only follow orders."

"What do you want? Money? Am I to give you money?"

"Woman, if you are offering me a bribe I could have you arrested right now. I'll pretend I didn't hear that."

"How is that a bribe? I just want you to release my sister. I have her baby here. Please don't separate them for the baby's sake."

"I think you need to keep your baby. She is doing just fine without the person inside." The guard left.

Johnny saw what was going on and immediately came to Susana's side.

"Oh, Johnny, I'm glad you are here," Susana turned to face hm. "Please tell Dad. Ana's going to panic, I need to see if I can communicate with her."

By now, Ana was banging on the door. Tina spoke, "Can you hear me?"

"I can."

"Listen carefully. Do you see the open windows we were talking about?"

"I do."

Move the garbage can to that wall under the window."

It was silent for a few minutes. "I got it under the window."

"Ana, you have to climb on that and pull yourself up to that open window. Can you do that? Meanwhile I'm going to get Dad to drive the wagon around the back and have Johnny see if he can climb to meet you. Are you okay?"

"I have to be. I'll try."

"Take a deep breath. The man said they wouldn't be back to open the door for maybe a few days. That's good. If we work quickly we will get you out. Stay calm."

"I'll try, Tina."

Ana thought for a moment. "Maybe if I put the lid upside down on the can, I won't slip off it. Trying as she might, finally, she was on the can. "That window is high. I can barely reach it and I don't know if I'm strong enough to pull myself up. I must, I have to, or I'm dead."

By now Johnny, Tina and Jacob were at the outside of the window. "Oh, here is an outside garbage bin. Help push it up to the window. We can stack a few together. Okay, there. I can easily reach the window. Ana, are you there?" Johnny hoisted himself up and halfway into the window. "I can see you. Here, let me pull your arms."

"I'm trying. David, that hurts but pull as hard as you can anyhow. I have no other choice but to get through this window. Please help me."

"I am. Here, okay, now we are getting somewhere." Ana's

body was coming through, resting on the window frame. "Okay, Ana, I'm pulling you through. Hold on as tightly as you can. Good, there we go."

Jacob was on the ground just beneath Johnny as he let her slide into Jacobs arms. "Good, Ana, you are safe. Get in the wagon and we'll be on our way."

"We should be okay Dad, the guard said it could be a day before the door would be opened. The last thing he did was put a sign on the door that said, "Out of order," and then he also said he was going to secure the station and close all exits. We need to get out of here."

Ana put her head in her hands, "I'm scared. I'm just beginning to realize what I'm putting you all through. You really should have left me. You have every right to do that. If I think about it, my parents are probably dead anyhow. Alexei is surely gone. What good is all this that you are doing for me? Who am I? Especially since, I am alone. Why would anyone care?"

"Ana, I made a promise to see you safely into Canada. I am going to do that."

"Why would anyone go through everything you are going through?"

"You heard what I said. I will do what I promised not only for you but also for Tina and you. You are the ones that will go with me to Canada. It isn't just about you anymore, Ana, it is about the three of us. It is our lives as well as yours. You have to hang in there with us. None of us will make it if you don't go with us."

Jacob was quiet for a moment. Then he spoke again, "You have to know there is no life here for any of us. We are all in this together to save each of our lives. Are your parents alive? I don't know that, but for the grace of God. There was a plan. If they were not shot, then just maybe there will finally be some kind of reunion."

259

"Come on Dad, let's just be out of here. We need to be on our way. You might want to know that we saw a little *bug* that had a red flickering light, in the bathroom. Do you think they heard us talk in there?"

"You didn't!" Johnny gasped. "That means they were listening to everything you said and what you did. What did you say and was it obvious that the baby wasn't Ana's?"

"That could have been the clue. I fed my own baby and they would have seen that! Traitors! Someone ought to hang them, shoot them and see how they like it!"

"Calm down, Susana. God is still in charge of our lives and He will see us through. It is dark and no one is following us. We have a good head start on them."

"With this horse I bought, I'm told he is the best they had and can lead in the dark and knows the way to the town we want."

"Uncle Jacob, where are we going?"

"Please, Ana," Tina exclaimed, "call him Dad. We've already made enough bad moves."

"I have a map. We are going close to where the ship docks. There are plenty of empty houses there."

"Who is coming for us, anyhow?"

"There is a group sponsoring us. I have our paperwork and they have theirs so when they come for us, we will know. I understand there will be a few other people that are also being sponsored just as we are."

"Does anyone know who I am?"

"It is my understanding, no one does. The man coming to meet us will know that it is imperative for us to get out of Russia quickly."

"Well, okay, Dad. If that's what I have to call you, I will. Won't they know when they see my paperwork, who I am?"

"No, Ana. Your name is changed to my last name. Your

date of birth is going to be 1906 instead of 1901. There shouldn't be any possible way once all the documents are signed and we've boarded the ship that anyone would know it was you."

"Lena already explained all of that to me after the party at the Opera, which now seems so long ago and almost as if I lived in a dream before. Oh how I wish it were a dream. This is definitely reality with an entire nation at war. So, I do know what I have to do."

"The authorities will only know what we tell them so you must call me Dad."

"Sounds easy enough for me."

"Good, then that's settled.

"I have one question. How will my family ever find me if they are alive and do manage to escape?"

"They know our plans and Nicholas had the passports made accordingly, he would know. Be aware though, it has taken us a couple of years to get this far. It may take them longer than us to get out of Russia. We are being sponsored but it may be very different for them. Ana, no matter what, we will always be your family.

They rode in the wagon continuing on the journey with their horse supposedly knowing where to lead them. Tina started talking, "I don't think they'll be looking for us anytime soon if what that guard told me is true."

Ana wasn't so sure, "I still feel skittish but moving on makes me feel more secure."

Johnny spotted a house that didn't appear to have any residents for the moment. "Jacob, what's that? A house? Let's check it out." They walked around it to be sure it would be secure from the outside.

"It looks vacated. Ah yes, the soldiers have been through here already. They've looted everything and left it in shambles."

"Why don't we check to see if we could stay overnight?"

"Let's you and I do that Johnny. Make sure there is no one in there. It might be a good stopover for the night. Tomorrow we'll be able to see better to find our way in the daylight."

Susana, the baby and Ana were quiet for the moment. "Your baby is sound asleep through all of this."

"Yeah, she's been fed plus the wagon ride puts her to sleep."

At least we are on our way now. I don't think they'll be looking for us anytime soon.

"Thank God for that. I do hope we will be safe here."

"You and me both. Enough is enough, Tina." It seemed like an hour before Jacob and Johnny came back. "Why so long?"

"We just cleaned it up a bit. It should be okay for now but we need to leave by day break."

"What Jacob is saying, is it looks like a soldier's stopover? We don't need to be here when they come back."

It was an old stone structure, no worse for wear. However, at some point, the front door had evidence of a break and entry. Boot marks and bullet holes riddled the door.

"It smells of death, Dad."

"I don't think that. It smells musty, but let's just sleep a few hours. The sun will be up shortly and then we'll find where we are going"

Fatigue had set in big time. It wasn't but a few minutes before everyone was asleep. That is until the baby awoke. She was crying uncontrollable. "She hasn't done that since we started this escapade."

"Feed her, Susana. Maybe then she'll settle down."

"She doesn't want to eat. I really hope Maya isn't sick."

"I think she's tired of being kept quiet."

Before anyone could think, they could hear the pounding of

boots on the ground.

Ana spoke up, "What's that noise?"

"Unfortunately, I also hear that. Let's be still. Maybe it will go away."

Ana was now whispering and interpreting the Russian, "I can hear what they are saying. They are coming. They know someone is in here. They are going to check it out."

"Oh, God, save us from this too!"

Tina looked up, "Look, the door!"

Lena covered the baby's ears as the door fell with a loud crash. Maya cried and began wailing while Susana tried to comfort her. Two Soldiers dressed in full gear with one hand on their muskets still in their holsters, as they drew the swords with one swift movement crisscrossing them as they continued to block the entrance. Not a question, it was the Red Army and this couldn't be good. This had instantly become a dare for anyone attempting an escape. The stench of beastly unkempt men was almost enough to send anyone into convulsions. There they stood in tattered uniforms daring anyone to defy them.

No one said anything.

Finally, the Soldier with the scar under his left eye said, "You are trespassing into our territory. Give us your names and what business you have of being here."

The other soldier in his crude demanding voice, "Your business, state your business!" echoed through the empty house, "Don't even think of leaving. If you do..." they smashed the sword blades together making a thunderous sound, "if you do, you will then understand the stench of death."

Ana by now decided having come this far through the never-ending struggles at every turn, one more incidence would not do. She stood up and demanded that they retreat. She spoke fluently in Russian, "Leave my family alone. You have done enough and you will let me out of here! *Теперь перейдите к.* Tina couldn't believe her eyes and ears. As the family huddled together knowing this might very well be the end of their journey, all now would be for naught. Whether Ana could stand her ground, it didn't really matter anymore. No one else knew what to do.

Ana spoke again, in Russian, "Kill me if you dare! God is with me and He will keep me now. I am walking through that doorway and you had better not dare stop me. God will be your judge."

Then without hesitation, Ana walked through the barricade. In total astonishment, the guards muttered, "Кто эта женщина и кто ее Богу за то, что она не может пройти заграждение?"

Jacob finally whispered, "Surely they will kill her."

Johnny was not to be pushed back. He jumped up from his seated position and ran to the door. "Ana, are you okay!"

"I am."

The guards left without a word.

"I heard you speak Russian to them."

"I did."

Ana's heart was pounding. It felt like it could burst if she didn't figure a way to calm herself down. "It wasn't even so much what I said as it was what God showed me to do. Think about it, they would have killed us. What had I to lose? They would have killed us all. I do not want any of you to die on my account. I've had enough and I've come too far to allow them to take our lives now. I know for certain God will see us through to where it is we are going."

"What did they say when you walked through?"

"Who is this woman? Who is her God that she could walk through our barricade?" Ana was desperately trying to calm herself down.

Jacob stood with her now, "Ana, God indeed enabled you.

If you wish, speak Russian. God will show you when and where. Thank you, Lord. We might just as well get ready and find the apartment we are all to be at until the next ship arrives."

Everyone was too tired to say or do anything but pack up the few belongings they had and climb on the wagon to find the directions. "Dad, you said you have a map, do you?"

"I do. Can any of you read it for me?"

"I always do that for you. Let me be your navigator, besides Susana needs to tend her baby." Ana was only too happy to involve herself in doing something as practical as reading a map. There had been a way too many emergencies with people trying to find her, capture her or even kill her. Whatever, but it had to be God that was seeing her through everything. Still, she couldn't forget Gypsy Wanda's prediction. She knew it was wrong but there it was. She knew now for sure that God wanted her to make it out of Russia.

Somehow, Maya was peaceful now. She loved being handed over from person to person. She never tired of all the love she was getting. However, the journey was not over yet.

Chapter 37
The Shake Down 1924

"See this map? The instructions have it all laid out for us with the address of the apartment we are to be at where our contact will make connections."

"Will we have to pay for that?"

"They've included the voucher for the Hotel room where we must wait for the authorized personnel from the ship when it docks. According to this information, we could be held over for at least a week, maybe two."

Finding the hotel was the easiest ordeal they had to figure out since the beginning of this journey with Anastasia's help in reading the map. Finally, everyone had settled into their new housing situation to wait.

"What do we do until then, Jacob?"

"We still have some rubles but I don't know how long it will last us. I should have accepted all that Nicholas was offering, I did accept a little."

"What are we going to do for food while we wait?" Johnny was in earnest now.

"Get a job? We don't even speak Russian. All our lives we've just spoken Friesland Dutch, German and some French."

"If you can speak Friesland Dutch you are close to speaking English. The language is very similar, easy to figure out. We never did speak Russian. Come to think of it, Dad, why didn't we choose to speak Russian?"

"Tina, we always thought that when you lived in an ethnic society that speaks the way we do, why learn? Not so wise a move now that we are in this situation."

"Truth is, Jacob, speaking the language of the people instead of cloistering ourselves would have been smarter."

Anastasia walked out the door, when she heard, "Where are you going, Ana? Please come back." Tina was pleading with her but she just continued to walk. After a few minutes of checking out her surroundings, she saw a large stone building. It appeared to be an active factory with working men coming in and out. She crossed over the gravel road, looking for the entrance when she saw a man standing on the outside, smoking a cigarette. "May I help you?

Anastasia spoke in Russian, "My father and brother need to work so that we can afford to buy food and milk for the baby."

Amused that a young woman would want employment for her family, the man said, "Yes, of Course."

"My family doesn't speak Russian very well."

"I'll see to it that they understand."

"How do you pay your workers?"

"We pay cash after each day."

Ana came back to the Hotel to give them the good news. Tina asked, "Where have you been? We were worried about you."

"You men need to see this man at the factory, he wrote his name on this paper. He will hire you, Uncle Jacob and Johnny. They will pay on a daily basis so you can buy food for us while we wait."

"Do they know who we are?"

"No, and they don't need to. They said they need your help.

Please, don't be afraid. I know God is in all of this."

"I'll go. It doesn't matter whether anyone else will come with me. I will go." Johnny knew what he had to do. For the next few weeks both of the men worked earning enough for food while they waited.

The family amused themselves watching the baby grow. Soon she wasn't only crawling and stumbling but attempting to walk. That delighted everyone. On the sunny days, they played in the grass near the front porch afraid to wonder too far.

The family was sitting at the table after dinner, preparing to relax as they waited for the next ship to arrive at the docks. When someone knocked at the door, "Oh, this might be the man we are waiting for."

"I didn't see a ship at the pier yet. It can't be."

Johnny opened the door, facing a man dressed in black pants and a leather vest over a tan shirt. "Is Jacob available?"

Jacob stood behind Johnny, "That's me but who are you?"

The man ignored the question. "You must come to this address. Bring the gold bar. Do not refuse if you want to leave with your family. I expect to see you at seven hundred hours tomorrow."

The man left.

"What are you going to do? Who knew?" asked Tina. I thought that was to be your inheritance from your parents?"

"That it was. I have never met my sisters' husbands, so I don't know if any of them are these men. Why would they do this, they all were given their own inheritance years ago. The gold bar was always passed on to the eldest son but because my father left his home for Russia, Grandpa gave him his inheritance. Then he gave it to me when he died. My sisters are the only people who would know."

"Your sisters could have done this to you? You can't be

serious, Dad?"

"My intent was to take the three of you to Canada. We would pay off the Mennonite Central Committee and find our new life. If you, Ana would want to join your family in France, you could have done that. You could make your own way if you wanted.

Anastasia insisted, "Please don't worry about me. Either way, I'll be fine. If my parents are alive, they will find me."

Johnny insisted, "Keep the Gold, we'll fight for it."

"No, can't do that. They can have the gold. It will be what it is. I'm not going to be responsible for bloodshed. We are going to get to Canada safely. As far as the MCC knew, we were to work off the cost of the Ship and Hotel expenses anyhow. That will be what we have to do. Tomorrow, I will give them what they ask. Gold isn't worth our lives. I will go."

"How did anyone know we were even here? If they know, who else knows?"

"That's the problem."

"Do we trust them?"

"No, they would just as soon take the gold, tell Moscow where we are and we are done. Am I right, Dad?"

"I guess you are exactly correct, Johnny. We need to pray that our man from the Ship will come before they have a chance."

"It's too bad we couldn't disappear and wait somewhere else."

"We can't do that. This is where the man has to come for us. Just let's pray they do."

"I will never know if of my sisters sent these men or if they've already hurt them. Now it has become a life or death proposition and our safety is much more important."

Johnny added, "Even if these people are your sister's husbands, my wager would be the money won't go to them anyhow. They found out about the money and they wanted it. You really shouldn't give it to them."

"It is out of the question." With Jacob, when he felt enough was enough, it was over. No more talking.

The next morning Johnny went to work and Jacob complied. The address led him to an antiquated stone structure with stairs that led to a basement apartment office. Jacob laid down the gold bar on the desk noticing the men with rifles lying there. "Here it is. How did you know I still had this?"

"We know. Your eldest sister is my wife."

"Sorry, I never had the privilege of meeting any of you." At this point Jacob looked at the men more closely, "If I'm not mistaken, were you not the one dressed as a Chinese man?" Jacob hesitated. "And then the train, right?" He recognized both men. "How is your diamond mine?"

"The gold, Jacob, just the gold."

"How is my sister?"

"Leave the gold. Just go, Jacob. I don't want to see you again."

"How did you find me, anyhow?"

"We've been following you for a long time. We almost lost you at the train station and then suddenly, there you all were. We continued to follow. We don't know where you are going but since you are at the docks, with a Ship due to come in, we decided to move in."

The other man said, "Just go. I don't want to know where you are going or why. Just go. We will have enough trouble to hide this gold."

"Then why do you want it?"

"Who knows, maybe we'll catch another Ship and disappear. First, we have to find someone to forge papers. I wonder how you got yours? How does a Jew get exit papers?"

"Get out of here. Your sister says you do everything honestly. Just go and get out of here. I don't want to know any more."

Jacob left. He would never be sure if his family had betrayed him or only their husbands? Under Communism, it was hardly likely that the money would remain in their hands. They could as easily have to die for it.

Jacob returned to his family but said nothing.

"Are you okay, Dad?"

"I am."

"Can we talk about it?"

"No."

Chapter 38
The Milkman 1924

Just as the discussion had been dismissed, another knock came at the door. Jacob prayed he had not been followed back by his perpetrators. "Who are you?"

A young man stood there with a case of carnation milk in his hands. "I'm Allen. How is everyone?" In moments, everyone was introduced. "So, whom am I dealing with? Are you all coming with us to Canada? I am here to prepare you for the passage on the ship." He handed Anastasia the case of carnation milk.

"No, just Ana, Tina and myself. The others are only here to see to our safety."

Johnny grabbed the carton, "That's too heavy for you, Anastasia. I'll take it for you."

"Thank you." Turning to Allen, "You must be the man. We feel like it has been forever, since 1919 we've been on the move. We waited a year hoping everything would quiet down. No such luck."

"How has your journey been, then?"

"Don't ask. We are here waiting to leave before we face another hurdle."

"You said, another hurdle?"

"We've been accosted all along the way."

"Let's get right down to it. Here are the papers. Complete what you can and then I'll bring the Doctor with me who has to give you clearance. If all goes well, you will board when the ship has refueled and restocked."

"Does this mean our passage has been paid for?"

"It has been paid for by the MCC, an organization that is sponsoring your passage. When you arrive in Canada, you get to work it off. Then you are free to go as you please. Go where you want and do what you want. Of course, we wish that you would choose to worship with us and become members of our Denomination. That would please us."

"We do have a slight problem that has come up just yesterday. We have been followed and could have trouble. Can you take us out of here, somewhere for our protection?"

"You were followed?"

"Jacob had to pay a ransom. If we are found here waiting to board the ship, it could very well be over for all of us."

"We have been followed all along but each time we have been able to escape. I don't know how much longer we can hang on." Anastasia was sincere.

"Okay. I was given the impression of how imperative it was that you board the ship safely. The details of why were not given decisively. We have a holding place, or customs, that you will all go through anyhow. If you are in there, no one will have access to you."

Jacob thought for a moment, "That means we need to say goodbye to everyone."

"No, they can come with us. They can say their farewells when everything is approved. Why don't we do that right now?"

Gathering up their meager belongings they followed Allen to a large auditorium next to the docks. "I knew when the paperwork I received was signed by Nicholas II, this had to be very important. Have you discussed what your names will be on the paperwork?"

"We have. This one is for Ana. Okay, this should be Tina's and then mine. Ana's birth is 1906 instead of 1901. That should stop any questions."

"Good. When Russia becomes some kind of democracy, maybe then you people can all go back to your homes. Possibly even the Palace, huh, Ana?"

"I think I had quite enough and don't want to remember, not even to come back. It is just over. It would be different if the rest of my family made it through."

They sat there working through the papers. "Just one more hurdle, the Doctor will come and do the examinations. After that we complete the boarding passes so that you can all board this ship."

"It is Canada we sail for?"

"Yes, Quebec. However, we are only disembarking there. From there we will board the train for Manitoba. I'll come back here tomorrow morning after the doctor has done the examinations and he will tell me when all has been cleared. Then you will board with me."

"When you arrive in Manitoba, you will be assigned to a family. The two women will be billeted out to families where their employment will go toward that passage for the three of you."

Just as their group was nearing the multiplex immigration site, "Jacob, don't look now but isn't that some of the Red troops a few yards behind us?"

"What happens now, Allen? Can they accost us here when we are with you?"

Allen pushed the huge glass door open, "Hurry, get in there. I'll deal with them."

Before Allen could turn to meet his aggressors, the soldier had the sword at Allen's throat, demanding they be allowed to search the people already inside the building with the family watching in horror. "What now? It's over!"

"This is just too much. How much, God are we to take?" Tina collapsed on the floor. The family could only watch.

"You have no authority here. As it stands these people must first be cleared to sail on this ship. Those who are not sailing will be free to leave after our clearance is complete."

The soldiers began backing away from Allen as he turned to reenter the building. "That was a close call but we made it. We are in the hands of the Canadian authority now."

"Allan, has that ever happened before?"

"No, Jacob. It seems someone sent them. Could have been the men who took your gold."

Jacob was silent. He didn't want to accept the possibility that these men might have murdered his sisters. They cared for no one but the money they had stolen. No one would gain anything. Only lose, to those who stole. A symbol of what Russia had now become as a nation.

Susana helped Tina on her feet. "Are you alright, now?"

"I should be. That was too much."

Jacob asked, "Where do we go from here, Allen?"

"A couple of large rooms at the other end on this floor. Plenty of cots, showers and supplies you can help yourselves to. I will return tomorrow with our Doctor to complete your clearance. Do relax, tomorrow has to be better."

The night was quiet and rest came easy for by now no one had the energy to even as much as worry about tomorrow. The next day the doctor arrived and did the examinations.

"I'm afraid, Tina does not pass the blood test. She will need to wait behind. Has she anyone to stay with?"

Johnny answered, "She can stay us. Will she be able to take the next ship?"

"Just keep your papers, Tina. When you can pass the blood test, notify your family and either arrange for the sponsorship again or if they have the means, just send the ticket and you can join them."

"Susana, I want you to give this doll I've carried all over the country, to Maya. She can have it to remember me by. Maybe she will be the one to find me someday."

These were sad, yet happy moments for the family. They were happy to be freed from running but sad to be leaving family behind. Jacob made no comment for he knew what had been his lot in life. For him life could never continue in Russia, the land he had been born in. First his Dad had to leave Germany to save his own life, now he had to leave his homeland of Russia to save not only his life but also one of Nicholas's daughters. Yet, he knew God was in charge and God would see him through all of this.

It was soon after that when their *milkman* ushered the two, Jacob and Anastasia onto the ramp leading to the deck of the S.S. Minnedosa.

Anastasia turned to Jacob, "What's all that noise down there on the dock?"

The Soldier's hadn't given up. They wanted to gain entrance one more time, demanding that they needed to search the Ship for illegal passengers.

The Captain insisted, "You do not have proper paperwork to board this ship. It must come from Moscow and you have nothing. Be assured also, no one can board without proper paperwork. In the event that were to happen, they will be returned into your custody. Please stand back and we will give you the signal should we find that to be the case."

The First Mate appeared, "Captain, all paperwork is in

order as processed before boarding."

"Please continue."

The whistles blew and the ship began to pull out, the Captain saluted the Soldiers standing on the dock. Jacob breathed a heavy sigh.

Anastasia spoke up, "They had to try just one more time, didn't they?"

So, it went.

It would be days before Jacob and Anastasia would be settled enough on this ship to contemplate the future upon arriving in Canada. Life's journey had a way of not being over yet.

It was now only the two of them traveling and leaving Tina behind hadn't been Jacob's intent. Jacob knew that waiting for his daughter Tina wasn't a choice. He could not leave Anastasia behind and he would never go back on his word even if it meant death. He had lost his own daughter at least for a time but also the last of his possessions, the gold, but he knew God would see them through this as well. They had come through tremendous trying times and here they were. The next step would be for customs in Quebec to accept their documents.

Would their papers be accepted from a Country in turmoil? Who would be there to meet them? Would they recognize strangers? Jacob couldn't help himself thinking, the daughter of the Czar had become a slave for a time. That part was not what he had promised the Czar.

Other questions kept pouring through his mind. Would they be refused immigration? They had their papers but would Nicholas's abdication invalidate their paperwork?

Journey to the End

Chapter 39
Disembarking S.S. Minnedosa 1924
Debt Repayment

"Here are some options for you, Jacob. You will not be able to stay with Ana as she is required to be a "live-in" servant. Some of the money she would earn could go to an apartment for you and the remainder would go to debt repayment. There is another option. We can send you to live with the Amish Mennonites. They will see to your needs and in that way, Ana will only have to pay for her own keep and the fare to get you both here, thereby paying it back sooner. The choice is up to the two of you. Whatever works for you." Dr. Wiebe was the one assigned to billeting the refugees into places of employment.

"Also, Ana, you can choose whether you want to be a cook, a house housekeeper to clean and take care of children, or work in a clothing factory."

"I'd prefer to cook, Dr. Wiebe. I am a very good cook. The heavier work could easily be a problem for me."

"Okay, so we have you settled, in theory. I will check my list and call the family you would be best suited for. Then, Jacob, what would you like?"

Ana interrupted, "Please, if it would please you, get an apartment. Then maybe I can come stay with you on my days off."

"No, I'll gladly go live with the Amish. The debt is less and you will be able to get on with your life sooner than later. I know you want to marry and have a family. I wouldn't mind that in the least and maybe they will allow me to do something to earn some money. Also, if I can earn my own money I'll be able to take care of myself."

Tina's health had kept her behind and Ana worried that she wouldn't be able to earn the money soon enough to have her brought to join her Dad. She may have been Jacob's daughter but she was Ana's soul-mate. Probably the only one who could ever understand her without having to recount the past since past could be remembered no more.

Anastasia was hired to be the chef for a Jewish family. This was her first employment where she would have to prove herself not only to her employer but also to herself. Find out what she was made of. No one would know that she had been royalty in growing up, that Alexandra had allowed the sisters to cook, cleanup and serve even the servants just out of sheer pleasure. Now that she would have to work off the debt, it had become one of her greatest benefits to enable her to work as a cook for wealthy families. Before it was pleasurable volunteerism and now it was to pay the debt of her passage not only Jacob but also for Tina, so that when her health improved, she could come to Canada and not have to work for her passage.

She worked hard, day after day. Some of the people that employed her were orally abusive and she would have to request a reassignment from time to time.

In due time, Ana was able to repay the fare.

"Uncle Jacob, I have good news. I don't need any more money. Now I'm working for only myself only. How about you returning to Winnipeg and we'll find an apartment together?"

"I think, Ana, I will move to Vancouver where the climate

is mild. I won't have to labor over the hard-cold winters and the unbearable summers. It's time I get to retire. I now have the money so you don't need to worry about me."

"I want to send for Tina. I think I'll send the money to her so she can come and join me. How would you like that?"

"Wonderful. I do think you should send the money through the MCC for her passage. It will be quicker that way."

Ana did just that. She waited and waited some more. Finally, she contacted Tina and asked about the money, had it arrived?

Tina said, "The money came to the MCC but it was taken for another family on the waiting list. They felt that even though the money was designated for me, I wouldn't be strong enough to make the journey. I had the medical clearance but I don't know if I'll get it again. I'm not that well anymore but please don't feel bad. It is probably better this way. I'm still with Susana and Johnny. The baby isn't a baby any more. Everyone here is very good to me."

Jacob moved to Vancouver and often bragged how good the weather was. It had been an exceptionally mild climate, the best in years. Ana wanted to join Jacob but she stayed around town and visited with friends she had grown to know and others that were paying back debts for their own passage as well. They continued to work but for Ana, she was still longing for the promise of Gypsy Wanda. She wanted that man, she wanted a family and she wanted that longing in her heart to be settled conclusively.

Men came around. "Ana, how about a date?"

"A man of the cloth? Me?"

"Why not you? Could our love not grow?"

"Tom, I have to be me. How can I be that person I don't always want to be? Then, you are not blonde and you don't have blue eyes."

"You'll get over that. I need a woman like you to walk by my side. To care about people as you do and then care as much as I do about our walk in the Lord."

"It would be too hard to listen to the needs of the people. I would feel if I can't fix it, why am I here?"

"You aren't supposed to fix anything. You can't become codependent. God does the fixing. You are only supposed to love them in the Lord. Give advice where necessary. You can't bear their burdens for them but you can listen to them and show them how God can lighten their burden."

"I just don't know."

"I know. I love you. I know you can love me just as I love you."

"You walk that straight and narrow way. I don't want to be so confined. Like I said, I want to be me. Only I can do that."

Anastasia hadn't forgotten her past but she could share that with no one. That was why she wanted Tina to come. Tina would have understood.

Why can't I forget? She had to realize only God chooses to forget but we are humans. She thought that just maybe if she could meet that blonde blue-eyed man he might be the one to understand.

It was another one of those mornings just before Alexei would walk to the wharf. He would sit there and watch the anglers bring in the catch for the day. The manager of the restaurant he had become cook at would be there to buy the freshest fish for the day. Every time the Ship came in to restock and then unload passengers, he would watch.

Alexei had been running late this morning and thought, *I might just as well go directly to work and enjoy my cup of coffee.*

Then he had a strange nagging in his being. *Well, who knows, I've done this so often I wouldn't feel like my day had begun correctly if I miss this morning's Ship docking. A habit is a habit. I have to live in hope.*

One more time he watched people disembarking. He stood up to leave as the last people were disembarking. He took one more look, but this time he was talking audibly "What? It can't be? Olga and Tatiana? I would know them anywhere." He rushed up to the dock and called out.

"Did you hear that, Olga? Does anyone know us here?"

Olga looked at Tatiana, "It can't be?"

Alexei by this time stood in front of them. "You came."

"You are here!"

"I am, Tatiana. I'm on my way to work, but come with me and then I'll take you back to the house."

"What house?"

"Aunt Olga's. That's where I'm living. She said that if any of you come out of Russia, we were supposed meet here."

"Where is Aunt Olga, anyhow?"

"She and her husband moved to Denmark. They still think that Russia will settle down and then they plan to return."

"Sorry, Alexei, only in your dreams. That will never happen."

After introductions and leave from his employment, Alexei took his family home.

The weeks went by as they each shared their experience of how their journey was. The girls shared life in the convent and how they were able to make the boarding on the ship with the help of Sister Mary.

Months slipped by but Alexei had not forgotten as he continued to do his morning jog to the pier just before his shift would begin at the restaurant. Again, he watched day after day.

Alexei always wanted to live in the optimism of seeing the rest of his family.

"We are coming with you today, Alexei. We want to begin to wait with you."

"Why not let's make this a ritual of ours to come and wait when the ship comes in." Tatiana wanted to live in the expectation as Alexei did.

"Are you sure? You know what the news is coming out of Russia."

"How can that be true? You made it okay." Tatiana really did want to live in the anticipation of the future.

"That's what I say." Olga said. "I just have to live in the confidence that our parents will make it."

"I know what the news said but you know Moscow, propaganda is what it is and they thrive on it." Alexei insisted. "I have this gut feeling I had when you guys disembarked.

"Let's just believe and go expecting."

They chatted with the anglers at the wharf and just as they focused on the last of the passengers coming off the ship, "It is them!" Tatiana couldn't contain herself. "It is them! I'm sure of it."

"Where is Maria? They can't have come without her. If that is them, where is she?"

"Let's go see." Alexei reached the couple. Then there was the stare. He was about to ask for Maria, when he turned to glance around, and surely enough, Maria came to join them.

It was now a few years and many letters later from their Aunt and Uncle in Denmark. "Did you read this letter from Olga and Nicolai? They are moving to Toronto. Look at this. They want you, Alexei, to come live with them. If you do that, I want you to find out where Anastasia is." Nicholas was insistent.

"They are saying that they want you to go to Law school, if you would like to, of course."

"Again, if you do, please find Anastasia. I had told Jacob to send her back to us, here in France. I don't know what happened from there. Please find her." Nicholas was very wishful.

"Indeed, that would be exciting."

Chapter 40
The Foretold Happened 1928

For Ana, as she was now known, it was time to find a way to start her new life. With the little money she had left over, she was able to share an apartment with a girlfriend in downtown Winnipeg. The good news was she could choose whomever she wanted to work for instead of being assigned by the Mennonite board. Having to work double duty was over. It wasn't supposed to happen this way, but now that was over and at last Ana would have time to meet people.

"Well, Hilda, where are we off to tonight?"

"I need to get some things from the corner store. Let's go there and then maybe go to the local fountain for milkshakes."

"I like that idea."

Ana and Hilda walked to the store finding what they wanted. They were about to pay for their items when Ana noticed the storekeeper.

"Are you the store owner?"

"I am."

"Are you busy enough these days?"

"Right now I am. I do okay." Ana noticed that he was a tall

slim, handsome blonde man.

"You must be Dutch, from Holland, right?"

"Almost right. Apparently, my people came from Holland to Germany and then to Russia."

"Russia?"

"Yes, but our people left Russia when the Revolution first started erupting. They always said, anyone could have seen that it wasn't going to get better. I was born in America. Not sure exactly where but after I was a month old we came here. However, I went to Law School in Chicago but ran out of money. That's when I decided to buy this store. So far, it's done very well. At least it puts the bread and butter on the table. Tell me about yourself."

"That means you were out of the country before the revolution escalated."

"Certainly, before the Czar and his family were massacred. That only happened just a few years ago. I haven't paid much attention to all of what was going on. I'm here and they are there. Doesn't matter to me."

"Lucky man. Our family had to make it through all that chaos. Not a good sight."

"I hear it got ugly."

"You can't imagine."

"By the way, my name is John

Soon Hilda and Ana made their way to the local Soda Fountain for an outing every evening.

Much small talk occurred as both of them reminisced and began dreaming about the future. Would they marry and live in the country? Would they have children and how many?

Hilda said, "I'd like to marry a man with dark hair, preferably tall. What about you Ana?"

"Well, you know, I almost forgot. Before we left Russia, I went to see a Soothsayer in our village. I'm beginning to remember it like it was yesterday. Okay, I remember, Gypsy Wanda lived in a little black shack, kind of back, near the edge of the woods. Not far from our family's home. It was just before we got to go to an Opera Ball. I snuck out and found my way to her house. I just had to know what the news on the street was and what was happening."

"I can't believe you would do that."

"I swear, Hilda, I did."

"What did she tell you?"

"She told me I'd marry a tall blonde blue-eyed man."

"How about that, John, the store keeper is blonde."

"I'll bet he's probably married."

The two girls often frequented the store for odds and ends. However, matters of the heart were not to be ignored. Both Hilda and Ana began to make numerous trips to the local store and then off to the community theatre. They lived in the center of downtown so everything was easy access. As people do, the girls met men, but it seemed no one was very serious about anything.

"Ana, I thought you had a good suitor."

"I don't think Tom's the man for me. He's a preacher and I don't think I have what it takes. Like he's serious about stuff that I kind of tolerate. I want someone who will allow me to be who I really am."

"Tell me, you are always very secretive. Who are you, really?"

"That's the problem. If I marry someone like Tom, I'd have to 'fess up."

"Confess what? You haven't been evil in a secret life, have you? I wouldn't believe that for a minute. How could a preacher be so awful that you couldn't be honest with him?"

"Like for instance, he always says you can't play with the *spirits* and stuff like that."

"Ana, you and I know, if you play with fire you will get

burned and you will pay."

"Oh, I know what I believe. No one can confuse me. I'd be okay, but Tom didn't think that was such a good idea."

"You know he's right."

"You probably are right. The last I heard though, Tom already found someone else. That's history now."

"You know Ana, I think you just want someone who will make your heart pop out. Someone you are convinced you can't live without."

"Don't you, Hilda?"

"You mean like some prince who will come by on a white horse? Then you'll know you'll live happily ever after?"

"Don't talk to me about a *Prince*. I just want someone ordinary. I want to live an ordinary life and have children. Having my own babies to take care of. I'd like that."

"It's more than just babies, Ana. I always think you have to afford them if you are going to have them. You and I both know what it's like to have to work hard for our keep. I'd like to marry a rich handsome man."

"Where do you suppose on meeting men, Hilda?"

"Maybe at church?"

"Yes, but then you have to live by the rules. I like breaking them. I say we need to venture out."

"Where do you suppose we could go?" Hilda turned in her seat and happened to spot someone familiar to her. "Ana look, isn't that John."

"John who?"

"The blonde person from the store. Who's that person with him? I could be interested in him."

"Hilda, they've spotted us now."

"Hey, girls. I didn't expect you two to be here. Meet my friend George."

They made introductions and they would cross hands in the handshake.

Ana thought for a moment. This is the handshake. This is the man.

Chapter 41
The Call

———————

Anastasia was now married. She had finally found her tall handsome blue-eyed blonde that she had been praying for all these years. He was John the owner of the store she and Hilda had frequented so often when they had nothing better to do. She was now happy and blessed with a family of her own. The Sovereign God, not the soothsayer back in Russia, had finally come through for her. However, in her mind, she would always wonder about Gypsy Wanda.

———————

It wasn't unusual for the telephone to be ringing in the early evening. It was a party line so that meant conversations were usually very carefully crafted so as not to add to the community gossip column. John answered the phone, "Hello," but there was no one on the other line.

"Who was that, John?"

"Don't know. No one said anything so I thought I might just as well hang up."

"Maybe it was meant for one of the neighbors."

"It could be."

About five minutes later, the phone rang again.

"That is our ring. Let me answer, maybe they'll talk to me."

"Hello." Ana just listened and didn't say a word.

John insisted, "Hang up the phone. If they didn't talk with me, I'm sure they won't talk to you."

It had been just a few short minutes and then she carefully put the phone back in its cradle.

"I wouldn't have shown them the patience you did. Some kind of idiot wants to be a nuisance. You gave them too much time."

"I thought maybe I'd give them time to say something."

Nothing more was said as Ana busied herself in the kitchen arranging, and then rearranging everything. She couldn't dare show nervousness. John mustn't know, No one must know about this call. Fortunately, John wasn't in the habit of being very aware of Ana's mood. This time it was a good thing. Ana had found out years earlier she could never share her inner most thoughts and feelings with him. His habit was to show extreme anger or if he heard a story he was interested in he would tell everyone and of course, it needed to be enhanced. As a result, she learned very quickly to live with his irritabilities. She continued to keep her own life a secret.

Morning came and not any too soon for Ana. It was all she could do to keep from getting distracted while making breakfast for her family. It was then she announced to John that she needed to go downtown to get a few things they needed for the household.

John asked, "Couldn't you just go to our local grocery store instead of taking that street car ride to town?"

"No, I think this time I better go to town. I won't be very long. There is food in the fridge should I be delayed. Don't worry, I won't be long."

Soon, Ana was off on the local bus to the depot where the

transfer would be made to the trolley for downtown. Ana's mind was running a mile a minute. *Could this really be Alexei? How will I know? The last time I saw him I was in the Hospital in Winnipeg. I haven't seen him since. It's been years. If he was around here, why didn't he call before? Will I even recognize him? What happens if this is a trap? Could somebody else know who I am? John certainly never knew, I never told him anything. What about the children, would they have guessed? I told them so many stories and I always knew John wasn't even interested in my stories. At least I could talk to my children about everything. Children love to hear stories. Surely, they couldn't have put that stuff together. I left gaps in everything, I'm sure I did.*

Ana made the transfer to the trolley line. She had gone to these department stores so often by herself. This was the one time she would have wanted to bring a friend along. Even if she could, that surely wouldn't be a good plan. She would have to see this one through alone. *He said he would be sitting on the bench at the trolley stop at 10 am when the stores would begin to open. I hope I'm a little early so I can walk around and see him first. Oh, God, please help me now.*

Finally, she was at her destination. "Driver, what time is it?"

Seeing her nervousness, "You should only have to wait about 10 minutes before the store opens. Just wait at the bus bench, you'll be okay."

There was no one to greet her. Ana knew she was early but now her mind decided that it had to have been a hoax. He would have been waiting. Anyone would know that if they were meeting someone, they should be the ones to be early. Common sense was not now the thing to depend on. Her mind raced as her imagination continued to build in her mind. *I just wished I had told him to just forget it. I wish I had told him that I thought he was a hoax and I didn't have a brother whose name was Alexei.*

Ana was standing between the bus bench and the store entrance. It was already 10 am and he still wasn't there. She would just go in, busy herself and maybe peek out to see if he had arrived. He did say he would have a sport jacket on with a red tie. However, she had never told him what she would look like. It had been years since the two of them had been together and then for only about an hour in the hospital. Oh, sure it was Ana, who was supposed to call him. He had given her his card. Where would that card be by now anyhow? That was years ago.

Ana's mind wouldn't stop. She felt like she needed to run away. She knew she must just run away. *With my sense of direction, I wouldn't even begin to know where to go.*

Then, before Ana could turn around, she felt a gentle hand on her shoulder. It felt so comforting. Was that God giving her the confidence of the Spirit?

Then she heard that voice, "Anastasia?"

Ana turned to face that man, "Alexei!"

For a moment, both held one another. Ana wiped the tears from her eyes, all she could say was, "Where have you been?"

A stranger walked by, "I say, it must be a reunion for you two?"

Alexei answered, "Right on the money. It has been years."

Both Anastasia and Alexei just stood there facing one another. No one could say a word. Finally, Alexei said, "I'm so glad I found you. I didn't know what to say to you on the phone. My gut feeling was that no one knows about me so I thought just meeting you here, might be the best. I was sure I'd seen you here before when I was searching for your whereabouts. I figured if I had the correct phone number and when you answered I would know for sure, especially since I asked you to just to let me talk."

"I was beginning to think you were only a figment of my

imagination. That's why I told everyone in the hospital that you were an angel that had come to visit me. There was no way I could tell John. He is incessantly jealous of anything I do and always thinks I'm seeing someone behind his back."

"When I saw you here, you were alone. Why does he let you go to town alone?"

"That's the one time I get to be away. Sometimes I take my daughter and then he doesn't suspect anything but then when the kids are in school, I do come to town alone. It helps keep my sanity. Don't get me wrong, he is not a bad guy, and I love him."

The two of them walked to the department store restaurant to continue their conversation.

"I've come here often for a cup of coffee and a morning snack. It is pleasant."

"Why are you here? Not just to come see me?"

"I own the race track and I own a few prize horses. If you remember, but it was a long time ago, I said I was an Attorney in Toronto. I did tell you I was going to Vancouver and that was why I gave you my card."

"Many things happened since I saw you. That was part of the reason I talked John into thinking it was a good idea to move to Vancouver."

"I'm sure I can guess some of it from that visit in the Hospital. Beside all that, I am here and want to stay in touch. I have a house keeper that I want to introduce you to but she doesn't know anything either, I will be sending messages and tell you where we can meet."

They talked the time away. Then they set a day and time to reunite.

Ana did some shopping and soon boarded the trolley for home. *How do I keep this up with John? What if he finds out? Then I will never see Alexei again. I couldn't live with that.*

Chapter 42

Reunion or Deception

"John, I need to do some shopping at Woodward's, again. If you get hungry before I get back, there is food for you in the fridge."

John seemed to be okay with that and Ana made her way to town.

They sat and talked in the Restaurant at the back of the store.

"Tell me more, Alexei. I've lost so much of my life." Her heart ached to just hear anything of her sisters, her parents and really, how Alexei came about to even find her."

"Remember when I saw you in the Hospital, I said last time, I am an Attorney but since then I have invested in the purchase of this race track. I've always been interested in horses."

"I still miss Sparky. Remember him?"

"I do. I remember how you taught him so many tricks. Uncle Jacob wasn't always happy with you but you thought it fun."

"You mean, like when Sparky would pull Uncle Jacob's hat off his head and twirl it in the air and then catch it?"

"Yes, he'd stomp his front foot for however many times you told him to. Well, Alexei, horses are smart."

"But, you never rode him."

"No, I didn't. He pulled my wagon many times, though. He took care of me any time I needed to go somewhere. Even in the snow, he knew his way home even if I couldn't tell which way to go. I guess it was a couple of years before we came out of Russia after we all separated, so I had time to train that horse. You know, I still have that problem, knowing where I am. I have to look at the signs above the door in this department store so I'll know which exit to go out to catch the trolley."

"You have taken care of yourself very well. It is just so great to be with you again. For my part, I bought a few prize horses and they are doing very well for me. Here's what I'm thinking. I want you to come to the racetrack but I don't want you to gamble. That will be your cover for giving to you what our family has commissioned me to give you. It will be like an allowance."

"I can never do that."

"Why, this will be from our Dad. What is so wrong about that?"

"Can I ever talk to him or Mother again?"

"I'm not sure we can do that unless you could fly to France for a visit."

"With John, not likely. He doesn't like to fly but I can't even tell him."

"Anastasia, I don't want to lose you anymore. I know you can use the help, so please allow me to do that."

"How do you suppose I will explain this to my husband?"

"Tell him you bet on the horses and you won."

"Maybe I can pull that off. I have him believing I'm psychic anyhow."

"Not that Ana, you're not into stuff like Gypsy Wanda was, are you? If you haven't already paid for messing with the *spirits,* you soon will."

"Believe me, I'll already have paid. That's a whole other story."

"Let's work on the horse races. Do you think you can get away with that?"

"I think it will work for a cover. John will buy into that, especially if I'm not losing money."

"You think?"

"I can't take much money."

"We'll work that out."

They talked and talked until the time sped on. Ana suddenly said, "I'm late. I'm in trouble. How can I ever explain this to John?"

THE END

Bibliography

Alexander, Robert, *Rasputin's Daughter*, Publisher by the Penguin Group, 2006

Catherine the Great, Wikipedia, the free encyclopedia, 2011

Kostova, Elizabeth, *The Historian*, Little, Brown and Company, New York, Boston, 2005

Massie, Robert K., *Catherine the Great*, Random House, N.Y. 2011

Massie, Robert K., *Nicholas and Alexandra*, Random House Trade Paperbacks, New York, 1967,
        1995, 2000

Warnes, David, *Chronicle of the Russian Tsars*, Thames & Hudson, 1999

Facts in History and Historical Documents

Articles

1918: Chaos in Russia and German's Last Offensive
Hainsworth, Jeremy, *Missing heir to the Russian Throne*,
Riasanovsky, Nicholas V., *Russian Authoritarianism and Empire*,
1855 to 1900,
A History of Russian, Third Edition, Oxford University Press,
1977, p. 414
Russian history: From Empire to Communism
On this day: Russian in a click, Vladimir Lenin, April 16, 1917
Russia blames Chechens for Beslan siege
Valerian Obolensky, *Russians in Exile*, 1917

The Russians Discover a Spy Tunnel in Berlin, 1956
        "The Russians Discover a Spy Tunnel in Berlin, 1956"
EyeWitness to History,
        www.eyewitnesstohistory.com (2007)

A BETTER WAY

Romans 3:23
"For everyone has sinned; we all fall short of God's glorious standard."

Romans 6:23
"For the wages of sin is death, but the free gift of God is eternal life through Christ Jesus our Lord."

John 1:12
"But to all who believed him and accepted him, he gave the right to become children of God."

Romans 10:9-10
"If you confess with your mouth that Jesus is Lord and believe in your heart that God raised him from the dead, you will be saved. For it is by believing in your heart that you are made right with God, and it is by confessing with your mouth that you are saved."

John 3:18
"There is no judgment against anyone who believes in him. But anyone who does not believe in him has already been judged for not believing in God's one and only Son."

**All scripture is being quoted
from the New Living Translation of the Bible**

My advice to you: if you do not attend a church already, find a Godly church with a biblical Pastor that can disciple you.

God Bless,

Diana E. Linn
Author

www.ingramcontent.com/pod-product-compliance
Lightning Source LLC
Chambersburg PA
CBHW031217120726
47905CB00002B/371